MURDER DOWN THE LINE

A SMILEY AND MCBLYTHE MYSTERY

Murder Down The Line
© 2022 Bruce Hammack
All rights reserved.

Published by Jubilee Publishing, LLC
ISBN 9781737344391

Cover design: Streetlight Graphics
Editor: Teresa Lynn, Tranquility Press

MURDER DOWN THE LINE

A SMILEY AND McBLYTHE MYSTERY

BRUCE HAMMACK

1

Calls at 4:30 a.m. never brought good news. Former homicide detective Steve Smiley thought about ignoring it. If it had been almost anyone else, a recorded message would be their punishment. But this was Leo, and at this hour it wasn't a social call. The conversation lasted only long enough to make an appointment for a pre-dawn breakfast.

April Fool's Day and Houston's sky played a joke on the entire city. Steve heard rain splatter against the car's roof, windshield, and on the window by his head. No wonder the Uber driver was surly. He cursed the rain in some colorful, but unimaginative prose, and didn't volunteer to act as guide to the door of the Denny's on the frontage road of I45. As a result, Steve reached into the left pocket of his pants for a wad of five-dollar bills instead of in the right pocket, which held the twenties. After thinking about paying the man to help him inside, Steve thought better of it, and was soon glad he didn't slip the man an extra twenty. Not only did the driver not volunteer to help his blind passenger, he parked far enough away from the curb to ensure both shoes suffered flood damage.

Steve tapped and sloshed his way to the shelter of the building. An exiting customer flung the door open as he felt for the handle.

"Hey, buddy. Watch where you're going."

Steve stumbled back but didn't go down. "I'd love to watch where I'm going. Want to loan me your eyes?" He regretted the words the second they left his mouth. Self-pity had almost cost him his sanity, and it had no place in his life now. After all, he'd shown he could still solve murders, even if Houston P.D. had put him out to pasture.

"Oh. Sorry. I didn't see the cane. Do you need help?"

"No, thanks. I hope you have a raincoat or an umbrella."

"Rain slicker and a hard hat." An awkward three second pause followed. "I'm sorry I almost knocked you down."

"No harm." Steve extended his hand and received a grip from one of the thickest, strongest hands he'd ever shaken.

The next voice was almost as familiar as his own. It belonged to his former partner in Homicide, Leo Vega. "Any trouble, Steve?"

Steve knew by the tone of Leo's voice he was an inch away from giving the man a truckload of grief. Two truckloads if Leo thought the man had anything smart to say. He also knew Leo's blazer was unbuttoned and gapped open so the man could see Leo's gun and the badge on his belt. The testy reaction confirmed Steve's suspicion of something gnawing at Leo.

"No problems. This gentleman and I were discussing the weather, and speaking of, let's get inside and let this hard-working man get to his first appointment."

"Not my first," said the man. "I've been up most of the night trying to keep the lights on for people." A phone rang and the deep baritone voice answered with, "You'd better tell me it's still working." Driving rain muffled the reply. "Don't touch a thing. I'm on my way."

Leo placed Steve's hand on his arm and led him to a booth. The smell of coffee and bacon mixed with the sweet smell of syrup wafted through the restaurant. Dishes rattled and clanked as muted conversations joined to give the restaurant the sound of fifty voices pushed through a car muffler.

The waitress arrived with a coffee pot and two cups, filling them both to the brim. "There you go, gents. I'll be back in a few to take your order."

Leo moved Steve's cup. "Your coffee's at ten o'clock."

"Thanks. The next time you call wanting to meet, make it on a day Noah's relatives aren't building another ark."

"The weather fits what's going on."

Steve took his first sip of morning coffee, followed it by three more, and settled his mug on the table. "I have all day. Start at the beginning."

"You might have all day, but I don't. They're transferring me."

"Congratulations or condolences?"

Leo let out a harsh laugh. "Condolences."

Steve picked up his cup, brought the mug near his mouth, but spoke before he took another drink. "You're not making sense. Perhaps you're the one that needs coffee."

"I'm fully caffeinated. My day started at 3:30."

"Am I smelling departmental politics?"

"You guessed it. I'm being transferred to Cold Cases."

Something between a groan and a growl came from Steve. "Who did you make mad?"

"No one that I know of. We have a new wonder-boy lieutenant with a row of fancy diplomas on the wall of his office. Let's just say he has his own ideas of what a homicide detective should be, and it's not anyone pushing fifty." Leo heaved a sigh. "All I wanted to do was finish my time working in Homicide, get my kids out on their own, and find a beach somewhere."

Steve scratched his chin. "Are you sure you didn't make someone mad?"

"Nothing serious, but Wonder-Boy didn't like it when I helped you with that last case you solved."

"All you did was help Heather and me solve a murder. Why would he have a beef about that?"

"I did some of the work on departmental time. Also, the request for help didn't come from a law enforcement agency. It didn't fit into any of the boxes in his spreadsheet."

Steve shook his head. "Ahh. He couldn't take credit for work you did."

"He said he values team players more than anything, and my working on a case without his knowledge or approval set a bad example for the younger detectives."

Steve leaned back in the booth. "It's people like him that make me glad I work outside all the red tape. I'm sorry you're being transferred, but I don't know what I can do about it."

Their server arrived to take orders, which delayed Leo's response. Steve asked her to refill his coffee and ordered the Grand Slam, his usual. Leo surprised him by selecting from the heart healthy options and explained as soon as the server walked away. "If you ever remarry, don't allow your wife to go with you for an annual physical. You'll be eating oatmeal, nuts, and twigs for breakfast seven days a week."

"When does the transfer take place?"

"Today, and I'm the April Fool's joke. Lieutenant Chase waited until Captain Price was out for a knee replacement. There's no telling how long he's been looking to make changes."

"Are you the only one?"

"Two others, all of us on the backside of our careers. Hank Jenkins is going with me to Cold Cases while Frank Harley gets to fly a desk at some new diversion program."

"That's a lot of experience to lose. I can't believe the higher-ups are allowing it."

"I was the only squeaky wheel. Hank and Frank are tired of

4

getting calls in the middle of the night to go look at dead people. They both want to coast into retirement." Leo blew out a full breath. "If I could afford it, I'd turn in my badge today."

Steve gave his head a shake. "You know better than to base a decision like that on emotion. I'll admit that Cold Cases doesn't have the best reputation, but it might be a nice change of pace." He took in a deep breath and raised the tone and tempo of his words. "At least you'll still be working homicides. Who knows, they might give you a case that you can sink your teeth into and you'll find you like the challenge of solving old cases."

"Don't talk about sinking teeth into anything when all I'm getting for breakfast is oatmeal, yogurt, and blueberries."

Steve leaned forward. "I've always wanted to tackle a cold case, something that made a big splash years ago but left everyone stumped."

"Do you want to take my place at work today?"

"I wish I could." Steve snapped his fingers. "I have a wild idea. When you get your first case, let's work it together."

Leo hesitated. "I don't know. I already got chewed out and transferred for working with you. If word gets out—"

"I won't tell anyone. Will you?"

Leo laughed. "If I remember right, we never did put everything in the reports we turned in. I see no reason to start now." He paused. "Are you sure you want to help solve a cold case? What about Heather?"

Steve waved off the question. "Heather's up to her eyes working on a high-speed rail deal. We work on murder cases when clients bring them to us. We never said anything about cold cases."

"You also realize there's no money in this for you."

"You're forgetting how rich us pensioners are."

Leo didn't have a ready comeback to the joke, but he did have something else to say. "They expect us to solve cold cases from our desks. In at eight, out at five. Any travel is on my own dime."

Steve lowered his voice. "You're borrowing trouble. Scan and email everything in the file. We'll put our heads together on how to proceed. If we solve the first case, I'll buy you a proper breakfast. How does that sound?"

Leo tapped his fingers on the table. "Right now, I'd do almost anything for a stack of pancakes. Let's try it."

2

Heather checked her watch as she came through the door of her condo. Fourteen hours had passed since she'd left it that morning. She called for Max, her lovable, chubby, Maine Coon cat. No reply. "He must be with Steve," she murmured, as she deposited her briefcase on the bar separating the kitchen from the living room. She scoured the refrigerator for any leftovers not growing mold. No luck. Time to go next door and see if Steve's refrigerator yielded better results.

Instead of going out the door, she stepped into the dining room, knelt down, and pushed open the kitty door they had cut between the two condos. It helped that the floor plans of their condos were mirror images. "Is Max with you?"

"On my lap," came the reply. "You woke him up."

"I'm coming over."

"There's salad and lasagna if you're hungry."

Heather's eyes shot heavenward as she placed her hands together to offer a quick, "Thank you, Lord."

In no time, she'd discarded the pinstriped business suit and slipped into leggings and a hooded sweatshirt. House shoes completed the ensemble. She made the twelve-step trek from her front door to Steve's and entered without knocking.

Steve hadn't risen from his recliner in the living room. "Top shelf of the fridge. Eat all you want. Max and I stuffed ourselves."

She looked down at the ball of black fur covering Steve's lap. "Did you let him eat off your plate again?"

His reply held more bark than bite. "I'll have you know I only let him lick the plate after he finished his half can of cat food. He and I have the same opinion of this diet you have him on."

"You shouldn't have given him anything." She closed her eyes and waited a few seconds. "Sorry. I had a lousy day."

"You're not the only one. Did you notice I wasn't here when you left this morning?"

She sat on the couch, which placed her within an arm's length of Steve. "I was in such a rush to get to work, and it was raining so hard, I wasn't paying attention. Where did you go?"

"Leo called me. He needed to talk."

Heather's stomach picked that moment to remind her she'd eaten nothing but half a bagel that morning. The gurgling growl caused Steve to chuckle. "You'd better feed that dinosaur living in your belly. Start with the salad and I'll heat the lasagna for you."

Heather brought her bowl of salad and a bottle of Italian dressing to the bar. She wasted no time before digging in while Steve retrieved a microwaveable plate and scooped a generous portion of lasagna on it. She spoke between bites. "Be sure to put the cover on that when you heat it. There's nothing worse than having sauce and cheese splattered all over the inside of your microwave."

Steve shook his head, but didn't reply to her motherly instructions. Instead, he said, "Leo called at four-thirty this morning. We met at the Denny's past the airport."

8

She looked up in time to see Steve pull a handkerchief from his back pocket and catch a sneeze. "You're not sick, are you?"

"Head cold from getting soaked. The driver dropped me off in what must have been a small stream. I'll be fine by tomorrow morning."

"What's up with Leo?" She took an oversize bite of salad.

"The big cat is away, and a rat took his place."

"Huh?"

Steve spent the next few minutes explaining the politics of police bureaucracies and how Leo fell victim to a power grab by an ambitious mid-level supervisor intent on making a name for himself.

Heather rose and went to the microwave that had beeped a full minute ago. She retrieved the steaming plate of food and set it on the bar to cool. "Sounds to me like the new lieutenant is cunning. It's going to look like he did two of them a favor. That leaves Leo playing the part of a malcontent."

Steve nodded. "I had to talk him out of turning in his badge. He sees the transfer as a one-way ticket to nowhere. I can't blame him. For the time being, I convinced him to try it."

"How did you do that?"

"I bribed him. Said I'd help him with his first case."

Heather's surprise at Steve's statement was matched by the surprise of blazing hot lasagne on her tongue. Not knowing whether to spit it out, or try to chew and swallow, she chose the former. One advantage of working with a blind man was that she didn't need to follow all the social graces.

"You didn't allow it to cool, did you?"

She spoke after she suppressed the burn with a drink of cold water. "Next time, don't heat it so long. And what's this about you working on a case without me?"

"I had to pull Leo off a ledge. He has six kids, with one starting college next fall. His last child surprised both of them so it'll be a while before they're all grown. There's no way he can lose the retirement he's earned. I knew the bullet train was your top priority, so I decided to help with the first case."

Heather sat down and spread the lasagna around her plate to let it cool. "I wish you'd talked to me about this before you agreed to help him."

"You're welcome to join us, but this project your father roped you into is already taking up every bit of your time and energy."

Heather mangled the lasagna a little more. "You're probably right. It's not like anyone's life is on the line like our last case."

"It'll surprise me if anything comes of the case. All Leo's going to do is scan and email me the material in the original case file. My computer will transcribe most of the information, but there may be some things Leo will need to read to me over the phone."

Heather dug into her supper and didn't lift her head until she'd downed half of it. "Want to hear about my crummy day?"

"Sure. Let's get all the bad news out of the way."

"The Texas Supreme Court ruled today that the consortium my company is a part of can't use eminent domain to force property owners to grant us a right of way for the bullet train."

"I thought you already purchased the rights of way."

"There are still some strong holdouts. If we can't talk them into selling at a reasonable price, or find a workable way around, the whole deal may be off."

"What are you going to do?"

Heather shook her head. "I've scheduled more video conferences for tomorrow morning with engineers and investors. We'll try to come up with alternative plans. The problem now is that everyone knows we're close to getting all the land. The court's ruling tells the holdouts they have us over a barrel."

Steve scratched his chin. "I'm surprised the federal government hasn't already stepped in and built a high-speed rail between all the major cities in Texas."

"They've talked about it, and the feds have the power to invoke eminent domain. I think it's only a matter of time before it happens. We were trying to get there first."

"Perhaps the holdouts need to look at it as something that's inevitable. They can receive a fair price now from a private corporation or get what the government thinks is market value later."

Heather snapped her fingers. "You may have missed your calling. Want to go to Mattherson County and negotiate the sale of land for a bullet train?"

Steve held up both hands as stop signs. "Haggling over prices is something I always left for Maggie to do. She knew how to bargain with people. It helped that we were poor, and it was a necessity."

"I wish I could have known her."

Steve's Adam's apple bobbed as he swallowed. "Yeah. Me, too."

Heather looked down as Max walked toward her. His back arched and his stomach convulsed. She slid off her chair, but not in time. Max deposited a healthy portion of partially digested lasagna and black fur on the carpet. She picked him up and moved him to the kitchen's tile floor, where any further mess would be easy to clean up.

While petting him, she said, "If you don't stay on your diet, you're going to a kitty fat farm. How would you like that?"

Max responded by hiking his back leg and giving his under-carriage a wash.

Steve handed her a full roll of paper towels. She looked up from the ample pile. "I thought you said you only let him lick your plate."

"There might have been a little of my supper left on it."

"A little? I don't think so."

Heather scraped up all she could and went for the dishwashing liquid to work on the stain. "Hopefully this is the last April Fool's joke for the evening."

"That reminds me. Jack called. He said you missed your date with him tonight."

Heather groaned. "Next year I'm staying in bed on the first day of April."

3

It surprised Heather when Steve said he'd accompany her to work. Most days, he and Max stayed home, doing whatever suited them. Steve would have coffee, spend a half hour on a treadmill, catch up on news, keep in touch with old friends, or surf the Internet. Now and then, he'd dictate or revise something in a story he was writing. In the afternoon, Steve and Max were likely to take naps. Steve, because the murder of his late wife still haunted him and long periods of sleep didn't come easily. Max, because he was a cat.

A further surprise came when Steve stood outside Heather's front door, waiting for her to walk out.

"Have you been out here long?"

"I heard a crash. Were you trying to balance your phone, coffee, a bagel, and your briefcase again?"

"At least I didn't drop the coffee or the bagel. I don't have time to clean up a mess."

"Hand me your briefcase. I can find the car on my own."

The ride to the office went without conversation. Steve had wireless ear buds inserted while Heather focused on her mental list of things to do. When they arrived precisely at 8:00 a.m., the receptionists' phones were abuzz with incoming calls. Once inside the outer office, Steve was on his own. He could navigate the maze of offices as well as she could. He took the time to speak to the cadre of receptionists and to accept their offer of a Danish and coffee.

Heather left him to be doted on and went straight to her office, where her administrative assistant waited for her. "Your father is on line one. He's been calling for the last thirty minutes."

"I know. He called my cell phone three times while I was driving. Any other fires I need to know about?"

"They can wait. I'll be at my desk when you're ready for a full rundown."

The red light on her phone blinked as if daring her to ignore it. She picked up the receiver and pressed the offending button. "Good morning, Father. How's the weather in Boston?"

"Never mind the weather. Why don't you get to work at a decent time? The day is half over."

Heather's eyes rolled back. "I'm fine, Father. Thank you for asking. As for the time, I arrive at my desk at eight o'clock sharp, just like you've done for the past forty-three years."

Her father grumbled something about her needing to arrange her schedule to fit his. She thought about asking him to petition God to change the shape of the world and the circling of the planets around the sun, but he interrupted her thoughts. "What's wrong with that state you're living in? Why did those idiots rule against eminent domain?"

She counted to three before the words forced their way out. "You surprise me. I thought you'd been around long enough to know there are always risks in taking bold moves."

"Sarcasm doesn't become you, Daughter. What are you going to do about this mess you've gotten us into?"

"If memory serves me, you came to me with the offer to invest. How is this suddenly my problem?"

"You agreed to be point man... er, woman. The boots on the ground."

"And my team secured over ninety-five percent of the rights of way. It was your attorneys who promised a positive result from the courts on eminent domain. Perhaps you should have talked to some politicians and attorneys in Texas instead of listening to your team of Ivy Leaguers."

"We wouldn't have this trouble if this was taking place in a normal state."

Instead of arguing, she changed the course of the conversation. "Let's look on the bright side. We're close to pulling this off. I'm having a video call with the investors later this morning and I plan on painting this as a minor setback. I've had the geologists and engineers go over the route for workable alternatives if we can't get the holdouts to sell. The biggest deal-breaker is in Mattherson County. Unless the geologists can find another way, the line has to go through there or we're back to square one."

Her father let out a deep breath, a sign the storm would soon be over. His tone changed. "You may be right about my lawyers. They didn't consider the obsession your locals have for individual property rights. This will take a personal touch. You'll have to go to Mattherson County and appeal to the owner's sense of acting for the common good."

"That's not much leverage."

"Then find more. You're the private investigator. Investigate."

Steve came through the door, giving her an excuse to end the conversation. "Need to go. Someone I have to talk to just walked in. Give my love to Mother. I'll keep you posted." She hung up and puffed out her cheeks.

Steve deposited his computer on his desk before he approached hers. "Dear old dad?"

"You guessed it. He took a big gamble on the train project and he expects me to make it work."

"Wasn't it you who said you wish your father trusted you to make good in business? This is your chance to show him what you're made of."

Heather looked at Steve as he stood unruffled by all that swirled around him. After a delayed response, she said, "You're right, and this calls for quick action. I'd like to hire you, Mr. Smiley. I need to find out what makes the land owners in Mattherson County tick. Something is keeping them from selling the land for the right of way, and we need to find out what it is."

"I'm committed to helping Leo, but I'll be free after that."

"How long will that take?"

Steve lifted his shoulders and let them fall. "He'll send me the first case as soon as he can. I'm expecting it today."

"Good. You should have it solved in a day or two. We can go to Mattherson County later in the week. In the meantime, I need to call Jack, grovel, and play a round of golf with him tomorrow. I may have to fit two dates into one day."

Steve shook his head. "You two certainly have a unique relationship."

Phone calls, meetings, a long video conference, and a steady stream of messages delivered from Heather's administrative assistant took up the rest of her morning. All the while, Steve sat at his desk with white ear buds inserted, waiting for Leo's call. The only sound he made was when he asked Heather what she wanted for lunch. She waved him off, but he ordered her a salad all the same.

Leo's call came as Steve took the first bite of a sandwich that smelled like heaven in a bun. Heather absentmindedly stabbed an assortment of vegetables as she reviewed a multi-page spreadsheet and listened to Steve speak to his former partner.

Once the three-minute conversation ended, she looked up. "Does it sound like an interesting case?"

"When they said cold case, they weren't kidding. It's a murder from 1942."

"You're joking."

"I'm not, but I think the lieutenant over Cold Cases is. Leo said it's how they initiate new members into the team. They pick an ancient case that nobody's been able to crack and give it to the new guy to solve. After the detective gives up, they put the case back in a cardboard box and move on to cases with a better chance of success."

Heather got back to work, and Steve finished his lunch. It wasn't long before he grumbled under his breath. After he issued a loud huff, she went to his desk and asked, "What's wrong?"

"You tell me. My computer can't put words to the documents Leo sent."

Heather looked down, took the mouse from him, and scrolled through the screens. "No wonder. These are handwritten notes in cursive, or copies of faded typed pages."

"Probably copies from carbon paper," said Steve. "I'll need to find someone to read them to me." He paused. "That could be dicey. These are still confidential police reports. I don't want Leo to get busted on his first day."

"You could hire an attorney to help you."

Steve shook his head. "This needs to be done on the downlow. Who do I know that has the time and is completely trustworthy?"

"I could do it."

"You don't have the time. You haven't even called Jack."

"Oh, snap. I'd better take care of that right now before I forget again."

Steve's cell phone came to life by announcing an incoming call from Bella Brumley. "Bella, what a surprise."

"I've been trying to call Heather. Do you know where she is?"

Heather slapped her forehead. "Bella. I'm so sorry. We're leaving the office now."

"No problem. Did you remember I'm staying with you?"

Heather crossed her fingers. "Of course. I told Max his favorite television personality was coming to see him."

Steve chimed in. "We should be there in less than thirty minutes."

"No rush. Can't wait to see you."

The call ended, and Steve reached down and grabbed his cane. "Anything you need to tell me?"

"Bella wanted to surprise you. She's in a big fishing tournament this weekend at Lake Conroe. She and her film crew flew in from Florida today."

"So, you not only forgot to tell me, you forgot about her coming."

"Guilty on all counts, Your Honor. Let's get out of here."

Steve spoke again as soon as the elevator doors closed behind them. "At least I'll have someone I trust to dictate everything that's in the report Leo sent."

"I thought you wanted me to do that."

"You'll be too busy groveling with Jack. Call him on the way to the airport."

4

Bella sat on her suitcase at the far end of passenger pickup, looking more beautiful than the last time Heather saw her. Long platinum-blond hair woven into a rope ponytail hung over her shoulder. She looked like a Nordic princess in stretch jeans, a football jersey and white canvas shoes. Heather wheeled against the curb and wondered how she'd ever forgive herself for forgetting the young woman who meant the world to Steve, and to her. She promised herself the next time her father called with a can't-miss business opportunity she'd decline.

Steve had his door open before Heather could put the Mercedes SUV in park. Bella's squeal bounced off the concrete and glass, causing heads to turn.

"Uncle Steve!"

It was an honorary title they'd settled on after Steve solved the murder of the man who'd kidnapped Bella when she was a child and raised her as his own. He was a big-game hunter who produced and starred in syndicated television shows. The world watched Bella grow from a gangly child to a world-class media personality. After his murder, she traded in her rifles and shotguns for fishing poles and now roamed the world with her film crew, catching and releasing finned creatures of every description.

Steve and Heather had also found Bella's birth parents and reunited the family two Christmases ago.

Bella enfolded Steve in her arms and kissed his cheek. She pulled away, but only a foot or so, took his hand and placed it squarely on her face. He used his sensitive touch to give him a visual picture.

"Have you grown another inch or two?"

She laughed like a schoolgirl. "Still at six-foot even. You must be shrinking."

"I wouldn't doubt it. I think my height is going to my belly."

"You look great. I bet you still have to use your cane to keep the women away from you."

Heather retrieved Bella's suitcase and rolled it to the back of the SUV while Steve and the closest thing to a daughter he'd ever have reunited. She stopped by the two who still stood on the curb holding hands. "I'm so sorry, Bella. I spoiled your surprise."

A hug and a few kind words told Heather she needn't worry about leaving Bella standing at the airport.

"Let's get out of this loading zone before we all get arrested."

Once inside the car, Steve asked, "Have you eaten?"

"I had a big breakfast at the hotel in Miami and bought some snacks at the airport. I'm good until supper." She paused. "Kate and I had supper together last night."

Heather wondered how Steve would react. Kate was the only woman he had shown any interest in since his beloved Maggie was killed. For now at least, Steve and Kate's relationship had cooled. Instead of pursuing an awkward discussion, he issued a huge grin and asked, "How does pizza sound?"

"Like old times. It's still my favorite meal." She poked her head between the two front seats. "Are you working on another murder case?"

"Funny you should mention that. If you're free this afternoon or tonight, I need to deputize you so you can help me. It's a cold case from 1942. My former partner, Leo, asked me to help him with it."

"Cool. We can talk and eat pizza and solve a murder. Just like we did when I lived with Heather."

Heather scoffed. "You stayed at Steve's most of the time. I grew tired of the same thing to eat every day."

"Are you helping with the cold case, too?"

Steve answered Bella's question. "Heather's tied up with a big deal that involves a bullet train between Houston and Dallas. No time for ancient crimes."

"It's a shame you two can't work together on the cold case. It sounds like Heather needs a break."

"I'll do something fun after I get the last few contracts for rights of way."

With everyone buckled in, they departed for the brief trip north to their condos.

Heather had to honk her horn to keep a woman talking on her cell phone from drifting further into her lane.

Bella spoke from the back seat. "I see the drivers around here didn't improve. It's not as bad in St. Thomas with Mom and Dad. They live on island time, which means nobody gets in a hurry."

"How are your parents?" asked Steve. "I sure enjoyed the Christmas I spent at their hotel."

"Yeah." Bella said wistfully. "That was a great holiday. They really wanted you to come back last year. But they're doing fine. Business is good. They worry about me because I travel so much, but they understand that's how I make my living."

"I listen to your fishing show and try to imagine what it's like in each location."

"One paradise after another. I'm working on an idea of having a handsome blind man come fishing with me. How does that sound?"

"I think it might be a hit if you find a young blind guy who looks really cool in sunglasses."

"I may have one, but he's not blind."

Heather jerked her head around. "Let me see your left hand."

Bella shot her long arm forward.

"No ring yet, Steve."

"That's a relief. I was feeling really old for a minute."

"Don't worry," said Bella. "I'm not ready for that kind of commitment. Besides, I'll want you to run a full background check on him before I make any sort of commitment."

"I'll do it."

Heather wondered if Bella was joking. She doubted Steve was.

STEVE WAITED UNTIL BELLA FINISHED READING EVERY SCRAP OF information in the case file before he commented. "Are you sure that's all?"

"I'm sure."

"It shouldn't surprise me." Steve shifted in the dining room chair. "In June 1942, World War II was in full swing. From what my grandfather told me, most of the able-bodied men had resigned from the police force and joined the fight. There weren't many detectives left. A patrol sergeant on the downhill side of his career investigated this murder."

Bella pushed her chair away from the table. "I need something to drink. Do you want another cup of coffee?"

"Not yet. Thanks anyway."

The refrigerator door opened. "Don't you have any soda?"

"Sorry. I would have stocked up if I knew you were coming. It's almost six. Let's order pizza and whatever soda you want."

"Do you still order from the same place?"

"Heather keeps coupons stuck to the side of the refrigerator with magnets."

Bella's laugh reminded Steve of tinkling bells at Christmas.

"That's what I like so much about Heather. She's worth a gazillion dollars, but is never wasteful."

"I don't know about the gazillion, but this deal she's working has more zeros than I can count. It's the most ambitious thing she's ever been involved in. She's worried."

"She'll get it done. I'm going to call in the pizza order. I'll get salad and breadsticks, too."

Steve didn't have time to respond before Bella was speaking instructions to her phone. After placing the order, she returned to the table. "Where do you start when solving an old murder case like this?"

"I'll start with the victim. His name was Rodney Wells. He was a second lieutenant in the army, an entry level rank for officers, so he'd not been in the service long. There was no separate air force back then, even though he was training to be a pilot. Since this is Leo's case, I'll call him tonight and we'll discuss things he needs to check on."

"Like what?"

"I noticed there weren't many newspaper articles about the murder. Someone shot him at the train station. There was only a brief obituary. Where is he buried? What about family? Where did he go to school? There's a chance he attended college since he was an officer. That's something else that will need to be checked. The reports you read said he wasn't married, and it didn't mention a fiancé. There might be a love angle to the killing if he had a steady girlfriend. Did he owe anyone money? There's always a reason for someone to kill. Find the reason and you're on your way to finding the killer.

But before you look for the killer, you find out as much as you can about the victim. That usually points you to the reason."

"But how will you find the reason when the guy's been dead so long?"

"There's a good chance I won't, but the graves of murdered people have a habit of making noises."

"That's spooky."

"Yeah. So is the thought of you getting serious about a young man. Tell me about him."

"He's back in St. Thomas. A little older than me, but not much."

"How much?"

"Seven years."

"What does he do?"

"He flies. Actually, he's the co-pilot on a plane that shuttles passengers to the surrounding islands."

"I may have to fly to St. Thomas and check him out."

"Really? That would be awesome."

"I said may. I never know when a new murder will pop up."

5

Heather saw light coming through the clear plastic of the kitty door between her condo and Steve's, an odd sight since he never turned on his lights unless he had company. She bent down, pushed open the flap, and hollered. "Is Bella with you?"

A gravelly voice answered, "What?"

Heather repeated the question.

"She's gone."

"Gone? When?"

"Come over. I'm not going to play twenty questions through a pet portal."

She let the flap slap shut and went to the door wearing a robe and house shoes. She grabbed the key to Steve's front door, which turned out to be unnecessary. Once inside, she found him leaned back in his recliner with his laptop on the table beside him. He didn't have on his sunglasses, which meant he'd been sleeping. "I thought you knew better than to leave your front door unlocked all night."

"I didn't. Bella left at 5:00. You didn't hear her get up and pack?"

"I was on a conference call to investors in Japan until nearly two, and dead to the world until ten minutes ago."

"She said for me to tell you thanks for the bed, and she'll catch up with you the next time."

Heather let out a huff.

Steve put on his sunglasses. "Don't blame her. You knew she was coming and didn't leave room in your schedule."

Even though she knew he was right and she should blame herself, that's not what came out of her mouth. "You could have at least hollered at me so I could tell her goodbye."

Steve grabbed the wooden handle on the side of his chair and jerked it upward, causing his feet to fall to the floor. He went to the kitchen. "You're not the only one who had a lousy night's sleep. I'm making coffee."

Heather grabbed his arm. "No, you're not. You take too long. We both need a good jolt to wake us up."

Steve settled on a bar stool and the next few minutes passed in silence as the extra-strong coffee filled the carafe. Neither spoke until they'd each downed half a cup. Heather led off. "Why did Bella leave so early?"

"She had to scout the lake with her crew. She needs to find where the fish hide and what bait to use. From what she said, that's just the beginning for a tournament. Then the camera guy and sound guys have to make notes on sunlight, backgrounds, angles, road noises, and a bunch of other things. It's a combination of art and science."

Heather raised the cup to her lips and mumbled. "I need to be kicked for not spending time with her."

"You could go to the weigh-in on Sunday afternoon and see her there."

"Can't. Another video conference with the company that's building the train engines and passenger cars. The cost estimates keep going up."

Steve shook his head but said nothing else.

Heather moved on. "You said you had a short night. Were you and Bella reminiscing?"

"She called it a night at nine. I got my days and nights mixed up and stayed on my computer until she came over this morning. She ate cold, left-over pizza for breakfast."

A shiver ran down Heather's back. "Yuk. How can she do that?"

"The same way you and I did in college."

"Point taken, but it turns my stomach now." She took another sip of coffee. "Back to the brief night. Why didn't you go to bed at a decent hour?"

"Besides being wound up by her visit, I wanted to start on Leo's cold case. It turns out there's a slight overlap between what you're working on and the cold case. On a hot summer night in 1942, Rodney Wells was gunned down as he got off the train in Houston. He grew up in Mattherson County."

"That is a coincidence. What else did you find out about him?"

"He'd just finished OCS and was visiting Houston before he went to pilot training school."

"Wait. What's OCS?"

"Officer Candidate School. He was a brand-new second lieutenant with a single yellow bar on his collar."

"Why was he in Houston?"

"That's a mystery at this point. He graduated from Mattherson High School in 1940. He used the time before the war to get in a few semesters at a junior college and worked at a small airfield in Mattherson. The army couldn't wait to get him in a uniform. From what I've learned so far, Rodney was quite the all-American, small-town boy."

"Did you get all this from the obituary from Mattherson's newspaper?"

"Some of it, but the obit from Houston's newspaper was more complete."

27

"That's odd."

Steve nodded. "It has me scratching my head as to why the Mattherson paper didn't play up the murder as much as Houston did. Only a small article with no picture. The *Chronicle* listed all the usual stuff and gave a list of surviving family members. I showed the article to Bella this morning. She said they had a photo of Lieutenant Wells in uniform."

"How did she describe him?"

"A hunk. Then she said he looked like a leading man in a black and white movie. Tall, dark, handsome and a glint of adventure in his eyes."

"I'd look for a woman. I can imagine a curvy blond falling hard for someone like that."

"The local paper listed no wife or fiancé in the obituary, or the write-up. Neither did the *Chronicle* or *Post*."

Heather went to fill her coffee mug and took Steve's with her. She poured as she spoke. "Tell me about the crime. Did anything stand out?"

"This is all from the handwritten notes from the cop in charge of the case. Rodney Wells's trip originated in Mattherson."

Heather interrupted. "That makes sense. There used to be a thirty-mile spur line that connected Mattherson to the main line."

"The official report said witnesses gave conflicting reports about who shot him. Some said a man, some said a woman. There were reports of German accents and one woman claimed she heard someone speaking Japanese. It was pouring rain, which didn't help things. The only reports that weren't disputed were that he fell down dead on the platform after getting off the train and that a .32 slug pierced his heart." Steve snapped his fingers. "One more thing. No one heard a shot, but two people remembered hearing a noise, covered by a loud cough."

Heather delivered the coffee. "Sounds like someone used something to silence the shot and covered the muffled crack with the cough."

"That's what I thought. We have to remember how noisy and crowded train stations were back then. Add the rain, the whoops of joy when people saw a relative or lover, and you have a recipe for chaos."

Heather looked at her watch. "I need to get going if I'm going to make it to the office on time."

Steve picked up his mug. "I thought you were the boss."

"That means I have to set a good example." She went to the sink and rinsed her cup. "What are you doing today?"

"I'll feed Max, take a long nap to make up for last night, and call Leo. He should know at least as much as I do about the case by the time I wake up."

Heather dried the cup and put it back in the cabinet. "Let me know if you want to go to Mattherson to poke around. I'll be going Saturday to talk to the property owner that's giving us such a hard time."

"This is Leo's case. I'm supposed to write a short story."

Heather was almost to the front door but stopped and turned on a heel. "Who told you to write a short story?"

"Kate."

"You talked to her?"

"She sent a message through Bella when they had dinner the day before yesterday." Steve lowered his voice. "Heather."

"Yes?"

"No matchmaking. I know you and Bella have been keeping in touch with Kate, and keeping her informed of the trouble I've had in finding a writing coach I can work with. My relationship with Kate will involve long distance help with my writing and nothing more."

Heather cleared her throat, walked into the cool spring morning, and grinned.

6

It was five-thirty in the afternoon when Steve arrived at the dive where Leo said to meet him. It smelled of old grease and spilled beer. The Uber driver received the fare, a generous tip, and left after giving Steve a pat on the back as he held the door open for him.

"Steve. You made it." The voice belonged to Leo, but it came with a slur. "Come on, buddy. Let me introduce you to the other cold cuts." He placed Steve's arm on his, walked him across a concrete floor, and delivered him to a table.

Leo gave first names only as Steve nodded greetings and occupied his hands with folding his cane.

"That's pretty slick how that cane folds," said a man named Sam.

Steve gave his head a slight nod. "It's like that credit card they advertise on television. I don't leave home without it."

Laughter came from four men.

Sam said, "We all remember you from when you were in Homicide. You were something else. The best of the best, but you didn't take the promotions offered after detective."

"I didn't want to become a professional paper shuffler. I take it this is a welcome party for Leo."

Another voice said, "Yep. He's now a part of the unloved and unwanted."

"That's why we call ourselves cold cuts. We work cold cases and they cut us out of the herd."

Steve nodded. "Clever."

"I poured a beer for you," said Leo. "It's at two o'clock high."

That earned a few chuckles from the group.

Steve found the mug and took a sip. Other smells overrode the beer to the point it tasted stale and dirty, but this party was for Leo. He'd pretend to enjoy it, even though he had no intention of leaving the glass empty.

What followed was an hour of office gossip, crude jokes, voices that increased in volume, and multiple pitchers of beer. Finally, Sam said, "That's all for me, boys. I'll leave it to the rest of you to help Leo with his case."

That comment brought about rough laughter from everyone, including Leo.

"What's the joke?" asked Steve.

A slurred voice said, "If you ever worked a cold case, you'd know. They don't call 'em cold for nothing. We don't get them until Homicide gives up. That means they chased down every lead. If a new lead or fresh evidence shows up, and the case is within ten years old, we're supposed to back off and let Homicide handle it. The brass wants their closure rate to be as high as possible. The department cuts us a lot of slack with closure rate."

Another voice said, "Yeah. A lot of slack."

Steve played along. "Give me an idea of how you'd go about solving a real old case; one sixty or seventy years old."

All laughed except Leo. "Like the one Leo is working on?"

Another voice said, "Perfect example. A soldier in the big war gets off a train down at the station. Someone pops him.

Every witness has a different story. A motorcycle cop makes some notes, and that's it. End of a life. End of story."

Steve nodded. "I see what you mean. Any witnesses would likely be dead."

Leo took his turn. "They gave everyone here this case when they came to the department's version of purgatory. No one ever got past first base."

"It's good training for Leo," said the man sitting directly across from Steve. "All we do is push papers around our desk, make a few phone calls, scribble a few notes and leave the office after putting in eight hours."

Leo explained. "No overtime allowed."

"Sounds like a cushy job," said Steve.

The most slurred of the voices said, "It's a soul-stealing waste of time. I'd like to see the name of a certain homicide lieutenant on the label of a cold case file some day." Murmurs of agreement followed from most at the table.

The term *soul-stealing* stuck in Steve's mind. He hated to see Leo trapped in a dead-end job, not to mention these once-motivated men soaking in self-pity and beer. Something needed to be done, but what? Steve leaned forward. "What would happen if you started solving cases?"

The one that sounded the most sober of the group spoke up. "Now and then we do. If it's a homicide, we get chewed out for not sending it on to what our lieutenant calls the real detectives."

"Why would he say that?"

"You'd have to know him to understand."

"He knows him," said Leo. "Jim Bounds."

"Ah. That explains it." Some men stuck in Steve's mind like chewing gum to the bottom of his shoe on a hot day. Bounds had large biceps and white teeth that he'd gladly use to either impress or intimidate. When Steve knew him, he was on the fast track to promotion. He wondered what Bounds did to derail his career.

The answer to the unspoken question came from the least inebriated of the group. "Bounds gave a female suspect a very thorough pat-down search at the scene of a wife-on-husband homicide. It turns out the woman he groped wasn't the wife, but the wife's attorney who called it in. If there'd been video, they would have canned him. As it was, they gave him an unpaid vacation, transferred him to Cold Cases and told him if they heard a peep out of him, he'd be gone. He took it to heart. In at eight and out the door at five. He likes it when we work on missing persons cases and not homicides. Keeps his door and the blinds on his office closed all day."

The mood had soured with talk of Jim Bounds. Chairs slid back and, en mass, the men left after wishing Steve and Leo a good night. In their wake, they left a cloud of despair.

"Now do you understand?" asked Leo.

"Yeah. You got a bum deal. So, what are you going to do about it?"

"There's nothing I can do."

Steve swiveled to face his long-time friend. "Bull. There's always something you can do. I know what you can do tonight."

"What's that?"

"Put down that nasty-tasting beer and act like the man I know you to be."

Leo slammed what sounded like his fist down on the table.

The next voice came from across the room. "Next time you do that, you're out of here."

Steve stood. "Come on. I'll call and get us a ride."

"Go ahead. I'm staying here."

It was time to change tactics, but dealing with a drunk, depressed cop wasn't the easiest thing to do. Steve played his ace in the hole. "If you don't leave with me, I'm calling Cariana. I'll tell her where you are and what you're doing."

"You wouldn't dare."

Steve chuckled. "Now that I have your attention, let's go somewhere that doesn't smell like the morning after a fraternity party and get something to eat."

The two men stood in the parking lot, waiting for the Uber driver. Steve turned to Leo. "I've been working on the case."

"What case?"

"The Rodney Wells murder case. Haven't you even looked at it?"

"Of course I did, and it didn't take long. Do you know how many people have handled that file? They all agree this is one where the killer got away."

"All the more reason for us to solve it."

"Impossible."

"Improbable, but not impossible. I'll bet you we find something tonight that no one else has discovered."

"What are you up to?"

"Trying to put a little hope back in you. Let's go to the original crime scene before we eat. Walking around will do you good."

"The train station?"

"Yeah. There's something I need your help with."

Leo let out a genuine laugh. "Is this déjà vu or that nasty beer that has me thinking we're really investigating a murder again? Let me get the file out of my car. I brought it with me, just in case."

The Uber driver took them to the train station. Leo flashed his badge and told the attendant he and Steve needed to go to the platform. When they arrived, Steve said, "Bella told me there was a diagram of where the body fell. Do you remember looking at it?"

"I have the file with me. There's a hand-drawn diagram and black and white photos. Wait. Did you say Bella Brumley described the diagram to you?"

"Yeah, but don't put that in your notes." He took a breath. "Look around. The tracks and the landing should still be the same as what they were in 1942. Get me close to where Rodney Wells fell to the ground."

"Nothing looks the same, but I'm guessing the opening in the center of the terminal is in the same place as it was. Let's go to the left."

Leo led him as Steve's cane swept an arc in front of him. "It should be right about here."

"Good," said Steve. "Now say Rodney Wells."

Leo did and Steve said, "I see red. I was hoping I wouldn't, at least not here."

Long ago, Steve realized he got the impression of the color red when he came to the scene of a murder and heard the victim's name. Bright red marked the place where the murder occurred. A clinical psychologist confirmed this ability and supplied the fancy name of associative chromesthesia to it.

Steve started walking parallel to the tracks. Leo caught up with him. "What are you doing?"

"Making sure that's where Wells died." He took another twenty steps and stopped. "Say his name again."

Leo did, and Steve shook his head. "Nothing here. Take me back to the spot."

After backtracking, Leo told Steve they'd arrived.

"Now walk me to the edge of the tracks slowly. Speak his name as we go."

"It's a good thing I'm still a little loopy. People are staring."

"Let them stare. We're almost finished. Say his name and walk slowly."

Step followed step, with Steve taking his time and Leo speaking the name of the dead man until the tip of Steve's cane dropped off the concrete.

"I think I understand what happened. Rodney Wells rode the spur line from Mattherson to where it joined the main line from Dallas to Houston. He stepped off the train and someone put a pistol to his back, fired the shot, and the assailant disappeared into the crowd. Rodney took a few steps forward, fell, and died."

"That sounds about right," said Leo. "That still doesn't tell us who shot him."

"No, but let's keep thinking about it. Was the shooter waiting here, or had he been on the train with Lt. Wells all the way from Mattherson?"

"He could have gotten on the train anywhere along the line."

"True," said Steve, "but he must have known Rodney, or at least had a good description of him."

Leo cleared his throat. "I have to admit this took away the beer-buzz, but I can't put you're seeing red in a report. I need hard evidence or we're at a dead end."

"You have a place to start."

"Are you serious? Do you think there's still records of the passengers on a train during World War II? Even if I find names, they're all dead."

Steve shook his head. "You're not getting it. The job of a homicide detective is to find out who killed someone. It doesn't matter if the assailant is alive or dead. It's about following the leads until there are none, and then searching for more."

"I thought it was about seeing justice done."

"Keep it simple. You're a detective. Start doing what you're paid to do. Take the thread of information you have and pull it until it either breaks or the whole thing unravels and you find the killer."

Steve added one more thing. "I don't know about you, but I could use a chicken-fried steak with lots of gravy."

"I'm all in on supper, but you haven't sold me on pursuing this case with much enthusiasm. I'll give it a few days. If nothing new turns up, I'll be looking for something else to do with my life."

"Make it a couple of weeks, and you can't count the weekend."

Leo laughed. "I feel like I'm buying a used car."

Steve pulled out his phone and told it to call Heather. She answered on the third ring. "What are you doing in Houston?"

"I'm with Leo. We're going to dinner. I left Max plenty of food, so don't let him con you into giving him more."

"Thanks for taking care of him. I'm still at the office."

Steve rubbed his palm against his cheek. "How did you know I was in Houston?"

"Bella put an app on our phones that lets the three of us track each other. She didn't tell you?"

"That little scamp. I wonder what else she did to it."

"She changed my ring tone to reggae music." Heather paused. "Was there something you needed?"

"I'm coming with you to Mattherson if the offer is still open."

"I'm leaving Saturday morning. Is that good with you?"

"I'll be packed and ready to go."

7

Heather yawned and glanced to her right. When would she learn that her body and mind needed more than four hours of sleep? Steve had his suitcase packed and waiting by his front door on this cool Saturday morning. He even had a travel mug of coffee waiting for her. She'd remained silent until the caffeine brought her brain and tongue to life. "Tell me about your boys' night out with Leo."

"We went to the train station and discovered a trail of blood leading from a train to the spot where Rodney Wells died."

This matter-of-fact declaration caused Heather's head and her Mercedes SUV to jerk to the right. She pulled back into her lane at the sound of a blaring horn.

Steve cleared his throat. "It's best to drive in one lane at a time."

"It's too early for sarcasm."

"You should have known better than to stay out so late with Jack."

She lowered her voice. "I wish I'd been with Jack instead of on another teleconference."

She needed to change the conversation before she said

something she'd regret. Steve had thrown her a curve ball with talk of a murder that didn't include her. "Did you and Leo make any progress on the murder case?"

"I saw red on the platform leading to the tracks."

"You could still tell after all this time?"

"Yeah. Kind of spooky, huh? I guess as long as I know the victim's name, I can tell the spot. We determined someone shot Rodney Wells on the train or when he stepped off."

"Wells? The Wells Mansion is the name of the B&B we're staying at tonight. The hotels looked sketchy and had critical reviews, so I booked us rooms in what looks like an antebellum mansion."

Steve responded with a grunt, followed by silence.

Heather used the time to give thought to how the week had passed. It was all a blur of getting up before dawn, fielding phone calls, emails, texts, and video conferences with long-winded, demanding investors. Chief among the time-stealers was her father. A massive wave of guilt and regret washed over her as she thought about how the frenetic activity had pushed Jack so far into the background that she wouldn't blame him if he traded her in on a Labrador retriever.

The miles passed and Heather's mind vacillated between thinking about how she would pull off the land deals and hating herself for agreeing to spearhead the project. She came back to the present when Steve turned to face her, and asked, "What time can we check in?"

"Three o'clock."

"We should be there well before noon. What are we going to do all afternoon?"

"Lunch, and I have a meeting at 1:30." It then dawned on Heather that she'd not taken Steve into consideration when she made the appointment.

Steve spoke into his phone before she could formulate a plan. "Search library hours for Mattherson, Texas."

The voice came back and informed them the public library would be open from 9:00 a.m. until 6:00 p.m. weekdays and 9:00 a.m. until 4 p.m. on Saturday, and 1 p.m until 4 p.m. on Sunday. That answered the question of what he would do this afternoon.

One thing about Steve that she admired was his ability to let things roll off of him. She sometimes wished he'd blow up at her, but the stoic streak in him prevailed. Also, he cared deeply for certain people and Heather counted herself lucky to be near the top of that list. He showed this by asking, "Who is your appointment with?"

"A woman named Belinda Mattherson and her husband, Johnny. They're the holdouts. From the little research I've done, she's the sixth or seventh generation of the man that founded Mattherson. They named the town and county after him."

"And her husband?"

"He's an attorney."

Steve shook his head. "No wonder the price of land keeps going up."

"True, but there's something he doesn't know. My geologists and engineers gave me a supplemental report. There's a tract of property next to the Mattherson land that could work as an alternative route. It's owned by a couple named Craig and Mindi Palmer. The Palmer name is also big in Mattherson county."

"Old money?"

"Old by Texas standards, about five generations. I've set up an interview with them tomorrow afternoon at their home."

The miles clicked by before they turned off the interstate and headed west to complete their final thirty-mile journey to the city of Mattherson. Heather pulled into the parking lot of a convenience store and used her phone to locate a restaurant. The only one that earned four stars or more sat halfway down the block on the town square, directly across the street from the front door of the county courthouse. She'd noticed the town boasted a population of nine-thousand, but she wondered now if some creative counting included dogs, cats, and chickens.

She circled around the limestone courthouse, looking for a parking spot and taking in the town's vibe. "There's at least four buildings on the town square that are looking for tenants. I wonder what keeps this place going?"

As usual, Steve had the answer. "They still produce a little oil. There's also cattle ranching, lumber, and a couple of prison units within driving distance that employ a fair number of people. Many of the ranchers and farmers supplement their income by leasing their land to hunters. There's a nice lake out west of town that's being developed."

"Here's a spot to park," said Heather as she waited for a tan half-ton pickup to back away from the curb.

The 1960s sign on the front of the restaurant read *Trudy's Cafe*. A subtext read *Best Pancakes in Texas*. Heather wondered about the veracity of the claim. Are there official pancake judges in Texas? She wouldn't be surprised if there were.

After being seated and looking over a menu, Heather ignored the claim to best pancakes and played it safe with a chef's salad. Steve behaved himself and ordered a hamburger, which came with enough fries to share with her.

The first major snag of the day occurred when Heather asked the server named Traci for directions to the public library.

The woman, not yet twenty, had a substantial baby bump and answered with a confident, country voice. "It's a block off the square on Pecan Avenue, but I don't think it's open today. Miss Velma's not over her surgery yet, Miss Ruby's twins came down with chicken pox, and the three ladies that volunteer went to Dallas for some sort of four-day prayer and fasting conference."

The server left, and Steve took a sip from his glass of water.

"If you can find me a park bench to sit on, I'll be fine until you finish your meeting." Distant thunder rolled. "Or I could wait in the car for you."

"Nonsense," said Heather. "You're coming with me into the meeting. I'd be interested in your impression of the attorney and his wife. I'm looking for some sort of leverage I can use to convince them to sell at a fair price."

Before they left, Heather got directions to their B&B and left a generous tip for Traci. It turned out that Belinda Mattherson's real estate office was two doors down from the cafe.

She and Steve stepped inside the real estate office as a streak of lightning and the accompanying crack of thunder caused the receptionist to let out a squeal. A more mature, bespectacled woman looked over the top of her glasses and her computer screen. Her gaze of chastisement focused on the young woman who'd squealed before she turned to Heather. "May I help you?"

"Heather McBlythe to see Mr. and Mrs. Mattherson. This is my business partner, Mr. Smiley."

"They're expecting you. I'll need to make sure there's another chair for Mr. Smiley."

The ice in the woman's voice extended beyond that shown to her co-worker. She had an ample supply of chill to go around.

While they waited, Heather noted the office staff of two appeared busy with stacks of files on their desks. She wondered if this was a ruse to make the office appear more prosperous than it really was. Surely in this small county there wasn't a real estate boom.

The woman reappeared from down a long hallway. "Please follow me."

Heather led Steve to a spacious office that bristled with photos of the woman behind the desk at various civic events and ribbon cuttings. She focused not on these, but on a much larger collection of framed photos of two young men. One bore a striking resemblance to the woman before her with raven hair and eyes that looked like black buttons. The second young man with his common features looked like a younger version of the man who sat on a leather couch against a far wall. If they were Belinda's children, it would seem she favored the dark-haired boy. His photos outnumbered the other boy by three to one.

The man rose from the couch and came with hand extended. "I'm Johnny Mattherson." He waved a hand at the woman who hadn't risen from her executive chair. "This is my wife, Belinda. It's nice to meet you, Ms. McBlythe. Who have you brought with you?"

The wife broke in before Heather could respond. "For heaven's sake, Johnny. Drop the formality." She rounded the desk, shook Heather's hand, and held on. "I insist you call us Belinda and Johnny, and we'll call you Heather."

Steve held up his hand. "And Steve."

"Of course, Steve. We weren't expecting you, but like I always say, the more the merrier."

She issued a laugh that no one joined her in. "Why don't you and Steve have a seat on the couch? Johnny will move chairs over for us."

While Johnny hurried to do his wife's bidding, Heather took the time to inspect the couple. Belinda wore wedge shoes which lifted her a couple of inches past five-eight or so. The conservative business suit was one Heather recognized as coming from Macy's. Judging from the photos of the two grown children, Heather believed Belinda's age to be mid-to-late forties. The absence of laugh lines around the eyes testified to the work of a skilled plastic surgeon.

"I couldn't help but notice your family photos. Is your eldest in college?"

"Yes, those are our boys. Both are in college. Ryan, the dark-haired one, is the eldest and is finishing his second year of law

43

school at U.T. Brian is a freshman, going to college at the University of Houston." Pride seemed to ooze from the pronouncement of Ryan's name and educational status. Not so much with the youngest.

"You must be very proud of both of them," said Steve.

Belinda folded her hands in her lap. "I'm sure Ryan will carry on the Mattherson tradition of excellence."

Heather took the occasion to watch for Johnny's reaction to the slight to the youngest son. She also noticed Belinda used the singular "I" instead of including her husband in her prophecy of the eldest son's future.

Johnny remained unfazed, possibly because his gaze ran up and down Heather's form, stopping to linger at key points of interest. He even parted his lips and ran his tongue over his top lip. Her scowl did nothing to cause his eyes to avert. This would be an interesting negotiation.

8

To Heather's surprise, Steve kept the conversation going. "Johnny, I understand the town and county bear the name of your relative, Clovis Mattherson."

"You're misinformed," said Belinda. "I'm the direct descendant of Clovis, not Johnny."

"My mistake," said Steve.

Belinda flipped aside the apology. "Clovis Mattherson was a true pioneer who came from Tennessee when most of Tejas, that's what they called Texas back then, needed men like him. He formed a militia to protect the settlers from Indians and built a crude fort where the courthouse now stands. The Mexicans claimed the land but did nothing to tame it. He took up the cause of liberty and fought Santa Anna at the Battle of San Jacinto. His bravery helped to win independence for the Republic of Texas."

Johnny spoke up. "It also earned him a large land grant."

Belinda didn't appear pleased that Johnny had interrupted her, and launched into the history lesson again. "Clovis's son, Cyrus, solidified the land holdings and expanded them by a few thousand acres. The next generation produced Percivale

Mattherson, the first to go to college and study law. He later became the first judge in Mattherson County. The Matthersons set the mark for civic, social, and spiritual leadership."

Steve nodded in a way that communicated he understood and appreciated the contributions the family had made. "The town must be full of Mattherson descendants."

It was Johnny's turn to speak. "Not as many as you'd think. Belinda's patriarchs believed in the English way of passing down lands. The eldest son would inherit the estate and had a solemn obligation to keep the land intact. This resulted in most of the siblings moving away to seek their fame and fortune."

Belinda's voice took on a tone of wistful regret. "As times changed, especially during hard times, some would give or sell off the less desirable plots of land as they saw fit. The Civil War and the Great Depression diminished the family landholdings, as did some poor investments through the years."

Belinda lifted her chin. "Now, I'm in charge of what's left. As the leading real estate broker in the county, I'm tasked with insuring that the Mattherson name lives on." Her tone moderated. "Johnny, of course, plays an instrumental part in all transactions."

It became clear to Heather that it would be Belinda deciding all things related to the land deal. That suited her fine. The lip-licking husband would do as told. It was time to get down to business.

"I've come with an enhanced proposal for you to consider." Heather took it out of her satchel and handed it to Belinda. "It's a more generous offer than the first, and I've added an addendum that you might find interesting. I can leave it with you or we can discuss it now, if you'd prefer."

Belinda handed the documents to her husband in a way that made an observer think the pages might soil her hands. "I have two homes to show this afternoon and I don't want my mind cluttered with something I'm really not interested in."

"I hope you'll look at the addendum before you make a final decision."

Johnny turned to the last pages and moved his finger across the page as he read.

Steve launched into what Heather thought was small talk about the Mattherson family history. "Belinda, do you remember hearing talk about a soldier named Rodney Wells? He was killed in Houston during World War II?"

"No." The two-letter word came out too fast.

Steve remained placid as a lake on a windless day. "It was a wild shot that you'd know anything. That was way before either of you were born and he wasn't a Mattherson. It's so far in the past, I guess it no longer matters. Forget I mentioned it."

"Then why did you?"

Steve leaned back in a more relaxed position. "A friend of mine is a Houston homicide detective. He's assigned to reopen the case and see what he can do with it. Heather booked rooms for us at the Wells Mansion and we were wondering if the current owners were kin to this man. I wouldn't have mentioned it, but the last name made me wonder."

Belinda stuttered. Steve quickly added, "I was going to the library to see what I could discover instead of coming here, but I understand it's closed today." He flipped his wrist to show it was no big deal to him.

Heather added, "Yes, that's why Steve came in with me. I meant to drop him off, but..."

Belinda stiffened. "Closed? Are you sure?" Displeasure seasoned the words.

"Something about illnesses among the workers and some sort of four-day conference involving the three volunteers."

It was soft, but Heather thought Belinda used the term "Holy Rollers" to describe the volunteers.

By this time, Johnny had digested enough of the addendum to get the gist of it. "You need to read this, Belinda. If you refuse, they're making plans to sell the plots of land they've already acquired to Amtrak."

Belinda waved off the information like it might be a gnat. "The Texas Supreme Court made their ruling. They can sell to anyone they want to, but no one can force me to sell my land."

Johnny shook his head. "You don't understand. The project would be under federal jurisdiction, which would render the finding in State Court moot. They could use eminent domain to force you to sell."

"Over my dead body," shot back Belinda.

Heather put on her best poker face. "It needn't come to that. It's the desire of all my partners and investors to make this a privately owned and operated railroad. We've already made a fair offer and you now have one that we consider more than generous."

Belinda jerked the document from Johnny's hand and threw it on the floor. "This isn't an offer, it's extortion. You'll rue the day you tangled with a Mattherson."

Heather rose, as did Steve. "We'll be in town through tomorrow. It's my desire to keep the negotiations going until we come to an agreement that is mutually beneficial." She took Steve by the arm and led him out of the office and into the rain-scrubbed streets.

Neither talked until they reached Heather's SUV and their seat belts clicked. Steve chuckled. "You sure put her knickers in a knot."

"She deserved it, and so does her husband."

"Why him?"

"I've seen feral cats with more morals than that guy. He's the type of man that makes wives lay awake at night wondering if they should find a recipe that includes rat poison."

Steve responded by squirming in his seat, which caused Heather to laugh out loud. When she gained partial control she said, "To top it off, he's a pudgy guy the same height as me with a bald spot on the crown of his head that looks like the landing pad for a yarmulke."

It was Steve's turn to roar with laughter.

Heather glanced at the clock on the dashboard. It was good to laugh. Life and work needed to be put into perspective. "We still have an hour before we can check in. How does an ice cream cone sound?"

"Perfect. I'll have mine in a cup with hot fudge, little bits of peanuts, whipped cream, and a cherry on top."

On the way to the Dairy Queen, Steve spoke in an even tone. "Belinda lied about not knowing anything about Rodney Wells's murder. The stories in the Houston newspapers were much more complete than what I found in the local newspaper. It wasn't well-reported here in town, but it's hard to believe anyone who grew up here wouldn't have heard that story at some time or the other."

"It sounds to me like the Matthersons run the town. I wonder if they had someone spike the story, or at least edit it with scissors."

Steve had a habit of rolling his fingers on his right hand against his thigh or on a tabletop while he processed information. He ended the deep thought by saying, "Small towns can have big secrets."

It was one of those throwaway lines from Steve that stuck in Heather's brain. She'd come to this backwater town halfway between two bustling cities, hoping to check off one of the few remaining properties on her list. Steve came to help an old friend keep his career alive. On the surface, the only thing the two had in common was the railroad. She wondered if the tracks headed in opposite directions or if they might join at some point. She also wondered why Belinda Mattherson lied about knowing about the young soldier.

"Steve. Do you think Leo's case has anything to do with my trying to put together this railroad deal?"

He shook his head. "I don't see how it could, but I'm not fond of coincidences. Let's hope we have a talkative host at the B&B."

The Dairy Queen came into view and another thought pushed its way to the front of Heather's mind. Jack. "I'll go in with you and get your hot fudge Sunday, but I need to call Jack."

"Drop me at the front door. I can take it from there."

She turned off the SUV but didn't reach for the door handle. Steve must have sensed she wanted to talk because he didn't open his door.

"Why do I ignore Jack when I'm at home, but call him as soon as I leave town?"

Steve took in a deep breath and let it out. "A man Leo works with remembered me when I had my sight and I was working day and night in Homicide. He said I was the best detective in the department. He meant it as a compliment."

"I don't get it. That's high praise from a fellow cop."

Steve shook his head. "All I could think of was the number of hours I could have spent with Maggie but didn't because I was working."

He popped open the door and found his way to the front door. Heather swallowed a lump and reached for her phone.

9

Heather told her phone to call Jack and waited until the recorded sound of his voice gave instructions to leave a message. The apology she'd rehearsed needed to be said to him, not a machine, so she told her phone to call his office. As expected, his mother, the office manager and receptionist, answered.

"I'm sorry, Heather. Jack's not in the office this week. I thought you knew."

"Uh... no. Things have been so busy, we forgot to sync our calendars."

"He'll be back in on Thursday."

Heather's stomach made a gurgling sound, a sure sign of how regret affected her. She covered a burp. "I tried to get him on his cell phone, but it went to a recording. I'll try later."

"You won't have any luck. He's on a five-day Caribbean cruise."

Stomach gasses worked overtime. "Oh. Well. I won't bother you any longer. I'll catch him when he returns."

It wasn't the most awkward conversation she'd ever had, but it ranked in the top five. Now, her imagination took off like a banshee. Had Jack dumped her completely? She manipulated her phone to the calendar and checked to see if she'd posted anything about him taking a cruise. Nothing. The thought of him going by himself made little sense. Her mind considered a likely scenario. "He's frolicking in the blue waters of the Caribbean with some chesty blond. It serves me right."

She noticed her left hand had a death grip on the steering wheel. Releasing it, she grabbed the latch and threw open the door. Metal screeched and groaned as the door reached its full extension and kept going. Beside her, a rust-dappled Pontiac Sunbird almost stopped in time. The brakes may not have been the best on the car, but the horn worked fine.

After backing up and moving to the next parking spot over, a burley man wearing a stained white T-shirt climbed out. He wasn't smiling.

"I'm so sorry. I'll be glad to pay for any damages."

He examined the front of his car. "Ain't that bad. A salvage headlight lens will cost less than a hundred dollars. They're easy to replace." He looked at the door of her Mercedes. "I'd hate to see the repair bill on this. You're talking about multiple thousands. The hinges are bent and sprung and there's damage to the front quarter-panel. At least the glass didn't break. Let's see if the door will close."

It wouldn't, but he said, "I can get it closed, if you want me to. It won't be pretty and you'll have wind noise, but it'll get you where you need to go."

Heather threw up her hands. "Do whatever you need to make it where I can drive."

She followed him to the trunk of his car. Inside, it looked like an over-sized pack rat had cleaned out an abandoned shed. After shifting through the debris, he came out with two small wooden blocks cut from a two-by-four. He took them to her car, placed them in the door jamb near the sprung hinges and put his considerable weight against the door. Metal groaned. He opened the door fully, and the blocks fell to the ground. He again closed the door and this time, it latched.

"That's amazing. You're a lifesaver."

The man smiled. "Just a county boy who had a similar experience as a teen. I was in a hurry, backing through the woods. A tree was in my blind spot. Bent my door back worse than this one. My pa fixed it the same way. That old truck wasn't worth fixin' proper."

Heather opened the door and grabbed her purse. She took out three one-hundred-dollar bills and handed them to the man. He shook his head and held out his palm as a stop sign. "That's way too much, Ma'am. All I'd feel right takin' would be a hundred for my headlight."

"I insist. One hundred for your headlight and two hundred for labor."

"I'll meet you in the middle. Two hundred for everything."

"And twenty for the meal I've kept you from ordering."

The man gave a toothy smile. "You drive a hard bargain."

By the time Heather came inside, Steve had finished his mid-afternoon treat. She sat down without ordering.

"I sure hope the rest of this trip is better than how it's started out."

"What's wrong? No Jack?"

"I managed to get into a fender-bender while sitting in a parking lot."

Steve's eyebrows rose. "That's a good trick. How did you manage that?"

Heather related the incident to him. "Goes to show I need to get my head in the game."

Steve tilted his head. "Have some ice cream. It helps everything."

"Not today. My stomach went into acid overdrive."

Steve pushed his empty cup into the middle of the table. "Nothing like a fender-bender to ruin your day."

Heather sighed. "If only that was all. I tried to call Jack. He's on a five-day cruise that I knew nothing about. I'm having visions of him snorkeling with someone who looks like the cover girl on the *Sports Illustrated* swimsuit edition."

"He probably is." The words didn't have a speck of sympathy in them.

Heather stared at him. "That's not the most encouraging thing you've ever told me."

Steve shrugged. "Considering our proximity to Galveston, he's probably on one of the short cruises that leave from there. Have you ever been on one of those?"

"Can't say that I have."

"They go to Mexico, usually Cancun, Cozumel, Honduras, places like that. The cruise lines hook you into planning excursions. If Jack is snorkeling, he's doing it alongside fifty other people from the ship."

"All it takes is one."

"You're underestimating Jack again."

"How do you know?"

Steve ignored the question.

Heather looked up as a young man in his late teens came through the door, took a step to his left, and stood staring out the window. Heather leaned over the table and lowered her voice. "Unless I'm mistaken, the youngest Mattherson brother just walked in. He acts like he's waiting for someone to join him."

"Let's stay until he leaves. Think up a reason to talk to him."

The young man Heather identified as Brian Mattherson came on point. His focus seemed to lock on the shiny red car pulling into a parking place. It soon became apparent his interest wasn't on the auto, but on the driver.

Heather kept her voice low. "It appears Brian was waiting for a young woman. She's about my height, with short hair the color of wet sand, and large glasses that hide her face. They're both checking out the customers and staff."

Steve kept his voice at the same volume as hers. "Are they holding hands or standing close?"

"No, but now his hand is on the small of her back as they're walking to the counter to place their order."

The young lady behind the counter had a voice that carried to where Steve and Heather sat and beyond. "Hey, Brian. Hey, Amanda. What brings you back from Houston to this dump of a town? If I could, I'd move to Houston in a heartbeat and stay there."

Even with Steve's exceptional hearing, he said he couldn't make out Amanda's reply, but the megaphone-voice of the employee projected loud and clear.

"Are you both still loving college? It's a shame your parents won't let you go to the same one. What would you like today?"

Heather watched as Amanda summoned the server to lean over the counter toward her.

"Don't you worry about that. If either of your parents shows up asking about you, I'll tell 'em I ain't seen you. I guess you'll be wanting your milkshakes to go."

Both heads nodded.

Heather continued to whisper. "Do you still want me to talk to them?"

Steve shook his head. "I don't think they'd appreciate us delaying their departure. It sounds like they're fugitives from the parent-police."

Amanda backed away from the counter several steps and gave a furtive stare toward the road running in front of the restaurant. Brian turned and spoke loud enough for Heather to hear. "You go on. I'll meet you with our milkshakes."

Quick steps took Amanda to her car, and she didn't waste time leaving. The taillights of her car disappeared over a rise as a new Cadillac SUV wheeled into a parking spot. Out stepped a woman who appeared to be in her early forties. She walked with a stride that matched Amanda's.

Once inside, she drew near to Brian, who took a half-step back.

"Hello, Mrs. Palmer," said Brian.

She ignored the social graces and got right to the point. "Amanda's father knows you're in town. If you have any thoughts of seeing her this weekend, you'd better think again."

Brian's reply was weak in both volume and veracity. "Amanda's in town?"

Mrs. Palmer gave him a hard stare. The server placed two cups on the counter. "Your order's ready, Brian."

"Oh, no," whispered Heather to Steve. "Brian has two milkshakes. Amanda's mother will want to know who the second one is for."

Steve raised his voice, and not a second too soon. "Brian. Is my milkshake ready?"

Brian and Mrs. Palmer's heads jerked around.

"I appreciate you saying you'd bring it to me. Don't worry if it's not ready. Ms. McBlythe can get it for me."

Heather concluded Brian was a young man who could think fast on his feet. He stepped to the counter, grabbed both milkshakes, and walked to their booth. "Here you are." He bent close to Steve as he placed the paper cup on the table in front of Steve and barely whispered. "Thanks, mister."

Heather scooted out of the booth and approached Mrs. Palmer. "Excuse us for interrupting your conversation with Brian. I couldn't help but hear him address you as Mrs. Palmer. Would you be Mindi Palmer?"

"Yes."

"I'm Heather McBlythe and the man with me is a business associate, Steve Smiley. We have an appointment with you and your husband tomorrow afternoon."

She interrupted. "Only with my husband, Craig. He

mentioned in passing it had something to do with a high-speed train."

While Heather talked, Brian took advantage of the opportunity to sneak behind Mindi and flee the scene.

With hand extended toward their booth, Heather asked, "Do you have time to join us for a chat?"

"Not now. My daughter isn't answering her phone and my husband and I are concerned about her."

"Then I won't keep you."

Steve sat leaned over, sucking the frozen delight through a straw. He raised his head. "Good job. Mark up a victory for love."

"Don't mention love with me in a Dairy Queen halfway between Houston and Dallas, while Jack's swimming with mermaids."

"Get some ice cream. It helps solve all kinds of problems."

"I wonder if they sell it by the bucket?" She settled for a dipped cone and ate it so fast her forehead ached.

Steve rose from the booth. "It's after three. Let's get to the B&B. I'll be coming down from the sugar rush pretty soon and a nap would be nice."

The door to the Mercedes groaned in protest as Heather opened it. She told her onboard computer to chart the path to their destination. In the town of less than ten thousand, it took them eleven minutes to arrive, only because they got stuck behind a tractor. The computer showed the street they turned onto made a large hairpin turn. It sat on a bluff overlooking a small river, just past the city limits. They passed a massive art deco-style home with front and side yards measured in acres, not feet. It was beyond anything Heather expected to see here, and the sign over the front gate read PALMER.

At the top of the hairpin-shaped road, she slowed to a crawl as they passed a second massive Victorian home. It boasted intricate trim and manicured grounds.

"I never expected to see homes like this in Mattherson." She did her best to describe it to Steve. He responded with a yawn.

On they went until the third and final home on the street appeared. A newer wooden sign announced they'd arrived at THE WELLS MANSION Bed and Breakfast. The antebellum home stood proud to be counted among the other two homes on the block, even though it appeared a little down-at-the heels. Cracks in the curved driveway allowed grass to poke through, as if nature mounted a counter-attack on the once-elegant property. All three deserved the title of mansion, but only this one suffered the indignity of being a place where guests had to pay to spend the night.

Heather reconsidered her choice of accommodations, but realized she was being a snob. "It's just as beautiful in person as in the photos on the Internet." She gave Steve a glowing thumbnail description of the three-story multi-thousand square foot home.

He replied with, "I hope the bed isn't a left-over from when they built it."

As Heather and Steve approached the front steps and raised porch, the door above them opened and a man dressed in jeans, work boots, and a chambray shirt came toward them. "Howdy. I'm Leon Wells. You must be Ms. McBlythe and Mr. Smiley. Come on in and make yourself comfortable. I'll grab your bags and run them up to your rooms. My wife, Sara Jane, will be with you directly. Till then, have a seat in the front parlor. It's off to your right as soon as you get inside."

Heather immediately liked Leon. He had a broad smile, a workman's hands, and looked to be the type that had a hard time standing still. After selecting a chair for Steve to sit in, Heather looked around the room. It was like entering a museum with a chronological pictorial timeline of the history of the Wells mansion and oil wells lining the walls.

Before long, a petite woman in her late thirties arrived. Like her husband, she wore simple clothes and had hands with no evidence of pampering. Heather guessed Sara Jane's work involved little time on a keyboard. A friendly smile preceded a soft voice welcoming them. "It's so nice to have you both. I'm supposed to give you a speech Leon wrote about how glad we are to have you stay here, but I'm more inclined to let people come to me, if you know what I mean. I'm not much on small talk to begin with, but I'll rattle on with the best of 'em once I get going."

Steve spoke before Heather could. "I can't remember ever staying in a mansion. I've been looking forward to coming here and soaking in the home's history, the town, and the county. Have you lived here all your life?"

"Born and raised. Leon and I married right out of high school, and this is the only home he's ever known." She looked away from Steve even though he couldn't see her retreat into shyness. "Of course, we only take up the top floor since his parents have passed on."

While Steve carried on the conversation, Heather studied the room, and the photos in particular. She thought back to Steve's comment about small towns holding secrets. It must have been her imagination running away with her again, but as she looked into the eyes of the men and women in old black and white photos, she wondered what secrets they wanted to tell her.

10

Heather and Steve's rooms were on the second floor with en suite bathrooms. Sara Jane took extra time with Steve to make sure he could navigate his room and bathroom. Heather left the hostess to do her job and retired to her room with the stated intention of catching up with emails and phone calls.

"This is an enormous bathroom," said Steve, as he used his cane to explore.

Sara Jane explained. "Leon started making renovations to this home as soon as he was old enough to hold a hammer. He kept it from falling down throughout high school and sketched out the plans for a bed-and-breakfast when his parents' health failed. He took every second bedroom on this floor and turned it into an en suite bathroom and closet. It cut the number of rooms, but nobody wants to walk down a hall to a shared bathroom."

Steve turned toward her. "I bet you helped him, didn't you?"

Sara Jane's laugh was as soft as her voice. "I set my heart on that boy in the eighth grade and hounded him until he finally got eyes for me. I wasn't much use in construction to begin with, but I learned."

"Tell me about the three homes on this street. The way Heather went on about them, all three are mansions."

"You'd better sit down. This is going to take a few minutes."

Steve did as instructed and found the wingback chair along the wall opposite the door comfortable, even if it sat a little low for his taste. He cut Sara Jane off when she started with the original patriarch, Clovis Mattherson. "I did some research on the Matthersons and Belinda added to it earlier today when we met her and Johnny."

"Then I'll skip to the 1920s. There was a big oil boom that started in East Texas and spread west. Leon's great-grandfather, Samuel Wells, drilled wildcat wells. He came to Mattherson county before anyone beat him to it and made a deal with Judge Mattherson to drill. It was a win-win situation when he struck oil, but there was a problem. How would they get it to the nearest rail line? One idea was to transport it by road, but they weren't always passable. The second involved putting in a spur railroad line and tie in with the main line running between Dallas and Houston."

This was the history lesson Steve wanted, and he hoped Sara Jane wouldn't stop until it was complete in his mind. A family member's version might end up better than anything he could get at the library.

"That's where Joshua Palmer comes into the story. He was a Dallas banker with strong ties to the railroads that were criss-crossing the state. With money to be made, and his wife wanting to get out of the heat of Dallas in the summer, he opened a bank here and formed a three-way partnership in the railroad with Judge Mattherson and Samuel Wells. He built his wife a summer home which is one of the three Heather described to you. Mindi Palmer and her husband, Craig, live there now. He runs the company that delivers fuel to many of the gas stations in the area. Craig also inherited the land around the lake west of town. I hear he has big plans to keep building homes out there."

"What does Mindi do?"

Hesitation followed, as if Sara Jane either didn't know or didn't want to say. She finally found her voice. "Mindi is into just about everything that doesn't involve Belinda Mattherson."

"I smell a feud."

As if someone had turned a water tap off, Sara Jane ended the lesson. "I'll leave you now, Steve. If you need anything at all, call out."

"There is one thing more. I can navigate this room and find my way to the front parlor with no help, but I'd like for someone to guide me to all the common areas of the house. I don't want to stumble into anything, especially antiques."

"Of course. Tell me what to do and I'll be your guide."

The tour took much longer than Steve expected. Fortunately for him, his hostess forgot the abrupt ending to the history lesson upstairs as she led him from room to room. Sara Jane wasn't kidding when she said she could hold her own with anyone once she had something to say. She gave accounts of long-dead family members, especially those who lived in the home. "The Great Depression hit in the thirties and the price of oil dropped so much that it didn't pay to pump it out of the ground. Samuel Wells knew how to find oil, but he was no good at making investments. Like so many people during the big bust, he lost most everything. The story goes he sold most of his leases back to the Mathersons and the Palmers. From that time until today, the oil in this county has run hot and cold, mostly cold. The reserves weren't as rich as first thought and no one came out the big winner."

Steve swept the ground in front of him with his cane. "If I remember correctly, there's a door to my right that leads outside."

"Only if you turn right. If you go left, you're back in the main hallway that connects to most of the downstairs rooms, including the formal dining room, the library, the billiard room, what they once called a mourning room, the sunroom, and the parlor."

Sara Jane paused, and her voice took on a different tone. "Whenever I go into the billiard room, I imagine what it must have been like when Judge Mattherson, Joshua Palmer, and Samuel Wells retired to play billiards, smoke cigars, and drink brandy after an enormous meal. They had money to burn, or at least they thought they did."

Steve soaked in the home's history. "If only the walls could talk." He also thought about how things changed when the stock market crashed and fortunes turned into the smoke of yesterday's hand-rolled cigars. Times were good and the friendships strong. Was money the only thing that ruptured the three-way relationship or could there be other causes? Did the murder of the young soldier, Rodney Wells, have something to do with losing wealth? Tomorrow he'd call the public library to see if they were open.

A creaking stairway told Steve that either Heather or someone else was descending. The pace told him it must be Heather.

"There you are. It's almost six. Are you ready to find something to eat?"

Steve moved to the sound of her voice. "A light supper sounds good."

Heather drew near. "I hope Steve didn't prove himself to be too much of a burden. I realized I didn't take him on a tour of the house. He's a bit of a bull in a china closet until he gets the floor plan memorized."

Steve nodded in agreement. "A big, clumsy bull. I almost did a face-plant on the billiard table because so much of the base is open. My cane didn't hit it until it was almost too late."

He faced Heather. "I'd challenge you to a game, but you'd probably cheat."

Sara Jane chuckled and excused herself.

Instead of following Heather's lead, he stepped out at a snail's pace and whispered. "Not so fast. Turn into the billiard room."

Heather did as instructed and Steve whispered, "Close the door behind us." He waited until he heard the click of metal.

"What is it?"

"When Sara Jane was giving me the tour of the house, we came into this room. She rattled off the names and history of a series of Wells men, so she must have been looking at photographs of them. One of them is Rodney Wells, the murder victim."

"I see it. He was a handsome young man wearing his uniform."

"Sara Jane clammed up when I started asking questions about him."

"Why would she do that?"

Steve lifted his shoulders and let them fall.

"Do you want me to ask her?"

"Not yet. Let's see what we can find in the library tomorrow."

Heather scoffed. "If they're open."

"It'll be open if Belinda Mattherson has anything to say about it, and I believe she does."

THEY LEFT THE HOUSE AND AGREED ON THE WAY TO HEATHER'S car to try their luck at a restaurant named *Pancho's*. It came with a three and a half star rating, which outshone all but the cafe on the town square.

Heather led him to the passenger side door. As he opened it, he smelled new leather. "Hey. This isn't your car."

Heather waited until she was in the driver's seat before speaking. "I called the Mercedes dealership before I joined you in the Dairy Queen. They brought me this one and took the other in on trade. It's almost the same as the last one, only the latest model. The makeshift repair wouldn't keep out wind or rain, and driving around in a damaged vehicle isn't the image I want to project when I'm trying to land a big deal."

Steve's phone announced a call from Leo. He told it to answer and stated his former partner's name before asking, "Any progress on the cold case?"

"I was hoping you found something in Mattherson."

"There might have been a feud going on between three prominent families: Wells, Mattherson, and Palmer. It may be down to two families now, but I have a hunch that most of our answers will come from here. I'll do some more digging tomorrow."

The call ended, and Steve let out a huff sounding like pent-up frustration.

"What's wrong?" asked Heather.

"I'm getting nowhere in helping Leo."

"You will."

Heather put the car in park. "Let's go in and see what culinary delight awaits us tonight."

After being seated in a booth, chips and salsa arrived with a flourish from a dark-haired young man. Heather smiled her thanks and picked up the menu to read to Steve.

With their orders placed and a chip loaded with salsa halfway to her mouth, the loud jangle of her phone erupted from her purse. She heaved a sigh. "Hello, Father."

"Daughter, you were supposed to call me with an update."

"No. I said I'd call you if there was anything significant to report."

"Did you go to Mathews and meet with the holdout?"

"It's Mattherson, and yes, I met with them and gave them the revised proposal."

"How did they react?"

"As I expected."

"Which is?"

"The husband seemed reasonable, but the wife was adamant about leaving the land unmolested by a rail line. I can tell you this for certain. She's the decision maker of the two."

Steve tapped out the seconds of silence on the table with his index finger. Heather won the game of holdout.

"You must not have expressed yourself clearly, or didn't use the right leverage."

"I explained verbally and in writing that we preferred to strike a deal with them, but were prepared to look at other options, including approaching Amtrak."

"You overplayed your hand and scared them away."

Somehow, she didn't explode in a rage. Instead, she kept her voice low and spoke at a measured pace. "Since you weren't here, you don't know what transpired. Would you prefer I use a recording device and send you audio? No, that's not good enough for you. What if I use one of my tiny cameras so you can critique my actions and words?"

The phone went dead. She breathed a sigh that sounded like relief mixed with regret.

Steve cleared his throat.

Heather bristled. "Do you have something to say?"

"Yes. Did I order a tostada with my enchiladas?"

Heather burst out laughing. "That's not what you were thinking."

"No, but I'm confused. You formed your own company so you wouldn't have to work with your father. Oil and water mix better than you two when you talk about deals. I thought you said you'd keep in touch with him, but wouldn't mix business and family. What changed?"

"It's complicated." Her words sounded hollow, but the arrival of their food put further parent-child relationship issues aside.

The meal lived up to its star rating and Steve downed his with the usual abandon. He had a philosophy about Mexican food. If it wasn't to his liking, then mask it with hot salsa.

Once finished, he pushed his plate away. "I don't think either of us made much progress today. Are you planning to talk to the Matthersons tomorrow?"

Heather's response came after a long silence. "Only Craig Palmer. I'll let Belinda marinate for a while. How much do the families dislike each other? Once I know that, I might leverage them against each other. What about you?"

"I'll come with you to the Palmer's. I know it's a long shot, but Craig or Mindi might know something about the Rodney Wells murder. After that, we stop by the library, and then drive home. Max hates it when we're both gone for two nights."

11

Sara Jane Wells met Heather with a smile and a cup of coffee as she entered the dining room for what was billed as a signature breakfast.

The hostess pointed in the direction Heather had come from. "The third step from the top of the stairway to the first floor is our burglar alarm. It's squeaked for as long as I can remember. Leon wants to fix it, but I won't let him. It tells me when guests are coming. I count the number of squeaks and know how many eggs to cook. I'll keep other things hot in the oven, but a fried egg doesn't taste right unless it's fresh out of the grease. Same with scrambled."

Heather looked around. "Where's Steve?"

As if Sara Jane had choreographed the morning breakfast scene, Heather heard the distinct sound of a wooden stair tread moan and squeal as a person's weight caused it to flex.

"There he is. I'll have your breakfast on the table before you finish your second cup of coffee."

Instead of being bright and cheerful, Steve arrived unshaven. He'd attempted to run a comb through his hair, but shouldn't have bothered. Two cow-licks competed for worst in show.

"Rough night," asked Heather.

"Need coffee."

Heather bypassed the antique china cups with saucers and selected an over-sized mug to fill. "This should help."

Neither spoke until he'd downed half of the black stimulant. He settled the mug in front of him. "I can't let Leo down."

"That's what kept you up all night?"

"Mostly."

"What's your plan?"

Steve puffed out his cheeks. "That's the problem. Other than searching the library and asking every person in town, I'm down to putting an ad in the paper or asking for help on social media. I considered trying to find a local Veterans of Foreign Wars chapter. I'd go to nursing homes, but I'm afraid they'd keep me."

Heather couldn't help but chuckle.

Steve picked up his mug but didn't bring it to his lips. "You sound chipper today."

"I am. I shut down my computer and turned off my phone. With Jack out of phone range, I didn't see much point in keeping it on. It was only ten thirty. Best night's sleep I've had in ages. I watched the sun come up this morning as I started a nice, long run."

Steve took in and swallowed two more drinks of coffee. "I'm surprised your father hasn't called you."

"Not yet."

"Good for him. After breakfast, I'll follow his example of going silent."

"Will you be awake in time to go with me to the Palmers?"

"Of course."

"Be sure to do something with your hair."

"Bad?"

"Not if you want to look like a starving artist."

STEVE STOOD AT THE BOTTOM OF THE STAIRS OF THE WELLS Mansion with hands resting on the top of his cane. His suitcase sat beside him.

"Let me get that for you," said Heather.

"I'll get it myself," said Steve in clipped words. "I don't know about you, but I'm ready to leave this one-horse town."

His tone reminded her of thirty-grit sandpaper, rough and abrasive. This wasn't like him. "My bags and hanging clothes are all packed. We can leave as soon as we're through at the library."

He turned toward the front door. "They're closed again."

"Closed? I thought you said it would be open."

"Apparently, not everyone in Mattherson jumps when Belinda hollers." Steve pulled the door open and stepped onto the front porch. "A new recording told me they'd be closed another day." He huffed. "No explanation, no apology."

That explained his foul mood. Heather used her new key fob to start the car remotely. Once both were buckled in, she tried to put sunshine in her words. "Look on the bright side. You might get some useful information from the meeting we're going to, and we can always come back. Forget about what you can't change and focus on the Palmers."

Steve blew out a full breath. "I'm upset because Leo's counting on me to save his career, not to mention his retirement pension."

"All that means is we'll keep on our toes today and find out as much as we can. I'll need to come back sometime next week. Plan on coming with me and we'll spend as much time as you like in the library."

"I didn't know you were planning on coming back."

"That's because you don't negotiate big business deals. The only thing I'm after today is a commitment from Craig Palmer that he'll entertain a proposal to sell his land. Think of it as a first date."

Since the Palmer Mansion was on the same looping road as the Wells and Mattherson mansions, they had no time to continue the conversation. "We're here." Heather swiveled in her seat. "I'd like for you to start off with a conversation explaining why you came to Mattherson. I need to get a measure of Craig Palmer, to hear how he presents himself, so I'll know what tactics to use."

Steve reached for his door handle. "Tactics? Is this a business deal, your first date with him, or a military campaign?"

"Something between the three."

Heather didn't need to use the ornate knocker on the front door inscribed with the name Palmer in the polished brass. Mindi opened the door and bid them welcome with a wide smile. "Please come in. I do hope you'll forgive me for being so rude yesterday. That was the frustrated parent in me coming out. Do either of you have children?"

Steve responded before Heather could. "No, but I understand they are the biggest blessings a family can have."

Mindi nodded in agreement. "You're absolutely right, Mr. Smiley, but they can be prone to mischief, too."

"I heard that, Mother."

Amanda Palmer approached from her mother's blind side. "The British would say it's bad form to besmirch someone without giving them an opportunity to defend themselves." She moved in front of her mother and thrust a hand out for Heather to shake.

Steve spoke as Heather and Amanda traded handshakes and conspiratorial winks.

"You must be Amanda," said Steve.

Mindi tilted her head ever so slightly. "How did you know?"

Steve didn't miss a beat. "I'm doing research on the prominent families in Mattherson, specifically, the Matthersons, the Palmers and the Wells. We stayed at the Wells Mansion, and Sara Jane gave us some basic information about you and your family."

"How interesting," said Amanda. "Are you researching for a book?"

"Yes. It may eventually turn into a novel."

"Oh, so you're an author."

"Only an aspiring author. It's giving me something to do in my old age. I'm leaning toward historical detective fiction."

Amanda pushed her glasses further up her nose. "You've come to the right town and families. Murders, unrequited love, greed, and all manner of skullduggery echo from the graves around here."

Mindi's eyes widened. "Amanda, you shouldn't say such things."

"Mom, you sound like Belinda Mattherson."

Heather decided the young woman had brains and grit. Behind thick glasses, eyes twinkled with the mischief her mother had accused her of.

Amanda spoke with a high level of certainty. "If only a small fraction of the rumors are true, there'll be plenty of fodder to stimulate a juicy full-length novel."

"Nonsense," said Mindi. "This is a quiet place where nothing much ever happens."

The words were devoid of conviction.

Mindi raised a bejeweled hand to form a stop sign for her daughter. "You'll have to excuse Amanda. She's always been curious."

Steve interrupted her. "If you have time, I'd like to pick your brain about stories you've heard, especially any that resulted in someone's death. Nothing recent, of course."

"That would be awesome," said Amanda. "I have a collaborative project that will keep me busy all week, but I'm planning on coming home next Saturday morning." She looked away. "I'm such a dolt. You don't live here. Do you live in the Houston area? Perhaps we could meet somewhere the following week?"

"It may work out that Heather and I need to come back next weekend. If so, could we have a nice, long chat?"

"Perfect. I'll brush up on my stories. There's one that involves the murder of a soldier from Mattherson. Someone killed him in Houston. No one knows why he was there or who killed him."

Steve gave no outward sign of exceptional interest, even though Heather's heart skipped a beat.

"Hmm," he said. "An unsolved cold case. I think you've given me the inspiration I've been looking for."

Mindi held a hand out to direct Steve and Heather away from Amanda. "Craig is expecting you in the study. Follow me." She turned to her daughter. "I'll be up to help you pack. I want you back on campus before dark."

Amanda stepped toward Heather and extended her hand. "It was so nice to meet both of you. I hope you'll be able to come next weekend."

The handshake included a tightly folded piece of paper. Heather tucked her hand behind her back, away from Mindi's hawk-like gaze.

The study looked more like a windowless library with floor to ceiling bookcases on every wall. Furnishings also mimicked a library except for a large desk guarding a leather executive chair. Two club chairs for guests faced the desk. Three rectangular tables with four padded chairs each took up only a portion of the over-sized room. Overhead fixtures and bulbs provided bright, but not harsh, light.

The lone occupant of the room stood and rounded the desk as soon as Heather and Steve entered. His voice boomed a greeting. "Ah, Ms. McBlythe and Mr. Smiley, welcome. I heard voices and realized Amanda must have intercepted you. I hope she didn't assault you with too many questions. She's hopelessly inquisitive."

Heather approached and extended her hand. "Your wife and daughter are a delight, Mr. Palmer. Thank you for giving us some of your time."

Craig Palmer's frame matched his voice: large-and-in-charge. Heather believed him to be 6'4", perhaps a half-inch more. His hair must have been dark at one time, but was now fully gray. If he hadn't been a hundred-and-fifty pounds overweight, he'd be a distinguished-looking middle-aged man. He gave his wife a look of dismissal with a quick glance and a nod.

She lost no time in responding. "If you'll excuse me, I need to check on Amanda."

The click of the door announced they were alone. "Please have a seat," said the patriarch of the mansion. "Let's not stand on formality. First names only if that's alright."

Heather responded by speaking as she directed Steve to a chair. "Your home is magnificent, Craig. I wasn't expecting to see a library of this quality."

"We have Amanda to thank for that. She could read the newspaper when she was three and devours books like I do fried catfish."

Steve perked up. "You're a man after my heart. Give me a plate or two of whisker-fish fried in peanut oil and I'll purr like a cat."

Craig's torso jiggled when he laughed.

Heather looked over Craig's shoulders. "I see you made room for some of Amanda's accomplishments on the shelves behind you."

"She's a prodigy in academics, especially mathematics. She's only in her first year at Rice and already several private companies and government agencies are clamoring for her attention. All she needs to do is keep out of trouble long enough to graduate and she'll write her own ticket to success."

Steve leaned forward. "I don't think you have anything to worry about. She didn't impress me as a young lady that would get into trouble."

"There are different ways to get in trouble. I'm not talking about run-ins with the law."

"Then you must mean trouble of the two-legged male variety."

"You're living up to your reputation as a detective. Amanda's weakness is she thinks she's ready for a permanent relationship."

"Do you suspect her of having serious feelings about anyone?"

Craig placed his palms flat on his desk. "It keeps me up at night."

Heather knew Steve had more questions to ask, but Craig didn't give him the chance.

"Enough talk about family matters." His gaze shifted to Heather. "It's a small town. People talk. You researched land ownership at the courthouse. Some of the best land is mine, and the rest belongs to the Matthersons. I'm guessing the fact you're sitting here this afternoon has something to do with the proposed bullet train."

Heather held her head and gaze straight. "It's far from a settled issue, but yes, I'm exploring options for routes."

Craig laced his long, thick fingers together in front of him. "You spoke with Belinda and Johnny Mattherson yesterday afternoon. You didn't stay long. Now you're here. That tells me Belinda doesn't want to sell, and believe me, she rules the roost in that family."

Heather made no move to contradict or affirm anything Craig said. She now knew he had spies in the courthouse and around town, giving him reports about their movements.

75

Craig continued. "If you had signed a sale agreement with her, you wouldn't have asked to see me. Either Belinda won't sell her precious family land for the right of way, or she's holding out for more money. I'm betting it's the latter. Either way, you could see my land as Plan B for your project."

Heather leaned forward. "All options are still open. No verbal agreements. I'm here to explore my options. Would you be willing to consider further discussions about this issue?"

Craig's countenance transformed to one of pure business. "I'll consider what you have to say, but all negotiations come with an understanding. I demand complete discretion on your part. It's no secret that there's no love lost between the Matthersons and the Palmers. I don't want it leaked that the train might go through my property." He lowered his voice. "One more thing. Don't think you can use me to start some sort of bidding war. If I hear you're pitting us against each other to drive the price down, I'll keep my land and you can get swindled by the Matthersons."

Heather stood. "I'll put together a preliminary proposal this week. Steve and I have already discussed coming back so he can do research at the public library."

Steve also stood. "I was going to take care of it yesterday and today, but it's closed."

Craig walked around his desk but came to an abrupt stop. "Are you sure about the library being closed?"

"It was closed yesterday and there's a recorded message saying it's closed today."

A look of mischief nudged the corners of Craig's mouth up. He spoke, but it didn't seem to be directed to either Steve or Heather. "Belinda will have some explaining to do."

Steve heard the words, but only Heather saw Craig's expression of satisfaction. She asked, "I take it Belinda oversees the public library?"

"Perhaps not for long."

Heather changed the subject. "I'll be in touch this week and firm up a time we can meet next weekend."

"Excellent. I look forward to it."

Once in the car, Heather retrieved the folded note.

"What are we waiting for?"

"Amanda passed me a note. She made a point of keeping her mother from seeing it."

Heather read the note aloud. "We both thank you. If Steve hadn't said the shake was his, I'd be on my way to Oxford."

"I like her," said Steve. "She reminds me of Maggie. A mind of her own."

12

Heather mulled over the last few days as she turned off Interstate 45 and pointed her SUV west to Mattherson on a sunny Friday afternoon. After the frustration of the weekend, the first two days of the week flew by in catching up on projects she'd let slide the last month. On Wednesday, she completed a proposal for Craig Palmer and had a long talk with Jack after his arrival home. Determined to make things right and turn over a new leaf, she rearranged her day Thursday to play golf with him, and that evening they enjoyed a quiet dinner at his place. Friday morning, she slept late to ensure she'd be fresh for meetings with the Matthersons and the Palmers, went to the office for a few hours, and picked Steve up mid-afternoon. Heather smiled. After catching up at the office and spending time with Jack, she could feel her world begin to right itself.

Lost in her thoughts and with most of the trip behind her, Heather belatedly realized she hadn't inquired about Steve's week. "Did you or Leo make any progress on the cold case?"

Steve snorted through his nose. "Leo's ready to throw in the towel and I'm not far behind him. I acted like I had a hot lead in

Mattherson, instead of a quasi-interview with Amanda Palmer, who may, or may not, have something more than third-hand gossip. If I don't come up with a solid lead by Monday morning, he's turning in his badge."

Twenty-five of the remaining thirty miles to the Mattherson city limit sign passed without conversation. Then, Steve's phone sounded an alert for an incoming call. A mechanical voice said, "Call from Leo Vega."

He instructed his phone to engage the speaker option, which wasn't unusual if they were working on a case. "What's up, Leo?"

"Have you been listening to the news?"

"Not since early this morning."

"Police found the body of a young woman in Hermann Park last night."

Heather glanced to her right. Steve sat up straight. "Keep talking."

"Details are sketchy. I got curious and made a couple of calls. The victim is Amanda Palmer. I remember you talking about her this week."

Heather's stomach did a back flip. Steve let out a soft moan and spoke in a soft, reverent tone. "Have they notified the family?"

"There's a blackout. The most I could get out of anyone is her name and where they found her. A heavily wooded area of the park."

"How long had she been there?"

"When I say there's a blackout, that goes double for us has-beens in Cold Cases."

Steve slapped his leg. "Keep on it, Leo. Let me know if you find out anything else." The call ended without the usual banter.

They drove in silence for another mile before Heather broke the silence. "What do we do first?"

Steve stopped the rolling of his fingertips against his leg. "We wait and play dumb until they notify Craig and Mindi. All we can do now is keep our eyes and ears open."

Heather slowed to the posted speed as they passed the city limit sign. "I was supposed to drop the proposal off at the Palmer's on our way to check in. So much for my plans."

Steve's phone again announced Leo's name. This time, he didn't put it on speaker. The call might have lasted twenty seconds. He kept facing straight ahead as he slipped the phone in his shirt pocket. "HPD notified the press. That means the Palmers know. Let's go to the Wells Mansion and check in. We're far enough from Houston that they shouldn't have heard about Amanda yet. Tell me how they react when I tell them about her."

As Heather pulled into covered parking around the back of the house, her phone came to life. The caller's number looked familiar, so she put the device on speaker.

"Hello."

"Ms. McBlythe, this is Belinda Mattherson. I don't want to go into detail over the phone, but something's come up and we desperately need to talk to you. Leon told me you and Mr. Smiley are staying the weekend next door. I know our meeting isn't until tomorrow, but it's imperative you two come to our home the moment you get into town."

Heather had to think fast. "We're still on our way. I'll need to check with Steve before I commit." She crossed her fingers. "I'm afraid he didn't sleep well last night, and he's snoring like a hibernating bear."

Undeterred, Belinda plowed on. "Stop in the moment you get to town. I can't stress enough how important it is that you come without delay."

The call ended without a commitment to answer the summons. Steve responded by saying, "Good excuse. I'll remember to reverse roles with you sometime. You can be the snoring bear."

Heather and Steve made it as far as the swimming pool before Leon jogged toward them to help with their bags. "Sara Jane is waiting for you in the kitchen with refreshments. She doesn't do that for everyone. She took a real shine to you two last weekend."

By the time Leon made it back from their rooms, Steve and Heather had settled at a small table, eating warm apple pie and drinking cold milk. It didn't take Steve long to polish off his and Heather finished her half a slice soon after. Friendly chit-chat about the trip up I45 followed. With dishes taken away, it was time to break the news about Amanda.

Steve cleared his throat. "I'm afraid we come bearing bad news and there's no easy way to put this. We found out on the way here that Amanda Palmer is dead. The police in Houston are investigating."

Sara Jane covered her mouth with her hand, but that didn't stop a gasp from escaping. Leon stiffened. "How did she die?"

"We don't know details yet."

Like a ship on heavy seas, Sara Jane listed from side to side. Then her legs buckled. If Leon hadn't been observant, she might have suffered serious injury. As it was, he eased her to the floor. Her head lolled as she regained consciousness, while Leon encouraged her with soft words.

Wrapped in her husband's arms on the kitchen floor, she muttered, "What happened?"

The muscles in Leon's jaw flexed. "Let's get you to a couch."

With Heather on one side and Leon on the other, they brought Sara Jane to her feet and shuffled her to the nearest room with a couch, which turned out to be the library.

Once they had her settled, Leon turned. "I need to know what's going on next door at the Matthersons. I saw the cop cars and I know who they belong to. Do the cops suspect Amanda was murdered?"

Steve answered. "From what I know, the death looks like a homicide. Belinda called us as we parked and wants to see us as soon as possible, but we don't know what it's in regard to."

Leon's head dipped and shook. "Traci did research on you and Heather. She says you two are private investigators. Is that right?"

Heather answered the question. "Steve was a Houston homicide detective before he lost his sight. I was a cop and detective for ten years before I could get to the trust fund my grandfather left me and start my business. We're part-time private detectives who try to solve a few murders every year."

"I guess that means you'll be offering your services to Belinda."

"What makes you say that?"

Leon ran a hand down his whisker-stubbled face. "The Matthersons are no strangers to rumors of murders. Are you going to work for Belinda?"

Steve continued in a calm voice. "We just learned about Amanda's death on the way here, so we've made no commitment to investigate her death. No one has asked us to become involved, but that doesn't mean we won't look into it. We're both financially secure, so money won't affect our decision to take a case or not."

"You work for free?"

"Sometimes."

"I know how Belinda can be, and I want justice done for Amanda. She was like a second daughter to us. I can't pay you much, but I'd like to hire you before Belinda does."

Heather stood up a little straighter. "I'm not sure that will be possible."

Steve added, "It's not that we're telling you no. We need to gather information first. There may not be any reason for us to proceed if the police have already solved the case. Also, Heather and I have to agree that we want to take up an investigation."

Before Leon could respond, Steve added. "Given Sara Jane's state, I think it best Heather and I accept Belinda's invitation to go next door to hear what she has to say. We won't commit to anything or anyone tonight. We'll also want to talk to you and Sara Jane as soon as she's up to it."

Leon nodded and walked with them to the door. "There's a path that connects our yard to the Matthersons's. The families have used it for years. I'll make a pot of coffee. We'll be waiting for you."

13

As soon as Leon shut the front door behind him, Heather spoke in a loud whisper. "I know you. You're rolling over how to start the investigation in your mind." She placed Steve's hand on her arm and set off toward the well-worn path between the two massive homes.

"Who said I wanted to take the case?"

She let out a spurt of a laugh. "Amanda reminded you of Maggie. The old bloodhound caught a scent and here we are walking on freshly mowed grass. My plans are on hold and you think there may be a link between the cold case and Amanda's death."

Steve came to an abrupt halt. "The pace you're on tells me I'm not the only hound walking across these yards. Admit it. You wouldn't be able to sleep tonight if we didn't find out what Belinda has to say. Who knows, she might have changed her mind and wants to sell the right of way."

"You don't believe that for a minute."

"No, but you won't know until we get there what she has to tell us."

Heather mumbled a comment under her breath but kept

walking. After climbing several steps, she used an ornate knocker on the massive front door. Footsteps clicked across the floor and the door swung open. She looked eye to eye with Johnny Mattherson. This time he didn't undress her with his gaze, but motioned them inside with his hand. "Come in and prepare yourself. It's going to be a bumpy ride."

A circular marble entryway held a large, round table topped with a substantial vase of fresh flowers.

"Leave your jackets on the table. Belinda's running hot and cold these days, and today, she has ice in her veins. There's a roaring fire in the study tonight."

Steve slipped off his jacket, but Heather only unbuttoned hers. "We saw all the cars earlier. It looked like a couple belonged to the police."

"The sheriff and two detectives from Houston. They didn't stay long."

Johnny led them to the second door branching off from the entry. When the door opened, he took a step back. Belinda stood to the side of the fireplace, holding a glass tumbler filled with ice and something amber. "Good. You've come."

Johnny moved to a wet bar. Turning his head toward them, he announced, "The bar's open. Care for something over ice?"

Heather and Steve both declined. This seemed to please Belinda as she moved to the couch and sat beside a man wearing a moderately expensive suit. "This is Andrew Curry, an attorney from Palestine, the next county to the east."

A quick head to toe examination gave Heather a measure of the man. Dark hair, slicked straight back, touched the collar of his white shirt, a clean shave, and black lace-up shoes that reflected light from the overhead chandelier. Very professional, even at this time of day.

Johnny confirmed Heather's other suspicions about the man. "Andy is the best criminal defense attorney in this area.

He and I try to play a round of golf once a week. One of these days I'll beat him."

This brought the obligatory smile from the attorney, but nothing else.

As expected, Belinda took over. "Mr. Curry suggested we hire private investigators to help us make sure overzealous police don't ruin my son's life."

Heather asked, "Which son are we talking about?"

"Brian, the youngest."

Steve said, "You have us at a disadvantage. Why would the police want to ruin his life?"

Mr. Curry fielded the question. "If you haven't yet heard, a jogger found Amanda Palmer's body in Houston's Hermann Park. It didn't take long for the police to zero in on Brian. He had the good sense to call home and refused to answer questions when they detained him for questioning. A friend of mine had him released in less than two hours."

Steve interrupted. "You said the police have already come and gone from here?"

Belinda barely let him finish the question. "Two detectives from Houston. They were horrid... asking all kinds of leading questions. Brian is a sweet child who wouldn't hurt anyone. I called Johnny the moment they arrived. He said for me not to say anything."

Johnny raised a glass toward Mr. Curry. "Andy came as quick as he could get away. He told them we weren't prepared to say anything. We need detectives who know Houston. We made some phone calls and your names rose to the top."

"What are your expectations of us?" asked Steve.

The door flew open and in walked an elderly woman leaning heavily on a cane. Her hair was a stringy thatch of gray. She wore a tie-dye blouse, a flowing tan colored skirt and sandals. In her wake walked a half dozen cats.

Belinda sprang to her feet. "Mother. You know you're not supposed to be out of your bungalow. It'll be dark soon."

The woman gave a confused look and stated, "Why do you call me Mother? My name is Babbs, and my guests are hungry. There's no more paté for them, only the cheap dry stuff you keep buying." Her cloudy eyes stared at the fireplace. "Besides, it's never dark if you walk in the light."

The look Belinda gave her husband could wilt the flowers in the entry. "Johnny, did you pick up the order like I asked?"

Johnny took the glass from his lips. "Sorry, dear. Forgot."

A huff that communicated more than disappointment came from Belinda. "Can't you think of anything besides golf?"

Johnny took a long pull from his drink.

Belinda wasn't through. "Take Mother to her bungalow and make sure all the bowls around the driveway are full. And take all these cats with you."

The elderly woman issued an inappropriate smile. "No need to wig out, Belinda. Remember what the Beatles said, 'Give peace a chance.'" She flashed a peace sign and wobble-walked out of the room with Johnny and the cats following in her wake. All but one, who was doing a figure eight around and between Steve's legs.

Steve reached down and picked up the black and white cat. He stroked its head and said, "You missed one."

Belinda grabbed the cat from Steve's hands, took it to the door and threw it in a motion not unlike releasing a bowling ball. It skidded on the marble floor and bounced against her husband's leg.

Belinda returned. "Please excuse the interruption."

Heather nodded. "How old is she?"

"Eighty." Belinda came back to the couch, sat down, and cleared her throat. "Let's talk about your terms. I've consulted with Mr. Curry about the standard rate for private investigators, and I'm prepared to pay more than that, provided you give me daily progress reports."

Heather started to answer, but Steve talked over her first word. "What are your expectations of us?"

"It should be obvious. Gather evidence that proves Brian had nothing to do with Amanda's death."

"And what if the evidence we uncover points to Brian's involvement?"

The response came back fast. "You won't. But if you find something that is harmful to my son, I'll expect you to remember who you're working for."

Mr. Curry broke into the conversation. "What Belinda meant to say was, whatever you discover will need to come to me and not to the police first."

Steve unfurled his cane. "You've given us a lot to consider. Before we commit to anything, we'll need a day or two to do some preliminary inquiries."

It was a good thing Steve couldn't see Belinda's expression. It appeared she expected not only a quick answer, but one that fit her narrative of the employer/employee relationship. She shifted her withering gaze from Steve to Heather. "While you and Mr. Smiley are sitting on your hands, remember that I'm the owner of the land you need for your train."

It took every drop of patience and tact Heather could muster not to tell Belinda what she could do with her land.

Heather seethed on the trip back to the Wells mansion as cats scurried toward the back of the Mattherson's massive home.

Steve stopped her before they cut through the hedges separating the two properties. "What did you think of Babbs?"

Of all questions that Steve could have asked, that one wasn't on her radar. "I thought we were trying to decide whether to take a murder case or not."

"That's only a third of the reason we're here. Sure, there's a recent murder case, but also an old case that needs solving. And don't forget, you came to Mattherson to buy land."

Heather's mind was still on the coercion Belinda tried to use. "What does a geriatric cat-lady have to do with any of those?"

"I'll let you figure that out after you get over being mad."

Heather stomped her foot and gave voice to her thoughts. "You don't know how much it aggravates me when you do that."

"Do what?"

"Get logical when I'm ready to throw a fit. You make me think and it spoils everything."

14

Heather led Steve through the front door of the Wells mansion. Leon met them in the foyer with eyebrows pinched and worry lines creasing his forehead. "Sara Jane's still shook up, but she's in the library and doing better. Amanda was Traci's best friend growing up. It's almost like we've lost a child."

Leon pulled his hand down his face. "I'm being a horrible host. There's a fresh pot of coffee and cookies in the kitchen."

Heather volunteered, "Let me help you. I could use a cup, and I've never known Steve to turn down fresh-baked cookies."

"I can find my way to the library," said Steve. "Is Sara Jane still on the couch?"

"Still there, but sitting up. She even ate a cookie." He paused, but only for a tick of the clock. "What did you learn from the Matthersons?"

Heather placed a hand on Leon's shoulder. "Let's get settled with refreshments and we'll tell you what we know so far."

It didn't take long before the two detectives sat facing the couple, each on couches with a coffee table between them. Steve led off. "Belinda and Johnny called in a criminal defense attorney to advise them on how to deal with the police."

Sara Jane looked over her cup of coffee she was using to keep her hands warm. "Did the police arrest Ryan?"

"Not that we know of." Steve placed his mug on the coffee table.

Heather noted that Sara Jane had inquired about the elder son and not Brian. She filed the info away to discuss later with Steve then expounded on Steve's last comment. "They detained Brian, but he demanded an attorney. He's free, at least for now."

Steve gave his head a nod. "The fact there are two detectives here talking to the Matthersons, as well as the Palmers, tells me there's a good chance the cops believe Brian has some involvement in Amanda's death. What can you tell us about their relationship?"

Leon looked at Sara Jane, who nodded for him to answer Steve's open-ended question.

"The three of them, Brian, Amanda, and our Traci, were thick as children could be, especially Brian and Amanda. They wanted to include Traci, but it just wasn't always possible for her to join in." Leon looked around the library like he was searching for the right words to say. "The simple truth is Sara Jane and I worked hard for every penny, but there wasn't ever enough for Traci to keep up with the lifestyle that the other two families could give their kids. It's like they're in some sort of competition to see who can spend the most money on them."

Heather said nothing, but her mind raced back to her own upbringing, which included private schools, both in the U.S. and abroad. Equestrian training, lavish vacations, special tutors, finishing school, and all that money could buy. Her parents chose friends for her based on last name and financial status. Like Amanda and Brian, they groomed her to be the crème de la crème of society. Until, that is, she rebelled after graduating from Princeton, and became a cop.

Coming out of her musings, Heather heard Steve change the subject. "Tell us about Belinda's mother. I believe she prefers to be called Babbs."

For the first time that evening, Sara Jane smiled, but Leon shook his head. "Even in the richest of families, there's that one they try to keep hidden. Babbs Mattherson is the town's crazy cat lady, but she's not crazy. Just odd."

Leon looked at Sara Jane who gave him the nod of approval to continue. "She used to live in the big house, but a few years ago Belinda built Babbs a bungalow, behind the mansion. Some say it saved the Mattherson mansion from ruin, but I know Babbs keeps a clean house. There was another reason behind that decision."

Heather tilted her head. "With her mother still alive, doesn't that make Babbs the primary heir to the Mattherson fortune?"

Leon shook his head. "She used to be, but from what we've heard, she turned over the control to Belinda a few years after she married Johnny Gentry."

"Wait a minute," said Steve. "Heather told me Johnny and Belinda both go by Mattherson. Then Belinda told us last week she was the Mattherson family heir, which means he took her name? It's usually the other way around. Shouldn't her name be Belinda Gentry or Belinda Mattherson-Gentry?"

A scoffing laugh came from Leon. "Belinda followed in her mother's avant-garde footsteps. I'm not sure of the whole story behind Babbs's husband, but she kept her maiden name of Mattherson. Then when Belinda got married, she refused to use Johnny's last name and kept her maiden name. Rumor has it, she made that a condition of the pre-nuptial agreement, which she insisted on because he had a ton of debt from college and law school. He's not the best lawyer around, but he knew enough to fix things, so her legal name is Mattherson."

Sara Jane added to the explanation. "They say she made

Johnny change his last name to Mattherson. I don't know if that's true or not, but it's how he signs his name."

Steve took up his coffee and took a long drink. After putting it back on the table, he asked, "What's behind the feud between the Mattherson and Palmer heirs?"

Sara Jane sat a little straighter. "At one time the feud encompassed the Wells family, too, but that ended a long time ago." She paused. "At least most of the bad blood did."

Leon expounded. "Hard times brought out the worst in all three families. The Wells clan ran out of money when oil all but died off. The other two bought the leases from the Wells family for next to nothing. We were lucky to keep the house. Since then, it's been the Mattherson's and the Palmer's going at each other like two goats trying to push each other off the top of a hill."

"Who's winning?" asked Steve.

"It's hard to say. They've gone back and forth ever since the Great Depression. The Matthersons have the most land, but they're not as sharp in business as the Palmer's. If you'd asked me two days ago, I would've said the Palmer clan would pull way ahead in the coming years. But that was because of Amanda. That girl had a mind like nothing I've ever seen. She saved every penny as a child and started investing in tech stocks in the sixth grade. There's no telling what her portfolio looks like today. She took her father along for the ride. He's a smart businessman, but it's because she taught him."

Steve picked up his coffee cup. "What about the two Mattherson boys? What are their prospects?"

Heather noticed the muscles in Leon's cheeks flex. "The eldest is every bit as sorry as his mother. He's in the second year of law school and is supposed to come back and learn how to steal like his parents. The youngest tries hard and is plenty bright in his own right, but he's too much of an idealist for my taste. Always protesting something."

The slamming of the front door preceded the sound of footfalls going up the stairs, accompanied by sobs.

Leon and Sara Jane both stood and headed for the door. "You'll have to excuse us," said Leon. "Our daughter, Traci's home from the Palmers."

Their departure left Heather and Steve with coffee and cookies on the table before them. It didn't take long for Steve to grab two cookies and lean back. It wasn't unusual for him to say nothing for a while after receiving new information. Heather knew this would be a two cookie break in the conversation.

He surprised her when he took his time eating the first cookie and then asked, "What will you do in the morning?"

Heather sipped her coffee before answering. "We both need to do research."

Steve nodded. "I thought you'd say that. I'm going to hang around here and see if I can't have a private conversation with Babbs. Come get me for lunch and then you can drop me off at the library. I want to find out all I can about the late Rodney Wells."

Heather looked at the cookies, thought of Jack, her long-suffering boyfriend, and how she didn't need to overindulge. It took considerable willpower, but she forced herself to pass on the late-night treat. "Are you still thinking Amanda's murder has something to do with the old feud?"

Steve's shoulders rose and then fell. He immediately took a bite of his second cookie, which kept him from answering her question. After swallowing, he said, "I need you to go to the grocery store the first thing tomorrow morning."

"What do you need?"

"A case of expensive cat food. Make sure it's the best paté they have."

"I'll go tonight, so I don't have to rush in the morning. I guess you're not going to answer my question about the cases being connected."

Steve's shoulders rose and fell again as he put the last bite of cookie in his mouth.

15

Sara Jane began the morning by forgetting to turn on the oven before she put in the homemade buttermilk biscuits. Heather looked on as Traci bounded down the back stairway, realized her mother's mistake and pulled out the baking sheet.

"Mom, you need to let Dad cook this morning."

"Amanda's dad called late last night. Your father's already left to help the Palmers deliver fuel today. You go on to work. I'm fine; I can do this."

"Heather and I are in no hurry," said Steve. "I can wait a long time as long as there's coffee."

Traci came to where Steve sat. "I'd like to talk to you after I get off work today."

Steve gave his head a nod. "I'll try to find out more about what the cops in Houston are up to." He paused. "I can't make any promises, but I still have a lot of contacts on the force."

A firm hand squeezed his forearm. "You read my mind, Mr. Smiley. Thanks."

The back door slammed shut and Heather refilled her cup.

Steve broke the silence. "Heather, you may need to give Sara Jane a hand with breakfast this morning. There's a couple of detectives staying here and I don't think they want raw biscuits or burnt bacon."

"I'll be glad to help."

Sniffles came from Sara Jane. "I can't ask you to cook."

"That's good, because I'm not making any promises. The only class I ever failed was making souffles in Paris. Keep an eye on me and make sure I don't mess up."

This earned a chuckle from Sara Jane. "The closest we come to fancy cooking is french toast."

"My specialty. Let's tag-team breakfast and get those pesky detectives on their way."

Steve made it a point to keep the conversation light, ensuring Sara Jane didn't slip back into grief that might disable her. With Heather's skills and his ability to not let the banter drag, the meal was soon ready at the appointed time of 7:00 a.m. Heather helped her hostess ferry the breakfast dishes to a sideboard in the formal dining room, while Steve topped off his mug of coffee and joined the gathering. She retreated to the kitchen to bring out the coffeepot. By the time she arrived in the dining room, Steve had already found his seat and Sara Jane had given instructions on the self-serve breakfast. She then retired to the kitchen.

"I didn't realize there were other guests here," said the man sitting across from Steve.

"We arrived yesterday evening. Here on business."

"Who's we?"

Steve pointed toward Heather. "Ms. McBlythe and me. My name is Steve."

"I thought she worked here."

"Just helping," said Heather. "Things are a little scattered today."

Steve added, "Nothing like the murder of a neighbor to make things scattered."

"What do you know about that?" demanded the Houston cop.

"Not much. Only what I heard you and your partner talking about when you came in last night. You need to be careful when you stay in older homes. They're not known for being soundproof."

Footsteps of another man coming down the stairs caught Steve's attention. "That must be Bernie. It appears he still runs a few minutes late."

Before the first man could respond, the second stopped at the doorway. "Steve? Steve Smiley? Is that you?"

"In the flesh, Bernie. I was just talking with Greg." He paused and turned to face the man across from him. "You're Greg Long, right?"

A harsh tone accompanied the response. "Look buddy, I don't know you, and if there're questions to be asked around here, I'll do the asking."

"Back off, Greg," said Bernie. "This is Steve Smiley. He's forgotten more about solving homicides than you'll ever know."

"I don't care who he is. What's he doing here in the middle of our investigation?"

Heather spoke up. "He already told you what he and I are doing here. We're here on business."

"What kind of business?"

"That's none of your business."

Steve held up his palms. "You'll have to excuse Heather. After being a cop and a detective for ten years in Boston, she can be a little prickly this early in the morning. It doesn't help that she's an attorney, too. You know how snitty those people can be."

Heather shrugged. "I play nice most of the time."

Steve added, "She really does, unless she runs into someone who rubs her the wrong way."

Bernie sounded serious. "Has someone hired you to look into the murder of Amanda Palmer?"

Steve shook his head. "Not yet. Heather and I are looking into things that involve trains. It's nothing but a coincidence that the girl down the street was murdered. Do you really think it was one of the Mattherson boys?"

Greg Long must not have liked Steve's answer. "Expect a phone call from Lieutenant Chase. He'll be interested to learn a couple of ex-cops are snooping around his case."

"Have him call my attorney," said Steve.

Heather held up her hand. "That would be me. I'll get you a business card after breakfast."

"Let's go," said Detective Long.

"You go," said Bernie. "It's not every day I get a breakfast like this."

"It may be your last if you don't get a move on. Remember what happened to Hank, Frank, and Leo?"

The breakfast progressed without the surly detective, which put a whole different vibe over the meal. Bernie savored his food while Detective Long tramped upstairs, making no effort to be quiet.

Bernie dismissed the threat and its source with a flip of his wrist.

Steve turned to Heather. He spoke as if Bernie weren't there. "Your impressions?"

Heather gave her unvarnished opinion. "Greg Long is a jerk and a boot-licker to the lieutenant that's trying to take over the department."

"Yeah, but what about the death of Amanda Palmer?"

"It sounds like Brian Mattherson is on his way to jail."

Steve nodded. "If this feud goes as deep as I think it does, Craig Palmer gave Greg and Bernie an earful last night." He faced the elder detective. "Am I right, Bernie?"

"You haven't changed, Steve. I used to think you had some sort of psychic power."

Heather rose from her chair. "I need to make some phone calls. What are you going to do with all that cat food I bought last night?"

"I'm setting a trap for Babbs Mattherson."

Bernie chuckled. "Whatever you're up to, I'd like a front-row seat to see how it ends."

"Who knows, Bernie? You may get your wish."

16

S teve shifted in the wicker chair to catch the morning sun on his face. Despite a cool start to the April day, the weather forecast called for temperatures to rise and peak out at seventy-eight degrees. A perfect spring day.

The purring of a cat caught his attention as the feline nestled beside his shoe. "What took you so long? I've been waiting for almost an hour."

The sound of cats smacking as they enjoyed the paté spooned out on paper plates joined the chirp of birds and the natter of squirrels. Steve gathered by the hissing around him there were now more cats than plates of food. Cats weren't known to share well and it didn't sound like Babbs' friends were any exception.

"You guys love the expensive stuff, don't you?"

Thirty minutes passed and most of the hissing and smacking had stopped. Steve chuckled. "I guess everybody's cleaning their face and getting ready for a nap, aren't you? There's nothing like a kitty pool party." He sat up from petting the latest ball of fur to rub against his leg when he heard the sound of shifting bushes. He'd laid the trap. The scouts had arrived first, and now he'd get the chance to speak with their benefactor. "Babbs? Is that you?"

The cracking of a geriatric voice answered. "There you are, my darlings. Mommy couldn't imagine where you'd gone. And, look. This nice man brought you something to eat besides that cheap food Belinda foists upon you."

Steve pointed to a twin of the chair he sat in. They had the feel of wicker. Heather said the cushions on the seat and back were bright red and blue stripes. "Won't you join us?" The creak of the wicker told him Babbs had settled in. In his mind's eye, he pictured a dozen or more cats circling her legs with one or two jumping up to claim a place on her lap. As if on cue, a long-haired feline landed on his thighs.

"What's this one's name?"

"That's Reginald. He's usually stand-offish with strangers, but he's also the most inquisitive. You must have cats."

"Heather and I share one. His name is Max, and because I'm home most days, he and I have become best friends."

The purring increased. "You and that beautiful woman were at the big house last night. I didn't know you were staying at the Wells Mansion."

"Heather came to make a business deal with Belinda, but I don't think it's likely to go through. I'm here to do some historical research."

"Groovy. I've lived here most of my life. What are you interested in?"

Steve couldn't remember the last time he'd heard the term groovy used in a sentence, and it took him by surprise. He gathered his thoughts and said, "I'm trying to gather information on the big-three families of Mattherson. I've learned a little from Leon and Sara Jane about their family. They apparently went from riches to rags after the big oil bust."

The sound of cats hissing brought a quick response from Babbs. "Clarence, you and Pearl behave yourselves or you'll have to leave the party." After one more hiss, Babbs asked, "What were you saying? My memory isn't what it should be. I'm afraid the acid I dropped in the sixties might have killed off a few gray cells. The childhood memories are clear as a bell, but from the time the Beatles told me they wanted to hold my hand until I stopped following the Grateful Dead around the country, it's a blur."

"I understand those were turbulent days, completely different from World War II."

Babbs's chair squeaked again. "Pearl, there's no more lap for you, but you can rest on the arm." She paused. "I was in cloth diapers during World War II. There's not much I can tell you about that, other than what my parents told me."

Following her response, Babbs launched into humming what Steve believed to be a song made popular by Janice Joplin. After the musical interlude, Steve tried to get her back on track. "There was a mystery I found in my research about a member of the Wells family. Do you remember your parents or grandparents talking about a young soldier during World War II named Rodney Wells? From what I read in old newspaper accounts he was an officer training to be a pilot when he was killed in Houston."

Babbs slumped in her chair and took on the voice of a child. "Daddy's leather belt stings like a dozen bees." Her voice changed to mimic someone else. "Don't ask about Rodney. Don't say his name around your mother."

She launched into humming a different song, one that Steve recognized from the big-band era. The title came to him. "String of Pearls."

Steve needed to bring Babbs back to the present before he lost her completely to memories that seemed sharp as a honed straight razor. "I guess you heard about Amanda Palmer. Can you tell me about her and her family?"

Babbs sat up straight in her chair. "Amanda loved my

friends and was always kind to them. She and Traci are the granddaughters I never had."

"I heard she was exceptionally smart."

"Not smart. Brilliant. But not as pretty as Traci. That worked out well, because Brian isn't that handsome." She sighed. "I was hoping they might marry and put an end to the hard feelings between the Matthersons and the Palmers." She paused. "Do you think history repeats itself, Steve?"

He drug his hand down the side of his face. "It seems to, doesn't it?"

"Why can't people be more like cats? They fuss and fight, but it never lasts. Mostly, they give each other room to live. I know you can't see them, but Pearl is on the right arm of the chair while Clarence is on the left. Both are content now that there's no more food to fight over."

"Have the Matthersons and Palmers always had trouble getting along?"

"Hop down, my little friends. Mommy needs to make sure Belinda remembers to get you decent food."

To Steve's surprise, he heard Babbs manipulate a cell phone and begin a conversation. "Belinda. I know you're pretending to be too busy to talk to me. I'll not have my friends eating dry food. Do something about it."

After leaving the message, he heard a phone disconnect tone, giving Steve the opportunity to speak. "I have half a case of paté left over. Why don't you take it?"

"Thank you, but that's unnecessary. It's a game I play with Belinda and Johnny. They pretend to forget and buy the cheap stuff, hoping it will drive my friends away. I could call and have it delivered, but then what's the fun in not calling Belinda? She always gives Johnny an earful, and it's entertaining. Besides, that's not the deal I made with them when they built my bungalow. They'll have several cases delivered today."

Babbs spoke in a maternal voice as she rose from her chair.

"Come, my lovelies, let's go home and leave Mr. Steve to enjoy this gorgeous spring day."

"Thanks for the conversation and for allowing me to borrow your friends for a while."

"I'm afraid they've eaten all the food you put out for them." She paused. "Perhaps the next time we speak, you can tell me why you really came to Mattherson."

"I look forward to that conversation and to hearing more about the history of the three families."

Steve sat pondering the conversation. It was interesting how Babbs's times in the here-and-now blended with conversations with cats and mental trips to psychedelic images captured in her brain. Then, she'd return to the present with cogent answers to questions. Had the drugs of the sixties really taken their toll, or was the crazy cat lady putting on an act?

It took Steve several minutes to locate and collect the plates he'd put out for the felines. He placed them beside his chair and pulled out his cell phone. "How's your morning going?"

Heather let out a puff of a breath. "Slow. Investors are worried about the bullet train falling through. Did you catch Babbs in your trap?"

"We had a very interesting conversation. She may be an eccentric cat lover, but she's not crazy. I have a feeling there's a lot more to her than what you see on the surface.

"Come get me for lunch. Let's go back to the diner and see how Traci is getting on today."

17

On the way to lunch, Steve gave Heather a full accounting of his time spent with Babbs Mattherson.

Looking for a parking place on the town square at noon on Saturday proved to be a fruitless task. Farmer's market booths had the street in front of the cafe blocked, so Heather settled for parking on a side street a block and a half away. She pulled the new SUV next to the curb. "I'm confused. Are you saying Babbs is mentally competent to make her own decisions?"

Steve didn't reach for the door handle. "There's no doubt the drugs she took and the lifestyle she led fried some gray matter, but she understands as much or more than most people her age. Did you ever hear the expression from the sixties that said, 'Tune in, turn on, and drop out'?"

"Yeah. I remember it from old movies and documentaries."

"That describes Babbs during her twenties. She tuned in to the world of peace, love, sex, and hard rock music. She also turned on the drugs and spent years in a psychedelic fog. Finally, she dropped out of society. Of the three, I believe she outgrew the drugs, although it wouldn't surprise me if she still smoked a joint now and then." Steve held up a hand so she wouldn't interrupt him. "As far as being tuned in, she's completely aware of what's going on around her. She knows the games Belinda plays and I believe she can outplay her."

"What about dropping out?"

"That's her defense mechanism. Whatever things she finds distasteful, she avoids by taking on the persona of a burned-out hippie."

"Like the feud between the Matthersons and the Palmers?"

Steve nodded. "That and the family business."

Heather looked out the windshield and watched an elderly, bow-legged man wearing a straw cowboy hat amble toward the courthouse. "Did you ask her if she'd signed over her rights as heir to the estate to Belinda?"

"That didn't come up this time. I want you to look for the record of a civil proceeding where Johnny and Belinda had her declared mentally incompetent. I have my doubts you'll find one."

Heather turned to face him. "My staff looked at a lot of real estate transactions when they were researching the route for the train. I found a couple of property sales that had Barbara Mattherson's name on them. That would be Babbs."

Steve scratched his chin. "What about the more recent transactions?"

"Belinda signed everything after she married. Johnny always acts as her attorney."

Steve reached for the door handle. "I know what you're thinking. How can you find out for sure?"

"I'll need to keep digging."

The passenger side door opened and Steve unfurled his cane. "Let's get to the diner and check on Traci. Besides, I'm starving."

The midday stroll took only a few minutes, but they had to wait ten more for a table. While they waited, Steve's phone buzzed in the pocket of his short-sleeve shirt. All Heather could hear was one side of the conversation.

"Hey, Leo... Yeah, I'm making some progress on the case. I found someone who knows something about Rodney Wells, but I need to take my time with her or I'll scare her off. I'll go to the public library and do some research. What's new in the Palmer girl's case?"

Steve had his phone pressed close to his ear, preventing Heather from hearing Leo's response. It turned out all he added was that the cops were focusing on Brian.

Traci approached and said, "I have a table open along the back wall. Will that be all right?"

"Perfect," said Heather.

Traci led the way through the maze, with Heather guiding Steve. The young woman waited to speak until they plopped in their seats. "The special today is meatloaf. It's actually pretty good, if you like that sort of thing."

Steve held out his hand and found Traci's wrist. "Do you believe Brian is innocent?"

"He can be a hothead, but he'd never lay a hand on Amanda." She looked around at the crowded room. "I can't talk now, but I really need to speak to both of you. Brian called me. He'll be in town this afternoon."

Steve patted her hand. "We'll talk this evening." He lowered his voice. "It's essential for us to speak to Brian. Can you arrange that?"

Heather watched as Traci stood up straight, pulled an order pad from her pocket and spoke in a confident tone. "Can do."

"The special for me," said Steve.

"Make it two," said Heather.

Traci nodded and quick-walked to put their orders in.

Heather watched as Traci went about her duties. Steve leaned toward her. "She's an exceptional young woman. Tough as nails."

"It appears so. That was dangerous of you to test how she'd react."

Steve shrugged. "She's not only tough, she's one that will take decisive action. We need to decide if we're going to take the case or not. And if we do, who will be our client?"

"Not Belinda Mattherson or her slimy husband."

"Agreed."

Heather looked around the crowded room. "Since we haven't talked to the Palmer's yet, that leaves us with Leon and Sara Jane Wells."

"There's one more. She hasn't asked us yet, but she will."

"Are you saying you want us to work for Traci and not her parents?"

Steve nodded. "Believe me, Traci will insist we keep her parents out of the loop."

"What makes you so sure?"

"We'll find out tonight." He took a drink of water. "We may have to press her a little, but I'll bet lunch that Traci has a good reason for keeping her parents out of what's about to happen in this town."

18

Saturday afternoon passed with Heather fielding more phone calls from nervous investors and Steve retreating to his room. She imagined him sitting in a chair, phone and laptop at the ready. He'd regularly scroll through the news articles for any scrap of information on Amanda's murder. Then, he'd set the devices aside and recline on the bed, fingers laced behind his head... thinking, pondering, shifting through conversations and nuggets of information.

With evening approaching, Heather started the SUV as Steve buckled his seatbelt and turned toward her. "Let's grab a hamburger to go. We need to get back and have that talk with Traci and Brian."

Twenty-five minutes later, they sat by the pool as Steve attacked his burger, fries, and chocolate malt. Heather discarded the top bun and lifted her one course meal as if it were a slice of pizza. She pinched off a few bites for two wandering cats, but they turned their noses up at the mustard, onion, and pickle-stained bread.

"Traci should be here any minute," said Steve between bites. "She's bringing left over cookies."

"What about Brian?"

Heather watched as the two cats trotted back to the Mattherson property.

"He'll have to sneak out of the house. Traci wasn't sure how long before he can get away."

"Just as well. That will give us a chance to discuss our contract with Traci."

Steve held up a hand and spoke around a bite of his burger. "Hold off on that. She might not be our client."

"I thought we agreed on that."

The back screen snapped shut, causing Heather to turn toward the sound. "Traci's coming now. She's carrying a plate in one hand and rubbing her belly with the other."

"How far along is she?"

"I'd say at least seven months, possibly eight. I'm not good at guessing that sort of thing."

Traci placed the plate of chocolate chip cookies on a short table between a seating of three wicker chairs. "They're not hot and gooey, but a cold cookie is better than no cookie."

Steve nodded and reached. "That's been my motto concerning cookies for as long as I can remember. Anything new on when Brian might join us?"

"He's having supper with his parents and that lawyer they hired to represent him. He'll be over as soon as he can sneak away."

Traci settled into her chair and dry-washed her hands. "I understand my parents want to hire you to investigate who killed Amanda. I don't want you to work for them."

Heather waited for Steve to say something, but he remained quiet. She took his silence as her cue to speak. "Why don't you want us working for your parents?"

Traci's gaze shifted to the third floor of the mansion next door. "Do you know what it's like to live in a town where two families control everything?"

"I can't say that I do."

"My mom and dad work like slaves for both the Matthersons and the Palmers. We're probably the only people in town who haven't chosen sides in this stupid feud. Dad does all the yard work and most of the home repairs for both families. He also does other odd jobs for both. Mom cleans and bakes bread for each family. My parents never talk to them about the past or what's going on in town or the county. If it doesn't involve their present jobs, they keep their mouths shut. They've worked hard to walk the tightrope and they can't afford to be seen as taking sides with either family. Both could ruin my parents, and who would pay what this house is worth if they had to sell?" She paused long enough to take a breath. "Heck, they don't even vote for fear someone might find out and tell Belinda or the Palmers. If you agree to work for my parents, you'll have to ask probing questions. People will think my parents are taking one side over the other."

Steve leaned forward. "They'll think the same thing as soon as we ask questions and then they find out you're our client."

With her chin lifted, Traci said, "People won't suspect me."

Steve leaned back. "We try our best to maintain confidentiality with our clients, but it doesn't always work out."

"Why not?"

"We try to help the police solve the crimes we investigate. Sometimes they let things slip."

Heather added, "And sometimes people we interview blab what we talked about. I imagine in a town this size, there aren't many secrets."

"Are you saying you won't try to find out who killed Amanda?"

Steve shook his head. "I'm not saying that at all, but your family has too much to lose, and so do you. If we take you on as our client, it's the same as your parents hiring us. Heather and I were already in agreement that we'd look into this murder. I guess we can proceed without a client."

"But I want you to prove that Brian is innocent."

Steve shifted in his chair. "The job of a good homicide detective is to find the truth of what happened and why. We never set out to find anyone guilty or innocent, only to follow the evidence, no matter where it leads us."

Heather took her turn. "Hold on a minute, Steve. I'm not comfortable investigating and not having a client. I'm fine with working pro bono, but we agreed that every case must have a client and a signed contract."

Steve leaned back and steepled his index fingers. After a few long seconds, he dropped his hands. "Give me until tomorrow at noon. I'll have us a client."

"Who?" asked Traci.

"That's confidential," said Steve.

Her face twisted in a question as Steve kept talking. "From now on, the less you know about the case, the more protected you and your parents will be."

Heather added, "We need information if we're going to have a successful investigation. That means you'll need to be open and honest with us about everything."

"Everything?"

Steve's voice had a somber tone. "Everything."

Traci again faced the upper floor of the house next door. "I can't tell you everything, but I promise to tell you the truth about what I can."

Steve leaned forward and whispered. "Is Brian the father of your child?"

With a vigorous head shake, Traci said, "No, and that's the last answer you'll get from me about who my son's father is. As for Brian, he was head over heels in love with Amanda."

Traci hesitated. "Amanda cared a lot for Brian, but not like everyone thinks. She was such a unique person."

"Can you explain?"

"She didn't think like most people or have the same desires. In some ways, she was more like a machine than a human, especially with long-term romantic relationships."

Heather shook her head. "That's not the impression I got when we saw them at the Dairy Queen."

"You saw what Amanda wanted you to see. Brian was the perfect boyfriend for her in high school. Their parents wouldn't allow them to date, but all the boys thought she was off limits because they were always together. Then they went off to different universities."

Traci laughed. "Have you discovered yet that they shared an efficiency apartment? But the only thing that went on there was study. Amanda said the housing on campus was like living in an aquarium. No privacy for study in her room. She arranged it to where she and Brian were rarely there at the same time. He was interested in more, but I know Amanda wasn't."

Steve took over. "Did the two families know the truth about their relationship?"

"No, not even Brian faced the truth of it. Everyone but me thinks their lives were a remake of Romeo and Juliet."

Steve took a bite of cookie. Again, it was Heather's turn to ask questions. "Do you know how the feud started?"

Traci's long brown hair shifted over her shoulders as she shook her head. "It started out with money, but it's what people don't talk about that makes me wonder."

"Like what?"

"Don't you think it's odd that in each of the three families there're photos of people in their homes who don't get talked about much?"

Steve folded his hands in his lap. "Like a soldier shot to death in Houston during World War II?"

"Dad calls him Uncle Rodney, but he was really a great-uncle to Dad."

"Who else don't people talk about?"

Traci started with her pinkie and worked her way up her fingers. "The women include Babb's mother and Amanda's great-grandmother. I also tried to do some research on the wife of the founder of the town and county, Clovis Mattherson. I didn't get very far. It seemed someone came in and deleted all references to who old Clovis was married to."

Heather shifted in her chair. "That's assuming he ever married. I can think of many reasons she wouldn't be listed."

"Like what?" asked Traci.

"She might have died in childbirth someplace other than Mattherson, or he never married the woman. The mother may have been the wife of a friend that was killed in the Texas Revolution or fighting the original occupants of the land and he raised the child alone. Remember, those were hard days and the life expectancy for women and children was very low."

Steve said, "It wasn't unusual for the early frontiersmen to find companionship with Native Americans, Mexicans, or slaves they brought with them."

Traci laughed. "I'd like to see Belinda's face if you found proof there's a señorita, a Native American, or a slave in her bloodline."

"Is she that prejudiced?" asked Heather.

Traci nodded her affirmative answer.

The rustling of the bushes on the far side of pool caused all three heads to shift.

"Yoo-hoo. Pearl. Are you over here again?"

Steve hollered out. "Babbs. Come join us. You're just the person we need to talk to."

Traci rose from her chair, walked to Babbs and exchanged hugs. Heather couldn't help but notice the familiarity and compassion in the way the two women treated each other. She'd tell Steve about her observations later. He had a knack for taking little slivers of information like that and interpreting them in ways that brought clarity to the cases they worked on.

As Babbs sat in the chair Traci had recently vacated, she turned to Heather. "Have you seen Clarence and Pearl?"

Traci looked around the perimeter of the yard. "They were here a little while ago."

"I don't think they stayed long," said Steve. "They probably came looking for paté and only found scraps from Heather's hamburger bun."

Babbs settled back in her chair. "Those two are my most finicky eaters. It's only the good stuff for them." She paused. "That sorry excuse for a son-in-law didn't bring home the paté like he said he would."

Steve motioned to Traci. "Would you mind going up to my room and getting what's left of the cat food Heather bought?"

The expectant mother left to fulfill his request without a word.

"That's so kind of you," said Babbs. "I've put it off long enough. From now on, I'm ordering my groceries online and having them delivered. Belinda isn't to be trusted, and Johnny hates my friends."

Heather wondered if it had more to do with a desire not to be bothered.

Steve spoke in a firm tone. "Babbs, it's time I came clean with you. Heather and I are private investigators. I used to work as a homicide detective in Houston, and Heather was a detective in Boston. I came to Mattherson to look into a cold case for a friend of mine. Do you know what a cold case is?"

She flipped the question away like it was a pestering fly. "I may be old, but there are more detective shows to watch these days than I can count."

"Since we've been here, three different parties have asked us to investigate Amanda's murder. We've turned them all down, but we now find ourselves in a quandary. We want to investigate, but we don't have a client."

Babbs's long gray hair fell across her shoulder when she nodded she understood. "Let me guess. Leon and Sara Jane want you to find out who killed Amanda. Traci does too, but she didn't want to involve her parents."

Steve affirmed the first two with a nod of his head.

"The Palmers probably didn't ask you, because they did their best to incriminate Brian and believe the police will arrest him." Like Traci had done, Babbs looked at the top floor of the Mattherson Mansion. "That leaves Belinda. She wants you to prove neither of the Mattherson boys had anything to do with it." She looked at Heather. "You want to help Traci, don't you?"

"Yes, but we told her we would go wherever the evidence leads us."

Steve joined in. "Like I said, we don't have a client. Would you be interested in hiring us to find Amanda's killer?"

Babbs folded her hands in her lap. "What will you charge me?"

"Nothing," said Heather.

Babbs shook her head. "You're a much better businesswoman than that. No wonder you're having trouble getting Belinda to sell you the right of way."

Steve rubbed his chin. "We want you to pay us in paté. One case to replace what we're giving you and another case for profit."

Babbs clapped her hands and cackled out a laugh. "That's a hundred percent profit. Too much. My father would roll over in his grave if I didn't get you down to a case and a half. He was hard as nails in business."

"It's a deal," said Steve. "Heather will put together the contract and have it ready for you to sign tomorrow morning."

The slamming of the screen door announced Traci's return and an end to the business meeting.

Traci returned with not only the cat food, but with an announcement. "Brian's on his way."

19

Traci pulled up another chair for Brian.

Heather asked, "Did Brian tell you how long it would be before he arrived?"

"It should be any second."

Right on cue, the thick hedges pushed apart and out walked a young man of college age. He wore jeans, canvas tennis shoes, and a T-shirt emblazoned with the University of Houston. Most of his straw-colored hair was in place as he approached with hands stuffed in the front pockets of his pants.

Babbs was on her feet and met him with a hug that conveyed genuine caring. He did not pull away as a tear slid down his cheek. The two whispered something to each other Heather couldn't make out. With linked arms, he guided his grandmother back to the gathering.

Traci rose as they approached and took her turn, giving Brian a hug that brought tears from both. When they finally separated, Brian said, "You look great. I always thought you were too skinny."

Traci gave him a pretend punch in the arm. "It doesn't look like you've missed many meals, either."

"I'm cursed with my father's pudgy waistline. I could do a thousand sit ups a day and never lose this roll." He grabbed the two sides of his waist with both hands to reveal love-handles.

The humor ended as the two stared at each other. As if instructed, they came together again in another hug. Words weren't necessary, as both found a silent way of expressing their grief.

After they wiped their faces, Traci got down to business. "Brian, this is Steve Smiley and Heather McBlythe, guests at the B&B. They need some information I think you can give them. I trust them and I'm hoping you'll help them."

Steve rose and extended a hand for Brian to shake. Heather remained seated, issuing a smile and a nod. "We hear you're in college. Is it all you thought it would be?"

"All I feared, and more. Much more." He raised his eyebrows in question. "I'm intrigued now. What brings you to Mattherson?"

"Business for me," said Heather, "but that's on the back burner for now."

Steve took his turn. "Heather's my next-door neighbor and part-time business partner. She brought me along so I could do historical research on the town and county."

Babbs spoke in a clear voice. "Sit down, everyone. I'll get a sore neck if I have to look up at you."

Traci took over and explained to Brian the expanded version of why Heather came to Mattherson. Brian gave Heather a sideways glance. "A high-speed rail line between Houston and Dallas would be awesome, but Mom is funny about selling family land. I don't know why, because there are sections that aren't good for anything but running a few head of cattle."

Traci then explained that Steve was interested in the three leading families in the county. She let out a false laugh, and said, "Or should I say the two leading families and the Wells. We lost the status of leading family a long time ago."

Brian faced Steve. "Are you a historian?"

"Not exactly. I'm a former homicide detective. Heather and I join up several times a year to investigate murders."

Brian's eyes widened. He turned to Traci. "Are they here about Amanda?"

"That's not why they came, but I'm trying to hire them to discover who killed her."

Steve spoke next. "Traci, you should know we've decided not to accept your offer. Another party has come forward and we've made a verbal commitment to that person."

"Who?" demanded Traci.

"That's confidential."

While Brian's head jerked around to face Steve, Babbs caught Traci's attention. If Heather hadn't been looking, she would have missed the wink Babbs gave to Traci. It only took a tick of the clock for Traci to put the pieces together. "Brian, these people are here to help. I've done a background check on them and they're the best. You can trust them. I really think you should help them."

Brian shook his head. "Dad and that lawyer he hired are both adamant. I'm not supposed to talk to anyone but them."

Heather spoke up. "That's the same advice I'd give you, but in this case, it's not the best advice."

Traci rubbed her stomach. "Listen to her, Brian. She's an attorney, and she used to be a detective. They know what they're doing."

"But..."

"But, nothing," said Babbs. "Do as Traci says. Steve and Heather share a cat. That's makes them double trustworthy."

Traci broke in. "I tried to hire them, my parents tried to hire them and so did your mom. They turned everyone down."

"Not everyone since they now have a client," said Babbs.

Steve took his turn. "From what I'm hearing from a contact in Houston, your arrest could be imminent. When that happens, you'll have no opportunity to talk to us. Your attorney will see to that. Heather and I need information from you tonight before it's too late."

Brian lowered his head. "I can't believe this is happening. I loved Amanda and would never have done anything to harm her."

Traci sat close enough to Brian to reach out to hold his left hand. "I know, Brian. Anyone with eyes could see you loved her. Don't be a fool. Your parents will do anything to get you out of trouble, but they aren't interested in who killed Amanda. Don't you see? The best way to get out of this mess is for Steve and Heather to find the person responsible."

She looked at Steve. "Sorry, Mr. Smiley. I didn't mean to interrupt."

"Forget it. You said what I was going to."

Heather leaned forward. "Brian, look at me. We can't make you talk to us, but I believe we can find the truth about what happened to Amanda." She paused. "But for us to do that, we're going to have to ask you questions that are deeply personal. If you don't want either Traci or your grandmother to hear the answers, you'll need to tell us now and we'll ask them to leave."

Brian's chin quivered, but he held it together. "I swear, I had nothing to do with her death, and I don't know who killed her or why."

Steve jumped in with a quick question. "Why are the police focused on you?"

Brian's shoulders slumped. "Amanda and I had a fight."

"When?"

"The day she died."

"Tell me about it."

With eyes shifting away from anyone looking at him, Brian said, "We were in the library. I got a glimpse of an incoming text on Amanda's phone. It said, *I'll meet you at nine on the street.*" He took in a deep breath before he continued. "I confronted her about it and she became defensive."

"Did anyone hear you arguing?"

A sheepish look came over Brian's countenance. "I lost my temper and Amanda wasn't one to back down from a fight. I guess you could say we caused a scene. In fact, they kicked us out of the library."

"What time was this?"

"About four-thirty in the afternoon. That was the last time I saw her."

"Did you call her later?"

"I tried, but she takes a while to get over things once she gets mad."

Traci held up her right hand. "I'll say. She got mad at me on Valentine's Day in the third grade and didn't speak to me until summer break."

Heather took her turn. "We've been keeping up with the story as best we can. News reports say they found her body in a heavily wooded area of Hermann Park, near Rice University. The police think that's where the murder took place. Do you know why she would go there?"

Brian shook his head. "We used to go there, but she didn't like the smell of the zoo, so we stopped."

"They didn't mention the exact location in the news reports."

Brian looked away as if peering into the past. "We'd go to the lake near the zoo, but only in the winter. I haven't been to Hermann Park since February and I can't see Amanda wanting to go there now that it's warm."

Steve looked like a college professor as he rubbed his chin and took in every detail. "Did Amanda have a car?"

Traci gave Brian a break by answering the question. "A new

Tesla, but it scared her to drive in Houston. If we went anywhere together, I'd drive us."

Brian looked at the ground between his feet. "Yeah, she didn't like to drive in the city. I was always reminding her to make sure her car had a full charge if she was planning on coming home. We seldom came home at the same time. What was the use? Neither set of parents allowed us to see each other. You saw last weekend how we had to sneak around."

"I'm surprised they allowed you to attend college in the same town."

Brian glanced toward his home and hung his head. "Yeah, we were too. They believe I'm still enrolled at the University of Houston. The truth is, I transferred in January."

Heather asked, "How did you pull that off?"

He shrugged. "They weren't happy about my choosing the U of H. Mom wanted me to go to an Ivy League school. I told her my grades needed to come up before any school of that caliber would accept me. In the end, I think she didn't really care where I went as long as I wasn't on the same campus as Amanda."

Traci joined in. "Amanda, Brian, and I put our heads together and came up with the plan for Amanda to start at Rice and Brian to go to the U of H, but only for a semester. At least it put them in the same city so they could see each other."

"I showed my first semester grades to Mom and Dad. We even made up a fake girlfriend for me. That seemed to satisfy Mom for a while."

Steve asked, "How did you keep your transfer to Rice from your parents?"

Traci lifted her chin enough for Heather to notice. "One of my mother's jobs is to pick up their personal mail and have it waiting for them on the big table in the entryway. I talked Mom into letting me pick it up when I get off work. I went through it every day and made sure nothing from Rice

University was there. So far, I've been able to catch everything."

Steve shook his head. "That's some conspiracy you three cooked up. What about paying for tuition, books, and all the other things?"

"That was easy," said Traci. "Tell them how you did it."

Brian nodded. "When I started at the University of Houston, I told Mom and Dad that I wanted them to put me on a budget and allow me to track my expenses through college. They were to provide the finances with the stipulation I'd never exceed the budget and ask for more money. I based my budget on how much it would cost at Rice and not the U of H. At the end of the semester, I'd stayed within budget and they didn't have to mess with paying any of my bills. After that, it was clear sailing. Mom stays super busy and Dad keeps up with Ryan more than he does with me. One less thing to do suited both of them."

Steve wasn't smiling when he scooted to the edge of his seat. "I want you to be perfectly honest with me. Were you or Amanda romantically involved with anyone else?"

"Absolutely not."

"Did Amanda ever talk about anyone having a crush on her?"

Brian shook his head. "Nothing like that." He paused. "Wait, she mentioned something about a guy that stalked her when she first arrived at Rice."

"Do you remember any details about him?"

"She told me not to worry about it and that she handled the situation. I think she reported him to the campus police."

"Did anyone hold a grudge against Amanda that you can think of?"

Again, he shook his head. "Amanda and me weren't the type to stand out. I guess you could say we were both kind of bookish and kept to ourselves. We didn't bother people or take part in any organizations. We weren't antisocial, but we kept to ourselves and focused on our studies. It may sound weird, but we both like to learn."

Steve sat back against the cushion and wrapped his right hand around the arm of the wicker chair. "I'm sure your attorney has already asked you to recount your actions on the day Amanda died. Start with when you left the library and keep going until you went to bed."

"I went back to my dorm and tried to call Amanda. I also sent her a bunch of texts, trying to apologize. My brother called and said he and Dad wanted to see me and Amanda."

"I thought your brother was in law school at the University of Texas."

"He is, but he was in town for an interview."

"What sort of interview?"

"A summer internship with some big firm. Ryan likes the action in a big city and to be around movers and shakers."

"Keep going," said Steve. "What did you do after your brother called?"

"The dorm was quiet so I read a couple of chapters, then got ready for dinner."

"Anything else?"

"Ryan said he and Dad would come by campus and then we'd go to Rice and pick up Amanda."

Steve nodded. "Because he thought you were still a student at the University of Houston. Right?"

"Uh-huh. I had to tell Ryan I'd pick up Amanda and meet them at the restaurant."

Heather noticed that Traci's gaze had shifted to the upper floor of the mansion next door. She brought it back down and looked away when she realized her action hadn't gone unnoticed.

Lost in thought, Heather missed Steve's next question, but didn't miss Brian's response. "I gave Ryan the address of a sushi restaurant that was halfway between the U of H and Rice. It was also on his way out of town. We met there for supper, but without Amanda. As usual, Ryan looked like someone that walked off the cover of *Forbes Magazine*. Dad had on a suit, too."

"What did you talk about?"

Brian let out a huff of air through his nose. "There's not too much conversation with Ryan and Dad. They talked, and I listened. Dad said Mom was on to me and Amanda. Then I heard all about the career that will set Ryan on the path for success. It sounded like a pep talk he and Dad worked out. They were pressing me about going to law school and moving back to Mattherson. Dad left after we ate. Ryan and I not long after. There wasn't much left to say."

Heather interrupted. "I'd have thought Ryan would come back home and work with your father."

"That's Mom's plan, not Ryan's. She won't know until it's too late it's not his plan."

"What time did you leave the restaurant?"

"About eight."

"And what did you do then?"

"Checked my phone to see if Amanda sent me a text or tried to call. She hadn't. Then I drove to my apartment."

"Wait a minute," said Heather. "I thought you'd be living on campus."

"I do. I also have an efficiency apartment. Do you remember what it's like trying to study in a dorm?"

"You pay for both?"

"Amanda and I split the cost of the apartment."

Traci piped up. "I told you about it."

Steve put a hand up for Traci not to speak and gave an explanation. "A good detective wants to hear as many versions of the story as possible. It's amazing how you can pick up subtle differences and extra bits of information."

"Oh. Sorry. I won't interrupt again."

Steve asked, "Does anyone know about the apartment?"

"Only Traci. The three of us promised we wouldn't tell anyone about it."

The sound of multiple vehicles coming down the driveway that bordered the property line furthest from the thick hedges brought all talk to an end. Heather and Traci rose to their feet as two men dressed in off-the-rack suits approached with coats unbuttoned. Next in line was a man wearing cowboy cut slacks, boots, a white shirt with a large metal badge on it, and a straw cowboy hat.

Heather said in a low voice, "Steve, the posse's here."

Somehow, Steve knew who to address. "Detective Long, I was wondering when you might make an appearance. Is that Bernie with you?"

"Can it, Smiley," said Detective Long. "You're close to going into handcuffs, too."

Heather stood with feet shoulder width apart, ready for battle.

20

Heather took a step forward and issued what she hoped would be her most withering glare. "You might like to know that I'm filming this and I won't hesitate to post it far and wide. If you have official police business to conduct, then do it and leave."

Long ground his molars but said nothing else to either her or Steve. Before he could take another step forward, Steve turned his head to face Brian. "If I'm not mistaken, these gentlemen do indeed have some police business to take care of. Stand up, Brian, and put your hands behind your back. You'll need to go with them peacefully."

Heather looked at Steve in surprise and added, "Don't forget what your father and your attorney said about talking to the police."

At that moment, Belinda and Johnny burst through the hedges, with Belinda leading the charge. By the time they reached the gathering, Detective Long had secured handcuffs on Brian's wrists.

"Release my son," shouted Belinda. She turned to her husband. "Do something!"

The sheriff held a folded document. "Sorry, Belinda. They have a warrant."

Johnny looked at the sheriff and then his wife. "There's nothing I can do."

"You're worthless. Why did I ever marry you?"

Johnny examined his shoes as Belinda turned to the sheriff. "You've known Brian since he was born. He's never had a ticket or been arrested."

The sheriff tilted his straw hat farther back on his head. "Actually, his record shows an arrest last September for disorderly conduct. As for tickets, you'll need to talk to Johnny about them."

Johnny took a step back. "I didn't want to bother you with any of those things. They were all trivial."

Belinda fumed, but turned back to the sheriff. "It's preposterous to think Brian had anything to do with that Palmer girl's death."

The sheriff resettled his straw hat on his head. "The law is the law, Belinda."

Johnny found his voice. "Can you at least insist he stay in Mattherson County?"

The sheriff shook his head. "That would only last a day or two. Then television crews and reporters would be swarmin' everywhere. They'd be asking anyone they could find to make a comment, and they'd start with the Palmers. Believe me, it's going to be bad enough with Brian being in jail in Houston. You don't want the press here in Mattherson."

Belinda took a step toward the sheriff. "Don't count on support if you're dumb enough to run for re-election."

By this time, the two Houston detectives had walked Brian to their unmarked SUV and secured him in the back seat. As their taillights disappeared past the corner of the Wells mansion, Belinda turned to face Heather. "Why didn't you stop this?"

Heather stuffed her phone in the front pocket of her slacks. "Why ask me?"

"Because I hired you to keep this from happening."

Steve interrupted. "We never agreed to take your offer." He turned to her husband. "Isn't that right, Johnny? There's no written contract, which we always require, and we made no verbal promise to find evidence to clear your son."

He nodded, but said nothing else.

Belinda thrust a tight fist with an extended index finger at Heather. Her voice sounded like flint hitting steel. "You're working for the Palmers, aren't you? You two are nothing but a couple of money-hungry gumshoes." She took a step forward. "Don't think I can't see right through you."

Belinda turned and faced her husband. "You almost had me talked into a deal with this fast-talker." Her attention turned back to Heather. "Forget your dream of a railroad. There will be no right of way through Mattherson County... ever!"

Heather kept her mouth shut, hoping Belinda wouldn't launch into Steve.

With shoulders thrown back, Belinda left the Wells's back yard mumbling a string of oaths and curses. When she couldn't find a break in the hedges, they received her wrath as well.

Before anyone could speak, Babbs broke into a Bob Dylan tune. She'd hum a verse and sing the chorus. In a strange way, it took some of the edge off the arrest and Belinda's reaction.

Traci rose from her chair. "I'm going to the Palmer's and make sure they know what's happened. I'd hate for them to hear some exaggerated account on television or read about it online."

"That's actually my job, but I'll give you a ride," said the sheriff. "It might be good if you're there for support after I leave."

The two walked to the sheriff's SUV and soon disappeared,

just like the two Houston cops and Brian. That left Heather, Steve, Johnny, and Babbs at poolside.

Babbs finished her humming and hefted herself from the chair with some effort. "Can't spring up like I used to. I'd best get back to my friends. It's past their supper time. Thanks again for the cat food. I'll make sure and tell them they have you two to thank."

"Our pleasure," said Steve. He waited a tick before saying, "By the way, Babbs, could we meet with you after breakfast tomorrow morning?"

"I don't see why not. Come to the bungalow. Clarence and Pearl will be glad to see you again."

Johnny asked, "Do you want me to help you get through the hedges?"

She gave him a sideways glance. "I helped plant those hedges. I know every limb and where each of my friends likes to hide in them. The answer to your question is blowing in the wind."

Heather watched as the woman hobbled her way through the hedge. It occurred to her Babbs gave answers that could be interpreted many ways. It might be a strange defense mechanism, but it seemed to work for her.

Johnny occupied the seat Babbs had surrendered. "I hope you don't mind, but Belinda is in a rare mood tonight, and I need to let her cool off before I go home."

Steve pushed out his feet and crossed them at the ankles. "Stay as long as you need to. I'm glad you're here; I've been wanting to get to know you a little better."

Heather wondered what Steve was up to, but played along. "You'll have to excuse Steve. He's a naturally curious guy. It's probably a holdover from all those years as a detective."

With chin lifted, Johnny said, "I've been around the block enough times not to be offended by questions. It comes with the territory of being an attorney." He gave her a wolfish smile.

"Here I am, trying to preach to the choir. I'm sure you get asked all kinds of questions."

Steve answered for her. "We sure do. Is there anything you'd like to ask us?"

The response came much too quick, as did the lecherous smile directed toward Heather. "Who's your client in Amanda's murder case?"

Without a hesitation, Steve said, "We've had three offers so far and there's still not a signed contract in Heather's briefcase."

It wasn't a lie, but Heather knew Steve had no intention of revealing Babbs.

It was enough for Johnny to peel his eyes off Heather's crossed legs and shift his gaze to Steve. "That means you haven't accepted the Palmer's offer yet."

"Neither of us have discussed investigating the death of their daughter with the Palmers."

Johnny let out a bray of a laugh. "That means Belinda threw one of her wild-eyed fits for nothing."

Heather had to bite her lip to keep from chuckling, but for a different reason than Johnny. Steve led the country lawyer down a road paved with Johnny's own false assumptions. She wanted to pile on while she could.

"I haven't talked to Steve about this, but I'm at a standstill in acquiring the land for the right of way. I need to get back to my office in The Woodlands soon and see what I can salvage."

Johnny waved his hand in dismissal. "Don't worry about it just yet. Belinda runs white hot when she's mad, but she'll calm down in a day or two. When I tell her you're not working for the Palmer's, I'll be able to get her to reconsider the sale of the property you need." He looked at Heather. "Of course, that will mean you and I will have to hammer out the details. It might take more than one meeting." Once again, he ran his tongue over his top lip.

Heather tamped down her revulsion and forced a smile.

"I agree with Heather," said Steve. "We need to leave tomorrow, or her cat will disown her. That leaves only tonight to find out the information I came to glean from a Mattherson."

"And what might that be?" asked Johnny.

"I ran upon a story about a young lieutenant in the Army Air Corps in World War II who was murdered as he got off a train in Houston. His case was never solved."

"Why are you interested in that?"

"I'm an aspiring writer. It sounds like a good premise for a novel. You know, a sharp young female detective solves a cold case that occurred way back when."

Johnny pointed at the Wells Mansion. "That young man grew up in the home you're staying in. His name was Rodney Wells."

"That's him," said Steve. "Second Lieutenant Rodney Wells. What do you know about him?"

With a shrug, Johnny said, "Only rumors that he and Babbs's mother were an item in high school."

"Were the Palmers in any way connected?"

"Now that you mention it, I heard talk from an old-timer that the Palmers and the Matthersons were getting along when the war broke out. You've seen the old newsreels. Everyone pitched in together to win. It was the murder of Rodney Wells that rekindled the feud." He waved the issue away with a flick of his wrist. "Of course, I don't know much about it. I'm still considered an outsider since I've only been in Mattherson for twenty-five years."

"Do you know of any old newspaper clippings Belinda might have stashed that would help me in my research?"

Johnny's head swung from side to side. "Belinda keeps nothing that doesn't pertain to our boys."

Steve sat up straight. "That reminds me. We had a pleasant chat with Brian earlier tonight and I got a good read on him. It seems he thought the world of Amanda. I don't think he had anything to do with her death."

"You read him right. While most of the boys around here are into hunting, fishing, and the usual activities at school, he and Amanda spent their time reading, or going to church, or helping with benevolent projects. As far as I know, Brian never used drugs or even took a drink until he went to college. I can't believe the police arrested him."

Heather had been quiet long enough. "What did you and your wife think about his friendship with Amanda and Traci?"

He hesitated long enough that Heather believed he was searching for measured words. "Let's just say my wife and I agreed on how we'd raise our children."

Steve let out an inappropriate laugh. "I know exactly what you mean. Maggie, my deceased wife, and I used to fight like cats and dogs on how we'd raise our kids. I concluded that I'd be much better off if I followed her lead. You know the proverb, 'Happy wife, happy life.'"

"I'll drink to that," said Johnny. "How many children do you have, Steve?"

He sighed. "None. That was one part of our marriage that didn't go the way we'd planned."

Heather interrupted before she lost Steve in the sea of melancholy that he swam in when he lingered too long with Maggie's memory. She moved on. "What about your eldest son, Ryan? Tell us what he's like."

"That's easy. He has Belinda's dark features and is a good-looking young man. He likes to live, and he's full to the brim with confidence. I'm as proud of him as any father could be."

"He sounds like a chip off the old block."

"He and I think alike about most things."

Heather wondered if one chip off the block was the way he treated women. She watched as Johnny rose from his chair.

"I need to get home and call a defense attorney in Houston.

I know several, but would either of you have a recommendation?"

Steve beat Heather to the punch. "I used to, but that was years ago."

Heather added, "Most all my work in Houston is civil, not criminal."

It wasn't a complete lie, but it bordered on it.

"No problem," said Johnny. "I'll call the same one we used when the police detained him."

Instead of fighting his way through the hedges, Johnny made for the driveway, taking the longer way home.

Once he was sure Johnny was out of earshot, Steve said, "Sounded like he wasn't cutting through the hedge. He must not be in much of a hurry to get home. Can't say that I blame him."

As soon as Heather stood, her phone vibrated in her pocket. She looked at the caller ID, moaned, and put the phone on speaker. "Hello, Father. How's Mother?"

"You can call her and find out after you tell me what's going on there. Have you secured the rights of way?"

"No, and it doesn't look like there's much hope for the immediate future."

"Why not?"

"The police arrested one of the property owners' sons for murdering my alternate landowner's daughter. Nobody's in the mood to discuss business."

A huff of disdain preceded a long pause. "I'm receiving phone calls from investors. They're losing patience, and frankly, so am I."

Heather spoke before she thought. "Then buy me out and handle this yourself."

He lowered his voice. "You know better than to make a rash statement like that. You could lose out on the biggest deal of your life."

"Perhaps, but Steve and I have taken on a murder investigation and I can't be hands-on with the project until we solve the case. We've already started but you never know how long these things will take."

"Then you leave me no choice. What are your terms for the buy out?"

"A return of my initial investment and per hour billing for work completed by my company up to today."

"It's a deal. Send me the numbers."

"I'll notify my staff the first thing tomorrow morning with instructions to expedite."

"If it were me, I'd call them in and have them start tonight."

"I'm out of town, and you're not me."

The phone line went dead. It wasn't the first time that one had hung up on the other. She hadn't kept count, but was sure he was behind by a two-to-one margin.

Steve rose from his chair. "Let's see if there're any cookies left. If there are, we can heat them in the microwave. I like my cookies soft and warm."

"Do warm cookies help with all problems?"

Steve grinned. "Not all. Some require ice cream."

21

The smell of fresh-baked cinnamon rolls competed with the aroma of coffee as Heather descended the stairs of the Wells mansion. She entered the dining room with mouth wide open in a yawn and dug crusty matter from the corner of her eyes. Instead of gracefully lowering herself into a chair, she plopped down and yawned again.

Steve looked fresh, clean-shaven, and dressed for the day.

"I hope you look better than you sound," he said as he raised his mug of morning stimulant to his lips.

"Sleepless night."

"Uh-huh. I thought so. It would've helped if you'd eaten a couple of cookies and had a glass of milk."

She rose and went to the coffee service to pour her first cup of the day. "Your home remedies will have me with more cellulite than six menopausal women signing up for Weight Watchers."

Steve chuckled. "Not bad for someone who stayed up most of the night, but it's a mental image I can live without. Was it Jack you were talking to?"

"Yeah. He caught some of my wrath, too." She poured too much coffee in her cup and had to concentrate on not spilling it as she returned to the table. "I thought he was interested in hearing about the blow-up I had with my father. I think he was for the first fifteen minutes, but then I heard him snoring."

"I did something similar once to Maggie. I still don't know why she put up with me."

Heather looked into her overfilled coffee cup. "Relationships aren't easy, are they?"

"Speaking of." Steve whispered. "Can anyone hear us?"

Pans clanged in the kitchen. Otherwise, the house was quiet. "Not if we keep our voices down."

"We need to press Babbs about her mother's relationship with Rodney Wells."

"I thought you wanted to focus on Amanda's murder."

"The longer I thought about it, the more I believe they're linked."

Heather bumped a table leg, sending a small wave of coffee over the rim of her cup. While dabbing her mess with a paper napkin, she responded. "The crimes are eighty years apart. How could they be connected?"

"Not directly, but keep your eyes open today. I'm counting on you to give me full descriptions of what you see. After you have breakfast and get ready for the day, we'll visit Babbs and her cats."

Heather took her first sip of coffee by bending over and slurping. "Do we need to do anything else in Mattherson before we go home?"

"I don't think so. You need to get to your office and unwind your big railroad deal. We'll start fresh tomorrow morning. Ever been to Hermann Park in Houston?"

"Once. Jack and I went to the Art Gallery. It's a beautiful park."

"I want to make sure that's where Amanda was killed." He pushed his chair away from the table and stood. "I'll be poolside. Take your time with breakfast and getting ready. I have plenty to think about and I'm not sure how receptive Babbs will be to our questions."

"Do you think her memory comes and goes?"

"I'm sure it does, but what I don't know is how much of that is real and how much she does because she wants to be left alone with her cats." He unfurled his collapsible cane, but didn't turn to leave. "I'd like for you to record our conversation with her today."

"Is that necessary?"

Steve walked toward the door to the hallway that led to the back door. "She's trained herself to give evasive answers to hard questions, but there might be something important if we read between the lines."

When Heather heard the back door close, she went to the sideboard and helped herself to half of a cinnamon roll that covered a fair portion of her plate. She added a helping of scrambled eggs and a patty of sausage. Instead of enjoying the meal, her mind whirled around thoughts of her father and the railroad deal, a continuation of the same loop that played in her head most of the night. Had she made a terrible mistake? She pushed away the half-eaten breakfast and stood.

Across from her, a mirror hung between an oil painting of the Wells mansion and one of a train belching smoke and steam as it pulled into a long-ago depot boasting a sign that read MATTHERSON, TEXAS. She only glanced at the paintings, but took a longer look at the woman staring back at her. She had tired, worried eyes. The hair looked like a pack-rat had made its nest in it, and her mouth gave the impression she never smiled. "No," she said to the mirror. "It was no mistake to drop the bullet train."

An hour later, Heather joined Steve at the pool. In the meantime, she'd showered, fixed her hair, carefully applied makeup, packed, and most importantly, secured a supper date with Jack. Her world eased back into its proper orbit.

Steve lifted his head as she approached. "Glad to see you came to grips with your decision to drop the rail project."

She tented her hands on her hips. "Go ahead, Detective Smiley. Tell me how you deduced that."

"The pace of your steps. You skipped down the back steps and approached in what I'd describe as a confident stride. That told me you've given up second guessing your decision." He paused. "I also caught a whiff of your perfume. You must have called Jack and patched things up. I'm guessing you have a date tonight."

All she could do was shake her head in wonder. He might not have vision through his eyes, but he could see people in ways that astounded her. Instead of wasting her breath by telling him he was right, she took a step toward him. "Latch on. This train is going to see a cat lady about a murder."

Steve placed his hand on her arm and they soon found their way through a gap in the hedges that deposited them close to Babbs's bungalow.

Babbs, wearing a rainbow-colored tie-dyed T-shirt and a purple peasant skirt, looked up from filling a series of dishes with fresh water. "There you are. I thought you might have forgotten to come. Pearl and Clarence would have been so disappointed."

"Sorry we're late," said Heather. "It's my fault. I should have gotten up an hour earlier."

"Nonsense." She gave a sweeping motion with her hand. "I gave up on tracking time my freshman year of college. None of my little friends own a watch, so why should I? Let's go inside. I thought about offering you some nice herbal tea, but I don't have any fresh milk. My friends would be upset if I served tea and didn't offer milk."

"Don't worry about serving us tea," said Steve. "We're both morning coffee drinkers, and we've had our quota."

Heather chimed in. "I love your bungalow. It's the perfect size for you and your friends."

Babbs accepted the compliment without commenting and motioned for Heather to follow her.

On the way through the doorway, it pleasantly surprised Heather that a foul odor didn't overwhelm her. Instead, she walked into a living room that served humans well, and cats even better. Sprouting from the floor along all the walls was a labyrinth of carpeted poles, platforms, walkways, and hiding boxes for felines. The walkways even went over the doors and windows.

The arrival of strangers caused a stir among the colony of cats. The timid ones raced to gain elevation or disappear into closed-topped boxes with holes big enough for the kitties to slink through. Others, sleek and plump, lay on their perches, looking down on their "mother" and the two strangers. Heather's mouth gaped open until she spoke. "I've never seen anything so elaborate. Did you design all this for your cats?"

"Designed and helped build," said Babbs. Pride seasoned her words. "Leon did the carpentry while Sara Jane, Traci, and I did the finish work with rope and carpet scraps."

Heather remembered Steve and described the intricate kitty playground to him. Babbs interrupted her. "Let me take Steve around the room so he can touch what you're trying to describe. I once had a blind cat that I had to do the same thing with. After he knew the layout, he could go anywhere the others could. I named him Sampson."

It took ten minutes for Steve and Babbs to complete their lap around the room. At about three quarters of the way, Steve made an observation. "Any cat would love to come live with you. Do you go out looking for them?"

"Oh, no. They simply show up. Some don't like the rules I set for them and they leave."

"What rules?"

"The main one is everyone must go outside to potty. I'll not have my home smelling like a litter box. Next, I don't allow fighting. It helps that they must agree to being spayed or neutered."

Steve nodded. "I can see how that would cut down on the disagreements over who they cuddle with."

Babbs stopped and looked at the tile floor. "Males fighting over females brings grief... so much grief." The room remained quiet, as if the words needed to settle like dust on the floor. She snapped out of her silence and continued the tour. When she did, it was like she'd stuffed the memories in a closet in her mind and shut the door.

The tour ended at a doorway that led down a short hall. Babbs brought Steve back to a fabric covered chair, and she took her place in a short recliner that allowed her sandal-covered feet to touch the ground. "Steve, Clarence and Pearl want to say hello to you. I told them they could join you in your chair, but only on the armrests."

On cue, both cats leapt to the arms of the chair. Steve welcomed them each by name and stroked the sides of their faces. The two felines soon settled amid deep purrs.

Heather issued a word of warning. "You'll need to wash your hands before you go home. Max will be jealous if he smells other cats on you."

"He'll just ignore me. That's his way of showing displeasure."

Steve continued to pet both cats as he eased into a conversation with Babbs. "Tell me what you remember about your parents."

The corners of Babbs' mouth pulled down. "A lot of arguments behind closed doors. Separate bedrooms."

"Do you have anything that belonged to your mother and father you can show us? Perhaps a wedding photograph, or an old love letter?"

"Some people say photos steal a piece of your soul."

Heather realized Steve was getting nowhere fast with his questions. Babbs had put up her barrier to unpleasant memories. She scanned the room for something that might trigger a memory that wasn't so unpleasant. When her gaze landed on a bookshelf, Heather rose from her seat and moved to where a series of books stood at attention, spines facing out.

"Is this your high school yearbook?" Heather touched the red-jacketed memento dated 1961.

A pleasant smile returned to Babbs's face. "So long ago."

"Do you mind if I look at it?"

"Go ahead, but why would you want to?"

"You're our client. We like to know all we can about the people we work with."

This seemed to pacify Babbs, so Heather took the yearbook from the shelf, moved a chair next to her hostess, and thumbed through the pages.

Babbs gave a page-by-page account of the students attending the small-town Texas high school. It took about twenty minutes to make it through the yearbook. The young woman on the pages looked so different from the one in front of Heather, but that wasn't what struck her the most. The young woman living on the pages was the class valedictorian, the homecoming queen, and an all-around athlete. She had bright eyes, a disarming smile, and the look of a woman with a bright future ahead of her. One would never guess it by looking at the woman beside her now.

By the time Heather and Babbs ended the trip down

memory lane, Steve had questions. "Did everything change for you in the sixties?"

A wistful look came into Babbs's eyes. "Everything changed in the whole country in the sixties. The music, the clothes, and most of all, the drugs. In high school, I thought I was living on the edge if I scored a beer or shared a bottle of wine with my friends. College was an eye-opening experience. By the time I dropped out of grad school, I'd tried almost everything you can name. I eventually came out of the fog and moved back home."

"Is that when you married?"

"Uh-huh. They picked my husband, so it wasn't like a proper marriage. He served his purpose, received payment, and left without a word to me."

The words "served his purpose" rang in Heather's ears. "What do you mean, he served his purpose?"

Instead of answering, Babbs rocked side to side and hummed a tune Heather didn't recognize.

Steve offered a likely explanation. "When you came back to Mattherson, you didn't come alone, did you?"

Babbs stopped her rocking. "You're clever, Steve. Just like Clarence."

Instead of offering an explanation, Steve changed the subject. "Did both of your parents attend Mattherson High School?"

"Uh-huh."

"What was your mother's maiden name?"

"Dumont. Elsa Dumont."

"Do you have your father's or mother's yearbook?"

"Only Mom's."

"Would you mind showing it to Heather?"

Wide-eyed fear flashed across Babb's countenance. She rocked side to side again and hummed louder. Heather and Steve both asked two more questions that went unanswered.

They left Babbs in her chair, rocking and humming, surrounded by cats.

Once outside in sunlight, Heather asked, "What caused her to shut down like that? Was it all the drugs she did?"

"We need to make a stop at the public library on our way home. Let's see if we can find a copy of her mother's yearbook. There's something in it that haunts her to this day."

22

Heather brought her SUV to a stop in the near-empty parking lot of the public library. She met Steve at the front bumper and the two were soon inside and standing at the circulation desk. A woman greeted them. She looked to be in her mid-fifties with gray-streaked brown hair that hung down her back. A large silver cross dangled from a thin length of leather.

Steve did the talking. "We're doing historical research related to Mattherson. Could you help us find something specific?"

"I'll try."

"Are you the person in charge of the library?"

"I'm a volunteer, but I reckon I know how to find most anything that's here."

Steve gave a nod. "Do you keep copies of the high school yearbooks?"

"Sure do. Dating all the way back to the thirties. You can't check them out, but there's a table and chairs next to the shelves holding the historical documents of Mattherson County. Second aisle on your left, all the way to the end."

They thanked the woman and made their way to a far corner of the library. Once there, it didn't take Heather long to find the collection of yearbooks. She ran her finger along the dates until she came to the end of the 1930's. "We're out of luck. The yearbook for 1940 is missing. All the others are here, but not that one."

He huffed. "I was afraid of that. Grab the ones from 1939 and 1941. We're looking for anything on Babbs's mother, father, and Rodney Wells."

Heather and Steve sat side by side as she opened the yearbook from 1939. It didn't take long for Heather to find Rodney Wells. As she flipped the pages and narrated, she clicked off his accomplishments and accolades.

Steve summarized. "The junior year for Rodney Wells and James Mattherson. As for Rodney, there wasn't much he didn't excel in. He was a three-sport letterman, named first team all-district in football and basketball, president of the slide rule club, and was the boy voted most handsome."

Heather added, "Tall, with wavy black hair. I bet he's the one every mother wanted their daughter to marry."

"Perhaps not every mother. Tell me about James Mattherson."

"He had his share of accomplishments in sports." Heather looked up from a photo that pictured James peeking around the trunk of a tree. "Here's one Rodney didn't have. James was voted class favorite."

Steve quipped, "With the last name of Mattherson, it doesn't surprise me."

Before Heather could get Steve to expand on his statement, he moved on. "Go through the 1941 yearbook and see who stands out."

Heather took her time and carefully separated the pages as they had a tendency to stick together. She wondered how long it had been since someone viewed either of the yearbooks. By the time they reached the back page, the class of 1941 had one student that stood head and shoulders above the rest. The valedictorian, homecoming queen, head cheerleader, and voted most beautiful was Elsa Dumont, Babbs's mother.

"Tell me what Elsa looks like," said Steve.

"A honey-blond with a cameo face. Tall, with the legs of a dancer in the team photo of the girls' basketball team. One photo in particular shows her filling out a sweater in a way that would make other girls envious."

Steve rubbed his chin. "You said Rodney Wells was voted most handsome, not James Mattherson."

"James was a nice-looking young man, but not one that would cause a girl to swoon. Not like Rodney Wells."

Steve reached in his pocket, retrieved his cell phone and told it to call Traci Wells.

"Whoever you are, make it quick."

"Traci, it's Steve Smiley. I have a job for you. It pays a hundred dollars."

"Will it help Brian?"

"No guarantees, but I think it might."

"Will I have to do anything illegal?"

Steve couldn't help but chuckle. "Nothing illegal or immoral. A Mattherson High School yearbook from 1940 is missing from the public library. We think Babbs has a copy, but she became upset when we asked to see it."

"1940? That's a long time ago."

"It's the year your great uncle Rodney graduated. Do you think you might track down a copy?"

"I can try, but—"

Steve didn't allow her to finish before he upped the reward. "I said two hundred dollars, didn't I?"

"If there's a copy in town, I'll find it."

"Thanks, Traci. Call me when you have it."

Steve stood, saying nothing else except that it was time to

leave and Heather needed to get to her office. She led him to her car, and they began what proved to be a silent trip home for Steve because Heather's phone all but blew up with calls from her staff and concerned investors who'd gotten wind she was selling her position back to her father.

The traffic thickened as they approached the turnoff to her office building. Steve broke his silence. "Don't take me home. I'll have lunch at my desk and call Uber when I'm ready to leave. You have way too much to do without wasting time on me."

Heather gave a quick, "Okay." She followed this a few seconds later with, "I'm delegating most all the work required to get me out of the railroad business to my staff. By the time they get to work in the morning, they should have all they need from me to get it done. I'll be available to help you full time by tomorrow."

"Good. We'll go to Houston."

"It sounds like you have a plan."

"I wouldn't call it a plan. It's more like several things on a list that might, or might not, bring results."

Heather caught something in Steve's voice. She'd heard it before and likened it to a hound catching a scent. "Which case will we be focusing on?"

"Tomorrow we'll focus on Amanda's murder, but we may swerve into the cold case if we're lucky."

A jolt of excitement coursed through Heather. She loved to watch Steve put together pieces until they revealed the person who'd committed a serious crime and needed to face justice. This case differed from any she'd ever encountered. Did a crime committed so long ago have anything to do with a college student being killed last week? Steve was right. They'd have to be lucky to fit such an old puzzle together with a new one.

Steve pulled his phone from his pocket and instructed it to

call Leo Vega and pushed speaker phone. This wouldn't be a private conversation.

After some good-natured banter about who had the least to do, Steve got down to business. "Heather and I want to visit the place they found Amanda Palmer. Can you get away long enough tomorrow to show us the exact spot?"

A laugh dripping in sarcasm preceded Leo's words. "Let me check my calendar and see if I can fit you in. Well, bless my soul, it looks like I can. One thing about this job, it's not hard to get a day off."

"Good. If the first stop turns out like I think it will, we'll have another stop to make and plenty to talk about."

"I hope some of it's related to the cold case. If I don't get something soon to give the lieutenant, the file goes back in a box."

"Heather and I are driving back from Mattherson. We have plenty to buy you some more time."

"I guess that's a good thing, but right this minute, I'm not sure how much more of this job I can stand."

Instead of responding, Steve gave Leo an instruction. "Meet us at George's Diner, near Hermann Park at 11:00 a.m. I'd like to get started earlier, but Heather has a hot date tonight. I don't expect her to be fully functioning until ten-thirty."

Instead of arguing, Heather spoke loud enough for Leo to hear her. "Just for that, we won't be there until eleven-thirty. If I'm going to celebrate tonight, I want to do it right."

"What's the cause for celebration?"

"I got rid of a railroad."

As usual, Heather paid for lunch with an American Express business card, folded the receipt, and placed it in a compartment in her purse. One more slip of paper she'd give her accountant to reduce her taxable income. Once outside, Steve spoke to Leo. "Leave your car here. I chose this place because we'll have to pass it going to and coming back from where I want to go today."

Heather piped up. "I knew you didn't choose it for the food."

Steve grinned. "I wanted a place we could talk without yelling. Most places today are so loud you can't carry on a conversation."

Leo threw in his opinion. "With six kids, I'll take a free meal any time and place I can get it. Thanks, Heather."

Once in the SUV, Leo pointed. "Go to the second street and take a right."

Heather touched the navigation screen. "I already put in the address."

Leo sighed. "They must have made a mistake and left that option out of my fifteen-year-old Corolla. Do you two really think there's a link between the deaths of Rodney Wells and Amanda Palmer?" He cleared his throat. "Don't get me wrong. I appreciate everything you're doing and there's no doubt you gave me plenty to keep the investigation on Rodney going, but it was four or five generations ago."

Steve shifted in his seat. "Like we said, there's a good chance we'll never be able to prove who killed him, but I believe we're close to finding at least one person with a motive to do it. He could have done it himself, or hired someone."

"Right now, it looks like tiny specks of evidence and a lot of guessing."

"I look at it like we're collecting dots," said Steve. "If we get enough of them, we might be able to connect them."

"I'm trying to believe you, but I haven't been able to find a single dot in Houston."

"Yes, you did. You found an old train schedule that told you what time the train from Mattherson arrived on the night Rodney died."

Leo huffed. "Fat lot of good that did. That info was already in the sergeant's notes."

Steve faced the windshield. "Brick by brick. Little by little. That's how you build a case."

Heather put on her blinker. "If you boys are finished complaining, I'm turning into Hermann Park. Tell me where to go, Leo."

He did, and they turned into a parking lot surrounded by trees. He pointed to the far end of the lot, away from all other parked cars. "They took the crime scene tape down after the folks in blue paper suits processed it. It was a pretty quick job with the park supervisor pushing them to hurry."

After pulling into a space, Heather and Steve followed Leo to a spot close to the parking lot, but tucked in a copse of willows.

Heather stepped on a branch that let out a snap. "It always amazes me how perps can find isolated places in the middle of such public places to do their deeds. We're within shouting distance of a dozen people."

The tip of Steve's cane swept the tops of the grass and warned him of other trip hazards. "There's so much noise in the city that people rarely react to something they can't see. It's not unusual for them to ignore loud noises, even cries for help."

"It's somewhere around here," said Leo as he pointed to a spot behind a lone oak tree. "I couldn't get access to the crime scene photos, but stopped by before they took the tape down and talked to a patrolman."

Heather knew what to expect next, and she believed Leo did, too. When she stopped, Steve took his hand from Heather's arm as she spoke in a clear voice. "Amanda Palmer."

He moved several steps forward. "Keep saying her name."

She did as he continued to walk, making a search pattern.

When he'd walked back and forth and front to back on an imaginary square, he stopped. "This isn't the original crime scene."

Leo let out a low whistle, followed by, "Are you sure?"

"The color I'm seeing isn't bright red, but more like a pale rose. Her body was here, but this isn't where she died."

"That's not good news for the young guns in homicide." Leo scratched his chin. "I'm no better off now than before. If anyone says we know this isn't where Amanda died because you saw pale rose and not red, they'll laugh me all the way to my forced retirement party."

Steve took a step toward the SUV. "Let's go to Rice University and see if we can find other places where the murder might have taken place."

Leo laughed. "A blind guy looking for a needle in a haystack. I think we should buy lottery tickets on the way. If lady luck is going to smile on us that much, I want to cash in."

23

Heather didn't need to use the SUV's navigation system to find Rice University. A morbid thought crossed her mind. The proximity to the park made it handy to kill on campus and dump a body in the sprawling nearby park.

Leo gave instructions from the back seat once they crossed Main Street, which led to the heart of Houston, not more than a couple of miles from the campus. "Keep going straight. You'll come to a stop at College Way. It's a loop that runs through the university. You'll have to turn right."

"Do you know where she lived?"

"Steve told me."

Heather shot a glance at Steve. "How did you find out?"

"Traci called me yesterday afternoon. She knew where Amanda lived on campus and that she was studying engineering."

Leo added, "Steve called me last night. He wanted to make sure I was familiar with the campus. This street loops around to the Brown College of Engineering. That's where she lived."

"This is my first visit to Rice University," said Heather. "It's more spread out than I was expecting. I love how the trees line the streets."

Heather glanced in the rear-view mirror as Leo gave additional details. "Students come from all over the world. It's patterned after the English Universities in Cambridge with a different college for each discipline. This is only my second time to come to campus."

"What brought you here the first time?"

"I took a wrong turn and liked the scenery so much I drove around for twenty minutes. The university has their own police department, so HPD lets them do their own thing." Leo pointed after the road turned ninety degrees to the left. "There's a small parking lot off to your right. We might luck out and find an empty spot."

Heather crept through the lot twice before she saw someone approaching a Toyota Prius. She had a professorial look about her and carried a book bag stuffed to overflowing.

"You'll probably get a parking ticket if we stay here very long," said Leo.

Heather brushed away the warning. "The cost of doing business."

The three piled out and made their way to where the road bent another ninety degrees to the left. "We're now at Brown College," said Leo. "Amanda lived in the building up the road on our right."

Steve squeezed Heather's arm. "Describe what you're seeing."

"Huge trees line both sides. The branches are so thick they cover the street. None of the buildings are uniform. They're all multi-story and set back from the street."

Steve swept his cane before him. "It even smells like a university campus. They must have mowed the lawns this morning. Is there on-street parking?"

Leo spoke up. "Not much. This is a park-and-walk kind of place. Most of the parking for students is in remote lots."

"If someone driving a car wanted to talk to Amanda, what would they do?"

Leo looked up and down the street. "The easiest thing would be to call her and tell her to meet them on the street."

"I was afraid you'd say that. I was hoping there'd be a parking lot behind the building she lived in."

Heather joined the conversation. "I'd say the chances of Amanda being killed in front of these buildings are next to zero. Too much foot traffic and windows everywhere."

"I get the picture," said Steve. "It makes more sense for her to meet her assailant on the street and go someplace with them. From all accounts, she was a brilliant young woman with a fair amount of common sense. I think she knew her assailant and trusted them."

A group of four students walked past them on the grass. They spoke Arabic and were so absorbed in their conversation that they paid no attention to anything or anyone around them. Only one of them looked old enough to be on a university campus.

As Heather kept watching the foursome, they passed a makeshift shrine of stuffed animals, flowers, and photos. A young woman came from the nearest building with a single rose, placed it among the other offerings, and bowed her head.

"Let's have a talk with that student," said Heather. "I have a hunch she knew Amanda."

The three moved toward the collection of offerings to the memory of a student whose life ended much too soon. "Excuse me," said Heather. "I couldn't help but notice you placed a rose to honor Amanda. We're following up on the investigation the police are conducting. Did you know Amanda well?"

She looked past Heather to the two men accompanying her.

Leo dragged his badge case out of the front pocket of his shirt and showed it to her. "What's your name?"

"Sung Lu Lee. I go by Sunny. It's about time the cops talked to me. I lived across the hall from Amanda the last two semesters."

Steve stepped forward. "The police haven't talked to everyone on the hall?"

"Amanda's roommate said they grilled her, but she's a drama queen. They spoke to some of the others, but not to me, and I knew her better than anyone except Brian."

Heather took her turn. "We know Amanda was involved with Brian Mattherson and we've talked to both sets of parents. Were there any other men she was interested in?"

"Not really. I mean, she talked about a couple of guys in her classes, but she didn't date anyone but Brian." She looked at the memorial and shook her head. "I can't believe you think he killed her."

Steve took a half step forward. "We're keeping an open mind about that and checking other possibilities. Right now, the evidence is pretty convincing against him. Did you talk to her on the day she died?"

"That afternoon I did, about 5:30."

"What did you talk about?"

"Mainly about the calculus class we had together. She was scary smart and I was always picking her brain. But she also mentioned she and Brian had a silly fight earlier that afternoon. They were supposed to go out to eat with Brian's brother. She bailed on eating out after the fight and then regretted it. Amanda loved sushi. She could be moody like that sometimes."

"Did she have any enemies on campus?"

"Not that I'm aware of."

"Anyone stalking her, or hounding her for a date?"

"A few. You know how it is when first-year girls arrive. She filed a complaint with the campus police against one guy that wouldn't take no for an answer."

"Did she talk about anything else on the day she died?"

"Not really. It was after dark when she knocked on my door and said she had to run downstairs and talk to someone."

"Did she say who?"

"I assumed it was Brian."

"Are you sure?"

She took her time in answering. "I think she said Brian, but she talked real fast. Know what I mean?"

"Yeah, I do. Thanks. You've been most helpful." He paused, but only to take a breath. "There's something you can do for us, if you would."

"What is it?"

"Could you ask around, sort of on the down-low? We'd be interested to know if anyone might have seen Amanda getting into a car on the night she died."

She nodded. "On the down-low is a good idea. There are a ton of international students on campus. Some of them come from countries where you don't talk to the police. By the way. I think it's cool you're a cop. I mean, I didn't know they had blind detectives."

No one corrected her and Leo handed her his business card.

Heather became lost in her thoughts, filing away the interview in her mind. She tuned back in as Steve asked a question to no one in particular. "Let's assume someone picked up Amanda. We know they didn't kill her at Herman Park. That means they took her somewhere else. Where could they go?"

"Anywhere," said Leo.

"True, but they dumped her body in the park. Let's focus on the campus. Where could they go where nobody would think anything was amiss?"

Heather had the answer. "When I was at Princeton and I

wanted to get away from everything, I'd sit in my car. Sometimes I'd study and other times I'd catch up on sleep."

Steve grinned. "Maggie and I would do the same thing, but
there wasn't much studying going on." He turned to face Leo.
"Where's the nearest parking lot for students?"

"That would be the north lot and there's a secondary lot
next to it."

"Let's check it out."

24

They retraced their steps back to where Heather parked. She removed the parking ticket from under her windshield wiper and stuffed it into her purse. A few minutes later, she wheeled into the north parking lot and made a slow path between lines of vehicles. A movement in her rearview mirror earned her attention, and she brought her SUV to a quick stop. Sure enough, a new Camaro backed out, turned toward the exit, and left an opening. With the aid of a backup camera, she beat another car to the spot with no time to spare.

When all three stood near the bumper, she asked, "What's the plan?"

"Same as in the park," said Steve, "except this time I want to check every parking spot while you or Leo say Amanda's name."

Leo scanned the lines of cars. "This is a huge lot, and there's another one behind it."

"No one said this would be easy or quick."

Leo made a sweeping gesture with his hand. "At least it's a nice day for a walk. Lead on Heather."

She brushed her arm against Steve's, his cue to place his

hand on her arm and allow her to lead him. "Come on, blood-hound. Show this big-city cop how we do things in the country." She led Steve to the nearest car and said, "Amanda Palmer."

"Nothing. If you only slow down and not stop, this shouldn't take too long."

The lot had multiple rows of vehicles. They'd made it to the end of the first row when Leo spoke up. "Heather, it looks like the campus cops don't like you."

She turned around to see a uniformed officer slide an envelope under her windshield wiper. "I'll give them this much, they're efficient."

They continued walking past cars, with Heather saying Amanda's name. The patrol car passed, then backed up and activated his emergency lights. Leo said, "Let me handle this. You two keep walking."

Heather and Steve did as he suggested. With a quick glance over her shoulder, Heather saw Leo pull out his badge and allow the officer to study it. As the distance increased, Heather gave more volume to Amanda's name. Ten minutes later, they were in the next row of cars and Leo was closing the gap. The patrol car had disappeared.

"What did you tell them?" asked Steve when Leo's footfalls told him he was near enough to converse.

"Mostly the truth. I said you were private detectives, and I was a friend. I sort of stretched the truth when I told her a student's concerned family hired you to find out if an old boyfriend was stalking a female student here. All you had to go on was a vague description of the car and that it had a splotch of red paint on the bumper."

Steve leaned on his cane. "That story may be closer to the truth than you think. We found out when we were in Mattherson that Brian's brother, Ryan, and their father were in town the day before Amanda died."

Leo acted like a bird dog coming on point. "Now that's an interesting little tidbit. I've heard no rumors of that."

"I didn't think you had. Brian told us his attorney and father have him sworn to silence. That probably applies to Ryan, too."

Leo glanced away and brought his focus back to Steve. "Are you planning on letting the young guns handling the case know about it?"

Steve straightened his posture. "I just told a homicide detective. What are you going to do about it?"

Leo took a step back. "If I brought information like this to anyone in regular Homicide, my lieutenant would hang me out to dry. Remember, I'm only to work on cold cases. Are you trying to get me fired?"

Steve shrugged. "I'm confused. You said you wanted to quit. Now you're acting like being a homicide detective means something to you."

Leo pulled his hand down his face. "You're playing mind games with me. I thought you were trying to help me solve an eighty-year-old murder."

Heather answered for Steve. "We are. It just so happens a recent murder keeps getting in Steve's way."

Steve held out his arm for Heather to place on hers. "Let's keep walking and you keep saying Amanda's name."

Fifty minutes later, Heather had said Amanda's name in front of every parking space in the north lot. Leo fell behind, but still followed, looking either bored or lost in thought. Heather whispered. "I think Leo is at a crossroads."

Steve spoke with confidence. "He'll be fine. Watch him perk up when we find the spot of the murder."

They headed into the addition to the north parking lot, Heather leading Steve and Leo following at a distance behind. After saying Amanda's name six more times, Heather led Steve past an empty parking spot. "Amanda Palmer," she said. Steve stopped, dropped his hands to his side, and made a right turn.

"Say it again."

"Amanda Palmer."

He took a couple of steps toward the curb. "Again."

"Amanda Palmer."

Goose bumps rose on Heather's arms as she watched Steve's chin drop to his chest.

"This is it. I'm seeing bright red."

Leo's footfalls came in a hurry. "I know that look."

Steve turned. "I'm willing to bet my pension that I'm standing on the spot where someone killed Amanda Palmer."

It was one of those moments where all noise ceased, and the light breeze stilled. Heather finally looked at Leo. He returned her gaze with jaw muscles flexing. "I've never known Steve to be wrong. His ability to see red gave me the willies every time, and it still does."

Steve turned on his heels. "Time to go. We need to plan out our next steps."

Heather caught Steve before he bumped into a car. "Let's go back to where we had lunch. The food may be lousy, but their iced tea wasn't bad, and it should be quiet this time of day."

It wasn't long before the three were sitting in a booth as far away from anyone as they could get. Steve opened up. "The first thing we need to do is place Ryan Mattherson in Houston on the day of the murder. According to Brian, he came from Austin for a job interview at one of the top law firms. He told us the name of the firm, but that needs to be verified."

Heather said, "I know one of the senior partners with that firm. I'll make the call."

Leo tilted his head. "Be careful. We don't want word getting back to Ryan that he's a suspect."

Heather stood. "If there's one thing I'm good at, it's talking to wealthy lawyers. We pump each other for information and even tell the truth if it's something inconsequential, like taking on a summer intern."

Instead of staying in the restaurant, Heather excused herself and went to the privacy of her SUV. It took a while to get past the gatekeeper and catch the attorney between appointments.

Thirty minutes later, she slid into the booth next to Steve.

Leo raised his eyebrows. "Success?"

Heather forced herself not to smile. "Ryan Mattherson may have worn a nice suit to Houston, but he didn't interview for a summer internship with King and Weaver."

Steve drummed his fingers on the table. "Leo, can you get phone records on Ryan? I'd love to know if he called Amanda."

"I'll be dancing barefoot on the edge of a knife if my lieutenant finds out."

"I know. But can you do it?"

Leo smiled. "You knew I could before you asked. I'll cover myself by saying I'm following up on a lead with the Rodney Wells case. After all, there's quite a family feud still going on in Mattherson."

"One more thing. One of us needs to find out the name of the guy Amanda reported to the campus police."

Heather nodded. "I'll take care of that. Leo's neck is sticking out far enough. I'd hate to see that handsome face rolling out of his lieutenant's office."

"Good. Heather and I will do what we can to track Ryan's movements while he was in Houston."

"Do you want to tell me your theory about why you think Ryan would kill his brother's girlfriend?"

Steve turned his head, as if he was looking out a window. "Not yet. I don't want to influence either of you with one of my wild ideas."

Leo took a last drink of his iced tea. "Anything else for me to do?"

"No, but there is something else on my list. I need to find out if Ryan Mattherson is planning to go home to see his parents this coming weekend or if he's staying in Austin. Heather and I need to talk to him, and the sooner the better."

Heather snapped her fingers. "I know how we can talk to him and we can do it from the comfort of my office building."

A sly smile crossed Steve's countenance. "You're going to ask him to interview for an internship."

Heather rolled her eyes. "Don't you get tired of reading my mind?"

25

Steve sat in his recliner, deep in thought, with laptop at the ready. Two days had passed since their trip to Hermann Park and Rice University. He turned his head when he heard the sound of car doors closing. Voices approached. He closed his laptop, rose from his favorite chair, and went to the cat door in the wall separating his condo from Heather's. Bending down, he pushed open the flap. "Heather, are you handy?"

Insistent knocks sounded.

"I'm right here at the table, doing research."

"I have unexpected visitors. Keep listening. I might need you."

He moved to the front door and instead of opening it, pushed a button and spoke into an intercom. "Please state your name and purpose."

"Detective Long. Open the door, Smiley."

Steve turned the dead bolt, opened the door, and stood back. "Come in. Who's that with you?"

The voice that answered spoke in fast, clipped sentences. "Lieutenant Chase. I've heard a lot about you, Mr. Smiley."

"Don't believe everything you hear."

Steve moved to the dining room table and gestured with an open hand for the two men to sit. "I can fix coffee if you care for a cup. I guarantee it's better than what you get at the office."

"This isn't a social visit," said the lieutenant. "It's a shame you're no longer on the force. You had quite the reputation for solving murders. Some people say you're some sort of clairvoyant or mystic." Steve noticed the lack of sincerity in the last sentences.

"I got lucky." He paused. "You said this wasn't a social visit. You must want my help with a case. Let me guess, you've made an arrest and now realize you have the wrong person in jail. Those can be tricky. Lawsuits by fancy attorneys can ruin a career like that." He timed the snap of his finger with his last word.

"Tell me, Lieutenant, was it you who screwed up or Detective Long?"

"You need a new crystal ball," said Long.

Steve let out a bellow of a laugh. "I sold mine when I lost my sight, but that was a good blind guy joke."

The lieutenant backtracked out of political quicksand as fast as he could. "Please forgive Detective Long's misguided sense of humor. I assure you he'll choose his words with more care from here on."

Steve leaned back and sighed. "I remember when there was camaraderie, and cops could poke fun at each other without having to worry about hurting feelings. Have things really changed that much?"

Steve sensed the lieutenant had leaned forward. "That's why we're here, Mr. Smiley. Times have changed. We take it seriously when people impersonate police officers."

"I totally agree."

"Then why did you go to Rice University, pretend you and Ms. McBlythe were cops, and interview students about Amanda Palmer's murder? You're not on the force anymore,

Smiley, and you shouldn't be poking your nose in a murder investigation. Obstructing an investigation is still a crime."

Heather's voice came from the direction of the living room. "Good evening, gentlemen."

As expected, she'd gone out her patio door and entered Steve's condo in the same manner. She'd likely come without shoes and listened, pressed against a wall so the two policemen couldn't see her.

Chairs scraped against the tile floor.

Heather continued while the visitors remained mute. "Let's see. So far, you've ridiculed a man with a disability, accused him and me falsely, and issued a threat."

The lieutenant's voice told Steve he was standing. "There was no threat. I was stating facts."

Steve responded. "But your facts are wrong and your investigation is about as funny as your blind joke. Heather and I are licensed private investigators. We're hired to look into the murder of Amanda Palmer."

"Who hired you?" asked Long.

"Shut up," said the lieutenant.

Heather took a step forward. "Did you tell my client to shut up?"

"I wasn't talking to Smiley."

Heather shrugged. "Since you're here on official business, I insist you refer to my client as Mr. Smiley. As for naming our client, we ensure confidentiality, unless given permission. Our client wishes to remain unnamed at this time."

Steve added. "That's the attorney coming out in Heather. I'm a little more loosey-goosey, if you know what I mean. As for our client, I'll give you a hint. Several people in Mattherson wanted to hire us to investigate Amanda's murder."

"How many?" asked Long.

Steve tilted his head. "Several are more than two, and that's the last hint I'm giving you. If you were doing a thorough investigation, you'd already know who they are."

The lieutenant cleared his throat. "There's still the problem of you identifying yourselves as police officers."

"That never happened," said Heather.

"We have a witness who says you did."

"And I have a recording of the interview that proves we didn't. You, of all people, should know that witnesses often make false assumptions when being interviewed. Do you correct them? Of course not. It would disrupt the flow of information."

Steve pushed up from the table. "If there's nothing else, and you won't accept my offer of coffee, Heather will show you to the door."

"No need," said the lieutenant in an even voice. "We'll show ourselves out."

The faint sound of Heather's footsteps preceded her slipping into a chair opposite him. He opened his mouth to speak, but she beat him to it.

"I know I shouldn't, but confrontations like that get me totally jazzed."

Steve lowered his voice. "Don't get too jazzed. We have a problem."

"What's that?"

"If they tried to warn us off the case, what do you think they'll do to Leo?"

HEATHER OPENED THE DOOR FOR LEO, WHO STOOD WITH HIS BACK to her. When he turned to enter, he kept his head down and shuffled in. It was as if a malevolent extraterrestrial had attached a diabolical suction device to his soul and sucked out all the joy.

Steve moved to his recliner and shouted over his shoulder. "Is that you, Leo?"

"Yeah. Or should I say, what's left of me." He moved to the living room and plopped on the couch next to Steve's chair. He looked at the screen of the television that wasn't on and didn't shift his gaze.

"Your former lieutenant and Detective Long left about ten minutes ago. Were you waiting for them to leave?"

"I wanted to see if they were coming after you."

"Did they fire you?" asked Steve.

Heather winced at the abruptness of the question. Then she realized that was how Steve and Leo often communicated— with an economy of words that sacrificed tact for facts.

"Not quite," said Leo in a soft voice. "Suspended pending formal investigation."

"With pay, or without?"

"With, I think. They said nothing about docking my salary."

"Was it Lieutenant Chase?"

"He conned my lieutenant into doing his dirty work, but it's Long's report that will sink me."

As Heather took a chair facing the men, Steve nodded like he'd already read the script. "Doesn't surprise me. Lieutenant Chase kept his hands clean by not writing a report. Then, the two lieutenants got together and worked out a deal. Chase's star is on the rise and Lieutenant Bounds will do anything to get out of time out. Once Chase makes captain, your lieutenant will remind him he took you down. Chase is the one after your scalp."

"He's going to hang it on the wall of his teepee."

"Teepee?" said Steve in a teasing way. "Chase impressed me as an industrial loft kind of guy. You know the type. Fresh haircut every week, keeps his car detailed, and only dates skinny women with wide mouths and big teeth. None of them last long, after he tells them he's not ready to make a commitment. Five will get you ten that they dump him before he gets the chance."

"You're probably right, but this isn't making me feel any better."

Steve waved a hand the way a king might dismiss a servant. "You always worry too much. Nothing's changed yet."

Heather thought Steve's last statement needed softening. "Something they taught us in law school was to never celebrate or regret what you could have done until the jury announces their verdict."

"You should listen to Heather. She's smarter than both of us put together."

Steve stepped toward the kitchen. "Let's brew a fresh pot of coffee. We have a lot to discuss concerning the two cases."

Heather beat him to the coffee pot. Once the two men seated themselves at the table, Steve gave Leo a line-by-line account of the meeting with Lieutenant Chase and Detective Long. It wasn't a laugh, but a slow grin spread across Leo's face when he learned the two cops thought they might have to answer a formal complaint.

"Did you really tape the interview with Sung Lu Lee?"

"No, but Chance and Long believed I did."

A chuckle came from Steve. "Heather just made half the charges against you disappear, Leo. Your worry-meter should be down to fifty percent."

"That's not how it works. They'll find a way to give me a pink slip and take away my retirement."

The coffee maker sputtered its last hot drops. Heather did the honors and delivered the men a mug each.

Steve turned his mug until the handle sat at the four o'clock position. "You go first, Leo. Tell us what you found out about the student that Amanda filed the complaint against."

"A dead end. Word got back to the kid's father in Japan. My source said something about family honor. He didn't know what happened to the student other than he finished the fall semester and didn't come back."

"That eliminates one suspect," said Heather. She took in a deep breath. "I called the headhunter agency I sometimes use to help me find quality applicants. They specialize in attorneys and accountants. I told them to contact Ryan Mattherson and dangle a carrot in front of him for a summer job. He'll be in my office tomorrow at 10 a.m. Steve and I will let him sit for thirty minutes before we interview him."

"I wish I could be a fly on the wall for that," said Leo.

Steve was taking his first sip when Leo stated his wish. He resettled his mug on the table. "No need to turn into a fly. We can interview him in Heather's special room and you can watch."

Heather noticed the blank look on Leo's face, and provided an explanation. "I had a room built that's sound-proof and has a one-way mirror with a video camera pointed at the person I'm interviewing. Of course, there's also hidden microphones. This allows me to tape interviews and, if I think it's necessary, call in a body language expert to help me."

Steve added. "You can stand behind the glass and watch the interview, if you're not too busy."

"Let me check my calendar." He didn't move a muscle or even hesitate. "It appears I can squeeze you into my busy schedule. In fact, if it's a day that ends in y, I'm free for a long time to come."

"There you go again with worrying about something that may never happen. Have faith, my friend, and enjoy the paid vacation."

Leo cast an inquisitive gaze Steve's way. "What are you up to?"

"Trying to get your mind off the suspension so you can be of use to us."

Leo leaned forward and pointed at Steve. "I know you too well. You're up to mischief, and you won't tell me what it is."

"Welcome to my world," said Heather. "He has this irritating habit of hiding an ace up his sleeve. Don't worry, he'll let you know before he plays the best cards."

"I'd forgotten how he likes to play his hand. I can't tell you how many times he'd wait until the very last minute to tell me something that cracked a case. It looks like I don't have any choice but to trust him again."

"That's better," said Steve. "Heather will go to her office as usual, and you can pick me up here tomorrow morning at eight. We'll stop for breakfast and it will be on me."

"Why can't I be in on the fun?" asked Heather.

"You need to go to work, or you may need to sleep in tomorrow." Steve tapped his wrist where he used to wear a watch. "Shouldn't you be getting ready for your date with Jack?"

"Holy smoke. I've been thinking about these two cases so much, I forgot all about it."

26

The stack of notes rose to four inches and made Heather wish she hadn't come to the office so early. She had three hours before Steve and Leo arrived and another hour before the interview with Ryan Mattherson. Her mind slipped back to pleasant memories of yesterday evening with Jack. He went into greater detail concerning the recent cruise he'd taken with golfing buddies to the azure waters of the Caribbean. His descriptions of swimming with sting rays and scuba diving made her long to dig her toes in the warm sand and take a siesta in a hammock made for two. Someday they'd carve out a week and go on a cruise. Soon. Very soon.

She opened her eyes and noticed the piles of work hadn't miraculously disappeared. After heaving a sigh, she jerked the first note from the stack. Two hours later, she'd reduced the pile by three inches. Time and her absence rendered most of the urgent items not so urgent after all. Some went in the trash, while relegating others into smaller stacks for members of her staff to handle.

Three remaining notes caught her eye. All concerned verbal commitments for sale of properties related to the proposed high-speed rail line. The owners now refused to sell. Would her father blame her? Probably. She wanted to pass the notes to someone else who would inform her father, but that wouldn't do. Responsibility, like a mosquito bite, itched until she scratched it.

"No time like the present," said Heather. She used her cell phone so she could walk out the kinks in her back while receiving icy blasts from Boston. The phone made the metallic ringing sound.

"Yes, Daughter. What is it?"

"More trouble with the rights of way. At least three more landowners are reneging on their commitments to sell. I thought you should hear it from me. I'll send you their names and any more I receive."

Her father's voice had a note of defeat in it. "It seems those three aren't the only ones pulling out of the deal. Once word got out about the court decision, it drove a stake in the heart of my plans. I wasn't expecting the judges to rule so heavily in favor of private property rights. It appears Lady Justice blind-sided me."

The admission left Heather scrambling for words. She composed herself and asked a cogent question. "Does this mean the entire project is off?"

"It appears so."

"How big of a loss will you take?"

"Loss? There won't be a loss. You did an excellent job negotiating the purchases. All the land runs between Houston and the Dallas-Fort Worth metroplex. Land will go straight up in value in the coming years. I'll hold on to it until it appreciates and then sell. Land is the one thing they're not making any more of."

Heather looked out her office window and smiled. "I should've known you'd hedge your exposure. You're the best businessman I've ever met."

"I learned a long time ago not to trust politicians, and courts can be capricious. It was a good plan, and you did your best to make it a reality. But even the best plans need to allow for unforeseen events. Don't worry about me. I'll end up making a good return on investment, eventually. That means you'll be the big winner in the end. After all, you'll get everything when I'm gone."

"Promise me that won't be for a long, long time."

Her father's voice softened in a way that didn't happen often. "I'll do my best. Call your mother. It thrills her to hear from you."

The call ended, and Heather spent long seconds staring at her phone. Steve's words to Leo about the futility of worry came back to her. She'd lost sleep due to concern about her father losing reputation, not to mention a substantial pile of money. All the while, he trusted her, and she hadn't let him down.

Before she went back to her desk, Heather placed the call to her mother and began an overdue conversation. It didn't last long, perhaps ten minutes. Her mother wasn't an early riser and today she had her annual physical exam.

With a promise secured that they'd talk longer later, it was time for Heather to get back to work. She wrote a quick note on the last slip of paper marked URGENT and rose to deliver it, along with the other stacks. Her personal assistant would disseminate them to staff attorneys, accountants, and real estate specialists, her small army of problem solvers.

She returned to her office, expecting Steve and Leo to have arrived. It didn't matter that they were late. Ryan Mattherson had arrived early and was safely tucked away in the interview room.

Instead of waiting in her office, Heather grabbed a cup of coffee and went to the observation room with the one-way mirror. She'd given instructions to the receptionist to place Ryan there and to tell him she was running late. Once inside the observation room, Heather activated the camera and audio recorder while she observed Ryan's actions. She loved it that Texas wasn't a two-party consent state for audio and visual recordings.

The future attorney came dressed for success in a Giorgio Armani slim-cut suit, a crisp ultra-white shirt, narrow tie and shoes so shiny they reminded her of a seal's skin. His hair, the color of coal from the depths of a West Virginia mine, was worn stylishly long, with plenty of product to keep it in place. Dimples dug deep into each cheek when he smiled. He moved to the one-way mirror and checked his teeth and hair to make sure all looked perfect. This allowed her to take a close-up look at his eyes. Deep brown irises with specks of gold. Two gorgeous eyes, but they held no warmth. Venomous snakes bore more compassion.

A cold shiver went down her back when he ran his tongue over his top lip. Ryan's father had used the same gesture to communicate desire the first time she met him. How many times had father and son used this non-verbal gesture?

She pitied the women who'd responded in the past and those that would.

A knock on the door caused Heather to swivel around. Leo led Steve into the room and closed the door. Steve's former partner let out a low whistle. "This is quite the set-up."

"Heather likes to see how people react when given choices. Watch Ryan while she explains."

"As you can see, the room is nothing like the drab, spartan police interview rooms. This one puts a person at ease with soft colors and a comfortable couch and chairs. It intentionally looks like an upscale office with bookcases lined with a variety of fiction and non-fiction books in multiple interests and genres, ranging from comics to classics, to the tawdry and sexually suggestive. On the coffee table, there's a wide selection of magazines. There are business magazines along with those dealing with home decor, hunting, fishing, and one for car enthusiasts with photos of next year's ten most expensive cars. A small refrigerator sits in the corner with a note on the front giving permission to help themselves to water or a soft drink while they wait. On top of the squatty refrigerator there's a basket of single-serving bags of chips, chocolate bars, trail mix, or protein bars, but no sign giving permission to take. People have their choice of sitting at a small conference table, on the couch, or in one of three chairs facing the couch. As you can see, each chair is of a unique style.

"A clinical psychologist helped me design the room. Everything, including the art on the walls and the one-way mirror, gives choices to whoever is in the room. I want to know how prospective employees, clients, and sometimes suspects, act when they believe no one can see them."

Leo stared at Ryan as he moved away from the mirror. "What have you learned about this pretty-boy so far?"

Heather moved to one side so Leo could get a better view. "I'll let you and Steve form your own opinion. Tell him everything Ryan is doing."

Leo took up the challenge. "Up to now, he's been admiring his face and hair in the mirror. I guess he's had enough. He's at the wall on the far side of the room, looking at paintings and framed photos. It's a Hodge-Podge of subjects. The pencil drawing of a nude woman is his first stop."

Heather set the timer on her watch and waited. "He spent twenty-nine seconds staring at the drawing."

Leo nodded while he kept his gaze focused on Ryan. "He's moved to the basket of goodies on the refrigerator and is taking a bag of M&M's. It's going into his coat pocket. Now he's on the couch looking at a magazine." Leo let out a chuckle. "That devil. He took long looks at the first few pages, slid it inside a newspaper, and kept thumbing through the pages."

Heather kept observing Ryan, but directed her question to Leo. "Did you notice the magazine he chose?"

"I missed it."

"It's a car magazine that features chesty women in bikinis leaning against restored muscle cars. The newspaper is a week-old edition of the Wall Street Journal."

Leo turned to face Heather. "I wouldn't trust this guy with Monopoly money."

Steve rose from his chair. "I've heard enough. Heather and I need to interview him and see how many other character flaws we can spot. Is there anything you want us to ask him, Leo?"

"Yeah. Ask him if he killed Amanda Palmer. I know he'll deny it, but ask anyway. Also, see if you can get a confession out of him for killing Rodney Wells back in 1942."

Steve shook his head. "I might get the confession out of him, but I don't think it will stand up. Ryan isn't over a hundred years old."

27

Ryan stood as Heather and Steve entered the room. He neatly folded the newspaper around the magazine and placed them on the coffee table. Heather ignored the deception and deposited Steve in a chair facing the couch. She extended a hand for Ryan to shake and had to admit the young man made a good first impression with his handsome features, sharp clothes, and a firm handshake that lasted just long enough.

"Thank you for coming in, Ryan. I'm Heather McBlythe and this is Steve Smiley. I'd like to make this more of a conversation than a job interview. I loathe stuffy, cold interviews, so I want you to relax and ask whatever questions come to mind. You can ask us anything you want."

She could tell by the tilt of his head that he wasn't expecting this, but he rose to the occasion. "I have two questions, if that's permitted."

Steve leaned back. "Make it three, if you like."

"Why me? And how did you get my name?" He paused. "I'd also like to know the details of the job."

"I'll take these in reverse order," said Heather. "This is the first of what may be several interviews for a position as summer intern. We understand you still have another year of law school to finish and then will need to pass the bar exam. I assume you researched my company, so you already have a general understanding of what goes on here. My business plan is to find undervalued properties, businesses, and investment opportunities, purchase them for fifty cents on the dollar, and sell them for full price or more. Preferably much more. I demand success and reward it handsomely."

Ryan's right eyebrow lifted when she said the last sentence. She continued. "If selected, you'll first be working under the direction of two of my top attorneys. The first evaluates potential with acquisitions of properties and businesses. Next, you'll do hands-on work related to the development of, or liquidation of, the properties and businesses. I like to take failing companies and fix them, if the potential profits warrant it. Otherwise, we break them up into smaller pieces and liquidate them. Finally, you'll spend a third of your summer working directly with me. I'll teach you how to maximize profits and write ironclad purchase agreements and sales contracts that protect us from losses and litigation. You'll receive the same base pay as a starting attorney, plus a generous flat rate for overtime worked."

Steve spoke up. "Her last intern paid off her student loans before she finished law school."

The right eyebrow went up again.

Heather's response to Ryan's questions seemed to satisfy him, so she moved on. "I know I'm being vague about money, but it's really up to you how much you earn. You earn bonuses by the quantity and quality of work produced."

Heather pointed to the refrigerator. "Would you like something to eat or a snack?"

"No... no thank you."

Steve took over. "I'll answer your question about how Heather heard about you. She keeps her ear to the ground about top talent coming out of law schools. There's buzz going around about you. They say you have great potential and a killer instinct. That's a big plus for Heather."

Steve allowed the words to sink in while he went to the refrigerator and pulled out three bottles of water. He returned and placed them on the coffee table. "Heather mentioned you'd be working with three attorneys if you're selected, herself included. They each specialize in different things. Which one appeals to you the most?"

Ryan didn't hesitate. "Working with Ms. McBlythe."

Heather made sure she smiled. "Why?"

"I love contracts."

"Again, why?"

He looked at Heather. "You said it yourself. A well-written contract is how you maximize profits and keep them."

Heather gave him a bigger smile. "Perfect answer."

She didn't miss that Ryan failed to mention avoiding litigation. He'd likely take undue risks.

Steve took over again. "You also asked how we got your name. Your brother told us about you before the police arrested him."

Ryan blinked several times. "I don't understand. How did you—"

Heather cut him off. "It was a fortuitous series of circumstances. Steve and I went to Mattherson and stayed at the Wells Mansion. I was trying to acquire property for a bullet train project to connect Houston to Dallas. One evening, Brian came over with your grandmother and Traci Wells to talk to us. We had a nice poolside chat. He mentioned you had an interview with one of Houston's top law firms. I know the partners and how selective they are with summer interns. Their background checks are well known among the top firms. I knew if you passed their rigid standards and got a personal interview with one of the partners, that's one less thing I'll have to do."

Steve jumped in. "Brian said your interview took place the same day Amanda Palmer died."

"Mom called and told me about Amanda. There's no way Brian killed her."

"Did you see Brian after your interview?"

"He and Dad met me for supper away from campus."

"That's nice of your dad to drive all the way to Houston to have a meal with his boys."

"He's an avid golfer. It's not uncommon for him to drive to Houston, Dallas, or all points in between to play. All the stars lined up, and we met for a meal."

"What did you do after supper?"

"I drove back to Austin."

"Did Brian mention he was going to see Amanda?"

Ryan sat up straight. "Why all the questions about Brian and Amanda?"

Heather patted Steve on the leg. "You'll have to excuse him. Steve used to be a homicide detective. Any time he hears about a murder, he falls back into his old habits."

"Sorry," said Steve. "You probably wonder why I was in Mattherson to begin with. I'm interested in a cold case that involved a member of the Wells family back in World War II. Research brought me to your hometown." He snapped his finger. "That reminds me. I picked up a rumor that one of the Palmer girls was involved with Lieutenant Rodney Wells and her father killed him. Have you heard anything like that?"

Heather knew Steve had heard nothing of the sort. He counted on her to observe Ryan and tell him how he reacted.

Ryan's right eyebrow raised about three millimeters. "I wouldn't doubt it. There's been bad blood between the Wells family and the Palmers. We Matthersons don't play those silly games."

Heather fought the urge to confront him for telling such a whopper of a lie, but thought about how this interview was to extract information and get a read on his character. Confrontation would serve no useful purpose at this point in the investigation.

Steve leaned back in his chair. "This isn't the time to discuss ancient history, but I'd like to talk to you about this cold case in the future."

"Sure, but there's nothing else I can tell you."

"Probably not. I've been running into a lot of brick walls with this case." He waited a couple of seconds. "Still, you never know how something small and inconsequential will crack a case wide open."

Heather concluded the interview on a positive note for Ryan by telling him she would be in touch and they'd discuss the details of his next interview. She escorted him to the reception area where they shook hands and Ryan left after flashing a smile.

By the time she reentered the interview room, Leo had joined Steve and she heard him ask, "What's your impression of the future attorney?"

Leo sat on the couch. "Arrogant, self-absorbed, narcissistic, in love with money and himself."

Heather returned to her chair beside Steve. "Don't forget he's a liar."

Steve scratched his chin. "But is he a killer?"

"I wouldn't put anything past him," said Leo.

"Do either of you think he was trying to beat his brother's time with Amanda? Or does it make more sense that his parents sent him to break up a romance?"

Heather raised her shoulders and let them fall. "We know Amanda was smart, but that doesn't mean she wasn't vulnerable to a handsome face and a fast talker."

Steve leaned forward. "Ryan impressed me as one of those guys that looks at life as a constant challenge. He wants to be the best, the richest, the top dog and he'll do anything to get there. He was valedictorian of his class, but the reputation of being the smartest student to graduate from Mattherson High belonged to Amanda. She had the potential to be world class in whatever profession she chose. He lied about a job interview. His jealousy of her must run deep."

"Enough for him to kill her?" asked Heather. The question seemed somewhat rhetorical, so she added. "I don't see it. He's the type of guy that goes through girlfriends like he's eating sunflower seeds. I predict he'll have six or eight trophy wives, each one younger and more blond than the last."

Steve chuckled. "I'll have to defer to your feminine intuition about his choice of mates. Still, I'm having a hard time pinning a motive on him."

Leo said, "It doesn't take motive to get a conviction if you have physical evidence."

"I'm working on that," said Steve.

Leo cocked his head to one side. "What's that supposed to mean?"

Heather took a long look at Steve, who sat in silence. Finally, she gave her head a single nod. "It means this is the point in the investigation that he does something sneaky and doesn't tell us what it is until we're close to the end."

Steve stood. "I'll admit that I need answers to a couple more things before we go back to Mattherson."

"What are they?"

"We need to go over the recording of today's session with Ryan. I'd like to know how many lies he told." He took a step toward the door. "Leo and I are going to lunch. Do you want to join us?"

"I cleared my desk this morning and called Jack. We're playing a round of golf this afternoon."

Steve clapped his hands. "That's great. At least one of you took my advice about worrying. There's hope for you yet, Heather." He took a deep breath. "That leaves me and Leo going over Ryan's interview and verifying his statements. We'll spend the rest of today and probably tomorrow fact-checking."

"We?" asked Leo.

"Heather has plans. If you don't help me, who will?"

He kept walking with Leo shadowing him. "By the way. Have a bag packed, and be ready to come to Mattherson when I call you."

"When will that be?"

"Soon."

28

Heather slowed as a Mattherson school bus turned off the state highway and proceeded down a county lane. Unlike the two previous trips to the sleepy town, conversation flowed on the way. Steve presented each piece of evidence for examination and evaluation. They debated motives of suspects for Amanda's killing. Steve assigned a numerical rating on his unscientific scale that ranged from least to most likely. He mentioned the remaining pieces of information needed to bring the investigation to an end. Once they tied up these half-dozen loose ends, they'd know Amanda's killer. Knowing, and being able to prove, who committed the older murder would be more difficult. It would take equal parts skill and luck to unravel the eighty-year-old cold case of Rodney Wells.

They passed by the Dairy Queen where Steve had used well-intentioned deception to keep Brian and Amanda's clandestine rendezvous from Amanda's mother. Heather wondered if the brilliant young woman would still be alive if Mindi Palmer had discovered the truth and reported it to her overprotective husband. She remembered how protective and proud he was of their only child and could only imagine how devastated he must be.

One thing was for certain. If any member of the Mattherson family had a role in Amanda's death, the feud would rekindle with greater intensity.

Thoughts of what could have happened occupied Heather's mind until she turned onto the road that offered a street-view of the three mansions. She slowed. "All quiet at the Palmer's home, except for a church van parked in front."

Steve issued a single nod. "That will be a bereavement committee from a church making a delivery of meals." Steve sat a little straighter. "Those are some of the sweetest people you'll ever meet, and sometimes the nosiest. If you like casseroles, they're the experts."

"Why do you say they're the nosiest?"

"Not all of them, but there's always those who want to know the details of the death. They tend to probe for the inside scoop."

"You sound like an expert on the inner workings of bereavement committees."

"Maggie served on the one at our church. With me working such long hours, she kept me informed."

Steve's voice had dipped to something that reminded Heather of a dirge, so she brightened hers. "We're here. I'll drive around to the covered parking. This place is beginning to feel like a home away from home."

Pulling into the carport, Heather spied a familiar figure coming toward them. "Traci's here to greet us."

"Good. I hoped we could talk to her away from her parents. This may be our chance to scratch two items off our list."

A fretful voice greeted them. "Welcome back. Please tell me you've made progress on clearing Brian."

Steve met her at the front of the vehicle. "We know a lot

more than we did the last time we were here, but there are still questions that need answers. Are your parents home?"

"Mrs. Palmer called Mom to help put up food. It seems all the churches got together and set up a schedule to deliver food. There's a new shipment every day and Mom's been bringing home most of it. You don't need to go out to eat while you're here unless you don't like casseroles."

Steve asked, "There's only two people at the Palmers to eat it all, and I bet they aren't interested in food. What are you doing with the rest?"

"We packed our freezers, and I've been putting everything else in Ziplock bags and giving it away to people who live in the country. News of free food travels fast among those who don't have much."

"We'll take our bags upstairs and then have a talk if you have time."

"Dad's at the Mattherson's. Something about a water leak. All I have to do is catch incoming calls. I'll help you get settled."

The three moved to the rear of the SUV. Heather passed out suitcases to carry. "Does the landline transfer calls to your cell phone?"

"Sure does."

"Good," said Steve. "It's a perfect day. Let's get something to drink and talk by the pool."

Traci hesitated, glancing at the top of the house next door. "All right. I baked cookies for you."

After a brief interlude, Heather, Steve, and Traci gathered by the pool. A lone Bradford pear tree and fluffy clouds provided partial shade.

Traci set her glass of water on the side table that separated her from Steve. "I don't know if I can stand this much longer. Will you be able to prove that Brian didn't kill Amanda?"

Steve turned his face a little toward Traci. "Let me ask you a question. Does Brian enjoy fresh-baked Tollhouse cookies?"

"He loves them, but what's that got to do with what I asked?"

"Be sure to keep all the ingredients on hand. You never know who might make an unexpected appearance."

Traci breathed a sigh of relief. "I knew you'd do it. I just knew it."

A serious tone filled Steve's next words. "Heather needs to ask you some questions. We hope you'll answer them."

Heather pointed to the upper story of the house next door. "I noticed both you and Babbs frequently look at the top floor of the Mattherson's home. I've also noted the unease on your faces, perhaps even fear. Did something bad happen to you there?"

Traci shook her head. "I've been in the home many times, but never beyond the first floor."

Heather recognized the defensiveness in Traci's voice, but pressed on. "I believe you about that, but there's something about the top floor of that home that upsets you."

Traci looked straight ahead. Then, her eyes shifted upward to the house next door. "There's a telescope in an empty room on the third floor. They use it to spy on us." Traci's gaze bore into Heather. "Do you know what it's like to live thinking someone's looking at you all the time?"

It took little imagination for Heather to visualize Ryan or his father focusing on family and guests, especially women at the pool.

Steve brought the next question. "You said 'they' use it to spy. All of them?"

"All but Brian. He told me his mother watches us like a hawk, looking for something to criticize. It's good that trees block their view of all the bedrooms but mine. Of course, the two perverts focus on the pool."

Heather meant to ask another question, but Steve spoke

before she could. "I knew there had to be a simple explanation."

Without taking a breath, Steve asked, "Did you have any luck finding a copy of the yearbook?"

"Sorry. I looked in the library, the high school, I posted on social media, and put an ad in the local newspaper. If one exists, I can't find it."

"Thanks for looking. For that much effort, you earned the $200."

"No, I didn't. You asked me to do one simple thing and I couldn't pull it off."

"In investigating murders, the clues come with what you find and what you don't find. Someone went to a great deal of trouble to bury the past. That's important."

Heather reached in her purse, pulled out two crisp one-hundred-dollar bills, and handed them to Traci. She received them with a word of sincere thanks, glanced at the third floor of the house next door and beat a path to the back door.

"What now?" asked Heather.

"It's too early for supper. Let's go to the public library."

Heather stayed seated. "Traci already looked there for the yearbook. Is there something else you're trying to find?"

Steve unfurled his cane. "It's what we don't find that interests me."

The brief trip to the library went without incident, other than Heather slamming on her brakes to avoid flattening one of Babbs's cats. The tiger-striped juvenile left with nothing harmed but its nerves.

Once Heather explained the reason for the hard braking, Steve powered down his window. "That's one, kitty. You have eight lives left."

Because of the diminutive size of the town and its proximity to the three mansions, they soon arrived at the library. A statue of a man dressed in nineteenth century formal wear stood in front of the library, square in the path to the front door. The bronze image held three books under his arm and looked straight ahead, as if staring at the future. The concrete sidewalk divided around the statue and joined again on the other side of the edifice. Heather walked slowly and described the statue and the modest library. She then stopped and read aloud the brass plaque. "*CLOVIS MATTHERSON Founder of Mattherson and Mattherson County. Frontiersman, Hero of the Texas Revolution, Civic and Spiritual Leader.*"

Steve gave a harrumph. "From what I've learned of old Clovis, he took his spirits out of a bottle. I remember nothing about spiritual or moral leadership."

Heather walked around the statue with Steve's hand on her arm. "Revisionist history. It's alive and well today."

Steve stopped. "That's a good point. Does it say when they placed the statue?"

"Let me look." Heather went back to the front of the statue. "Fifteen years ago. The Friends of the Library, Belinda Mattherson, President placed it."

Steve responded with only a nod of his head.

Once inside, Heather led them to the circulation desk. A woman with brown, wavy hair that cascaded down her back greeted them.

"Do you have a section on local history?" asked Heather.

"We certainly do. Everything you want to know is in the Mattherson Room at the rear." She used her hand to point to the right, reminding Heather of a flight attendant giving safety instructions.

Once in the room and the door closed behind them, Heather asked, "Is there anything in particular you want me to look for?"

"Spend the next hour or two going around the room. Whatever catches your eye, give me a brief description and move on.

If you see anything pertaining to the three families, tell me what it is."

It seemed a strange request, but Steve wasn't averse to breaking convention in investigations.

An hour and forty-five minutes later, Steve issued a yawn. "That's enough. I get the picture."

"I'm glad you do."

"Give me your overall impression of what's gathered here."

Heather considered the question. "I found nothing that interested me."

"Nothing?"

"I thought I'd get a better feel for the town and county, but something's missing."

"Do you mean missing or incomplete?"

Heather snapped her fingers. "That's it. Missing and incomplete. Only positive stories are here."

"I thought the same thing. Did you notice the lack of material about the Palmer family?"

"Or the Wells's contribution to oil production." Heather looked around the room. "It's a shrine to the Mattherson family."

Steve stood and stretched. "This room has Belinda Mattherson's fingerprints all over it. Let's find the librarian. I have a question or two for her."

The woman that had directed them to the Mattherson Room pushed a cart of books down the aisle in front of them. Heather whispered to Steve. "Library worker straight ahead."

"Did you find what you were looking for?" asked the woman with waist-length hair.

"Only partially," said Steve. "We're staying at the Wells Mansion and were led to believe that three families are responsible for the early growth of Mattherson. Is that correct?"

"You must mean the boom years when old Mr. Wells came here and drilled oil. Mr. Palmer wasn't far behind and spearheaded the establishment of a railroad. It was only a spur line, but it put Mattherson on the map."

"We found plenty of information on the Matthersons and a few mentions of Mr. Wells's contribution to oil, but nothing on the Palmers. Why is that?"

The woman broke eye contact. "I can't say."

Steve took a tiny step forward and lowered his voice. "That's an answer that can mean two things. Either you don't know, or you do know, but are unwilling to speak. I believe it's the latter. Then, I ask myself why?"

He let the question dangle in the air until the woman broke the silence. "Look, sir, I don't know who—"

Steve didn't allow her to finish. "I think you know more than you're pretending to know. My name is Steve Smiley, and this is Heather McBlythe. Heather came here to buy land for a high-speed train, but that's all on hold for now. You knew about that, didn't you?"

"Please, Mr. Smiley. I don't want to lose my job."

"That's the last thing we want to happen to you. This is a small town controlled by two families and you have the misfortune of having to answer to one of them. Right?"

The woman's head dipped and came back up.

"Since this is such a small town and you work with the public, you can't help but keep up to date with all that goes on. That tells me you already know that Heather and I are private detectives hired to find Amanda Palmer's killer."

He kept talking at an even pace. "We already have enough evidence to make the police question if they arrested the right person. We came here looking for answers, and we found some, but not enough."

Heather took over. "It boils down to this: you can push your cart back to the Mattherson Room where we'll be waiting for you, or you can expect a visit from an unpleasant homicide detective from Houston."

The woman looked with pleading eyes. "I can't be in the room with you for long. Please."

Steve whispered, "We understand." He turned, letting his cane guide him back to the room.

In less than a minute, a squeaky wheel on the book cart announced the woman's arrival. Heather wondered what questions Steve would ask, and why he was so intent on speaking with the library worker. She didn't have long to wait.

Without a prelude or any attempt to put the woman at ease, Steve hit her with his first question. "When did Belinda Mattherson cull the resources in this room?"

The question caused the librarian's eyes to open wide. "How did you know?"

"Like I already told one person today, look for things that are supposed to be here, but aren't. The Matthersons may have founded the town, but oil and banking brought it to life. Belinda's name is on the plaque outside and she's done her best to make sure her family name remains prominent. In her mind, Craig and Mindi Palmer pose a threat to her."

Steve took a long breath. "It's important for us to know when Belinda went through this room and discarded all the materials that portrayed the Palmers in a positive light. That includes Amanda."

The librarian clutched her blouse, close to her heart. "Do you think Belinda had something to do with Amanda's murder?"

Neither Steve nor Heather answered the question. After a few seconds, Steve repeated the abbreviated version of his prior question. "When did she take the materials from this room?"

"Last fall. I've never seen her act like that. At first, I thought she was kidding. She wasn't. It took her two days to go through everything."

"Including a high school yearbook from 1940?"

"I pleaded with her not to take it. My relatives are in that book. I tried to find copies, but I heard she located every last one known to exist and burned them."

"Thanks," said Steve. "Heather and I will be going. You've been most helpful and you needn't worry about us telling anyone."

Once outside, Heather didn't speak until she led Steve around the statue. "Are you ready to wrap this case up and put a bow on it?"

"One more interview."

29

Heather met Steve in the hallway outside their rooms at the Wells Mansion. "Did you want to go out for supper or take Traci up on her offer to eat casseroles?"

Steve didn't hesitate. "I'll take food from church ladies any time I can get it. For potluck dinners and church socials, they whip up their best recipes and see whose food disappears first."

"I didn't realize cooking for a grieving family was a competition sport."

"Not as much as potlucks, but the cooks take pride in their work all the same." Steve didn't move. "Did you know there's a protocol when eating at a church social?"

"Do tell."

"The first time around, take small portions of as many things as you want, or until you run out of plate. When you finish your first round, go back and get another helping of the dishes you liked the most. Think of it as voting in a primary election and then choosing your candidates in the general election."

Heather walked to the stairway. "Sometimes it feels like I'm living in a foreign country."

Once downstairs, they followed the sound of voices until they reached the kitchen. Sara Jane greeted them with a tired smile. "I hope you brought enormous appetites. Traci can't give away food fast enough and I'll need new clothes if I don't slow down."

Traci came from the refrigerator with both hands full. "I'm dragging out as many dishes as will fit on the bar. Don't be bashful. Take a little of everything or a lot of whatever you want. We have two microwaves, so it won't take long to heat and serve." She took a breath. "Steve, come with me. I'll tell you what each dish is and you can say if you'd like to try it."

Steve waved a hand at her. "This isn't my first rodeo. I'll try a little of everything on the first go-around."

Heather looked at the row of selections reaching from one end of the bar to the other. It reminded her of the buffet on a trans-Atlantic cruise she'd taken as a teen.

Instead of going to the dining room table, Steve asked if he and Heather could enjoy their meal in the kitchen's breakfast nook. Sara Jane and Traci heated their food and joined them. With the first round of Steve's journey into epicurean bliss ended, Leon made his presence, and displeasure, known to all. His rant started before he entered the kitchen.

"Sara Jane, I can't take any more. We're putting the house on the market as soon as I can find a real estate agent besides Belinda." He entered the kitchen and came to an abrupt halt when he saw their guests. "Sorry. I didn't realize—"

Steve waved off the apology. "I used to tell my wife the same thing after I'd had a rough day."

Traci took over. "I'm finished. Take my seat, Dad. I'll heat your supper. Do you want a beer to help you cool off?"

Leon shook his head. "Iced tea or water. I've been running all day without a break."

Sara Jane patted her husband's hand. "Take a deep breath. You're home now."

"Did you eat lunch today?" asked Traci.

"No lunch or breakfast."

"Your blood sugar must be near zero. Some sweet tea and these casseroles will have you back to normal in no time."

"Don't bet on it." Leon made a slash in the air across his eyebrows. "I've had it up to here with Belinda."

Traci tented her hands on her hips. "Don't tell me she had you doing yard work again."

"She wants flowers to line her driveway this year, and she didn't want to hear about me helping the Palmers."

Steve settled his fork on his plate. "I thought you split your time between the two families."

"Everything changed when Amanda died. Belinda gave me so many priority chores to do that I haven't had time to detail any of their vehicles, let alone be of much use to Craig and Mindi."

Traci rubbed wide circles on her stomach and looked toward the house next door. "One day soon, karma will catch up with the Matthersons."

Steve's phone sounded an incoming call from Leo Vega. He told the phone to reject the call. "I'll get back to him in a few minutes."

The interruption changed the vibe in the room. Leon dug into his meal while Traci fumed in silence. They seemed to have traded roles as parent and teen. This left Sara Jane to keep up a conversation. "Could I get you something else, Steve?"

"No, thanks."

"What about dessert? We have four different pies and two cakes."

"Perhaps later. Heather and I need to return that phone call."

Traci led them out the back door. Once out of earshot, she said. "Please tell me it won't be much longer before this nightmare is over."

Steve leaned on his cane. "If this call and one more interview go the way we hope, it will only be a day or two."

"I'm trusting you more than you know."

Heather spoke up. "He knows more than you think. Don't worry."

Once settled in a lawn chair by the pool, Steve instructed his phone to call Leo. Heather looked to the third floor of the Mattherson mansion. The curtains were open and the bottom half of the window didn't reflect. The glass on the top half of the window kept her from making out anything but the legs of a tripod and someone standing behind it. She mumbled under her breath, "Get a good look while you still can."

Steve and Leo ended their banter by the time Heather brought her attention back to the phone call. Instead of activating the speaker option, Steve had the phone pressed hard against his ear. She could hear Steve's side of the conversation, but could only guess what Leo had to tell him.

"Did you have any trouble getting the video from Rice University?"

Heather crossed her fingers, hoping the news was good.

"Great. What about the make of the vehicle and the plates?"

Steve faced her and nodded.

"How did Captain Price react?"

Not being able to hear both sides of the conversation grated on Heather's nerves.

"I'll call you back tonight after we talk to our cat lady. Plan on a road trip tomorrow."

A short riff played, indicating the call ended. Steve pulled the phone from his ear and stood. "Let's pay Babbs a visit. Can you find a way through the hedges again?"

She grabbed Steve by the arm. "Next time, tell that phone of yours to go to speaker so I can hear."

"Sorry. Leo came through for us in a big way. I'll explain on the way."

Heather glanced at a particular window of the Mattherson Mansion. "We're being watched. Do you want to wait until it's dark?"

"They can look all they want. It doesn't matter now."

A DOZEN OR MORE SHINING EYES WATCHED AS HEATHER LED Steve to the front door of the bungalow. Babbs answered the knock and gushed a greeting. "Look, Clarence and Pearl, I told you they'd come visit you tonight. Come in. Come in."

Heather settled Steve in the same chair he'd occupied the last time they came to the modest home. The two cats wasted no time in leaping to the arms of the chair to receive strokes. "Hey, you two. Max wanted me to say hello. In fact, he sent you a present." Steve reached in the pocket of his pants and pulled out a sealed plastic bag.

Babbs's lips separated into a wide smile. "How thoughtful. It's two little stuffed toys. They look like mice."

Steve unzipped the bag and allowed each cat to get a good sniff of the gifts. Tails twitched.

"They're stuffed with catnip," said Heather.

With a flick of his wrists, Steve pitched the two toys halfway across the room. Clarence and Pearl went airborne in pursuit. They scooped their prizes into their mouths and scaled the kitty gym until they perched on two of the uppermost platforms.

Babbs responded with applause. "I haven't seen those two so excited since they were kittens." She shifted her gaze to Steve. "You're a good man. Cats can tell."

After rejecting an offer of coffee or tea, Steve got down to business. "We wanted to give you a progress report on our investigation. We know who killed Amanda, how they did it, and we believe we know why." He paused. "Let me amend that last part. We think we know why, but I'm convinced there's more to the story than we've been able to uncover. We need your help."

Babbs looked off into space. "I remember the first time I heard the Beatles sing 'Help'. It was late summer of 1965." She hummed the tune.

Heather wondered why Steve didn't say something to bring Babbs back to the present, but he remained quiet until she'd finished and brought her gaze back to him.

Steve scooted to the edge of his chair and used his serious, low-volume voice. "It's time for you to listen closely and answer my next question seriously." Again he paused. "Are you ready to put an end to the feuds?"

She looked away again. "'Yesterday' was on the same album with 'Help.'"

Heather bit her lip. Babbs was drifting away again into a world of days long ago.

"I know about the Beatles," said Steve. "My mother loved the early albums. I grew up listening to them. 'Yesterday' is a song about someone's true love leaving them and the devastating effects it had on the person left behind. That person was you. You believed you were whole with that person, but only half a woman without him. That's what you thought, wasn't it? You'd never be whole without Charles Palmer."

Her eyes pooled with tears. "Everyone called him Chuck. He wasn't strong enough to stand up to his father. All because of the silly feud."

"What did he receive for breaking up with you?"

Babbs took in a full breath and released it. "There's no fooling you, is there, Steve?"

Babbs sat up straight. "What did Chuck receive? Anything and everything a young man could dream of. He had to choose between obeying his father and grandfather, or someday marrying me. He never got down on a knee, but ours was so much more than puppy love. Both of our families would have disowned us, but we said we didn't care. At least, at first."

She let out a sigh. "It turns out he did care. Chuck chose riches over poverty, but he also negotiated a life away from Mattherson. He drove to California in a new Corvette and finished college there."

"What happened to him?"

All signs of the crazy cat lady were gone, as were the moist eyes after she dabbed them. "Chuck believed in family honor. He kept his promise to his parents and stopped writing to me. It wasn't long before I heard rumors of him dating other women. Years passed, and I kept hoping. Then, I read in the local newspaper they drafted him. With a college education, they considered him prime officer material." She scoffed. "They shaved his head, handed him a rifle, and told him to lead boys right out of high school into combat. Second lieutenants had a high likelihood of dying on their first mission in Viet Nam. He made it until his second."

"Is that when you dropped out?"

Babbs nodded. "I already had, but his death put me over the edge. I needed to make the hurt go away, but I didn't know how. California called to me. I wanted to be near the places he spent time. I thought the drugs would help. Eventually, I had to come home."

"You had a child on the way."

"I was so strung out I didn't know who the father was."

Steve reached out with his right hand. Babbs took it and held on. They dispensed with words for at least two long minutes. Finally, Steve said, "It's time you moved on with your life. You're a whole woman and you will need to be strong to endure what's going to happen."

"You're right. I've hidden behind the persona of a burned-out hippie long enough. The last time you were here, you wanted Heather to look at my mother's high school yearbook. I'll get it for you."

While Babbs retreated to her bedroom, Steve leaned close. "Cross your fingers for luck. We may be on the verge of solving Leo's cold case."

Heather and Babbs sandwiched Steve between them on a couch. Steve held the 1940 yearbook and turned the pages. Heather and Babbs browsed the pages and made comments on things of interest. After thirty minutes, it became clear that graduating senior Rodney Wells and junior class beauty Elsa Dumont were one of those couples that looked right together.

"Oh, my," said Heather. "How did this photo of those two get past the family sensors?"

Babbs tapped her finger on the page. "The yearbook staff put it in after the final review. That's at the old pharmacy downtown. They had a soda fountain and served sandwiches."

Steve kept his finger on one of the last pages. "What's important about the photo?"

Babbs spoke before Heather could. "It's an advertisement for the pharmacy. My mother and Rodney Wells are sharing a milkshake."

Heather added. "One milkshake, two straws, both of them with lips on their straw, heads almost touching, looking into each other's eyes. It's a cheesy pose, but there's nothing fake about the looks they're giving each other."

Steve moaned. "That explains it, but I still can't prove it."

"Prove what?" asked Babbs.

"That your grandfather killed Rodney Wells to get him out of the way. Your father had his heart set on your mother."

"Of course he did. She was everything a man of that era looked for in a wife and the Matthersons always get what they want."

An involuntary shiver came over Heather. Babbs didn't show any outward emotion.

"Do you have proof?" asked Steve.

She shook her head. "Not really, but it's believed that Grandfather paid someone to do the deed, and that the man he hired was on his way to the Pacific to fight the Japanese. He never returned home."

Steve turned to Heather. "We need to call Leo and gather everyone at the Wells Mansion tomorrow evening."

Heather petted as many cats as would allow her to while she waited on Steve and Babbs to finish their conversation. Babbs was ready to talk and apparently felt the need to discuss the musical transformation the Beatles went through with the *Sergeant Pepper* album.

They finally broke free of their hostess and began their trek across the backyard. After squeezing through the hedges, Steve took out his phone and instructed it to call Leo.

"It's about time," said his former partner. "Did you get enough to get me off the hook?"

"That, and more. We're gathering everyone tomorrow evening."

"At which mansion?"

"The Wells. It's neutral territory."

"Captain Price and I will be there."

Heather looked beyond the swimming pool and across the backyard. A familiar black SUV sat in the driveway leading to the covered parking. "Uh-oh. We have an unwanted guest. Detective Long is coming this way. He's smiling."

"If they take me, call Leo."

"What if they arrest both of us?"

"Call Jack when we get to jail."

30

The handcuffs cut into Steve's wrists. "Hey, Long. I don't mind wearing your bracelets, but these are way too tight."

"I warned you, Smiley. Interfering with a police investigation is a serious offense."

Heather's voice cut through the night. "Did you get an arrest warrant?"

"He's not under arrest. Mr. Smiley is being detained for questioning."

"Then take the cuffs off and question him."

"Because of the complexity of the case, all questioning will take place at our homicide office in Houston."

Steve broke in. "Don't waste your breath. He's only doing what he was told."

"Do you consider my client to be a high escape risk?"

"Departmental policy states: 'Persons detained will be mechanically restrained for the officer's safety.'"

Heather huffed. "It's also departmental policy to use other means of restraint in special circumstances. My client poses no threat of physical harm and he's incapable of escape."

"She's right," said a second voice.

Steve asked, "Is that you again, Bernie?"

"Yeah, Steve. I hate this, but we're following instructions."

Heather broke in. "Did your supervisor tell you to violate department policy by affixing handcuffs too tight and not taking into consideration that Steve is blind?"

Hands brushed against Steve's wrists.

"What are you doing?" asked Detective Long.

"I'm keeping the city from getting sued and you from losing your job. The senior detective here is me. I say Steve's hands are going to the front, and I'll determine how tight they're to be worn."

"Thanks, Bernie. You can catch me up on the office gossip on the way to Houston." He paused. "I doubt we'll make it to the interstate before you bring me back."

The elder detective led Steve to a vehicle. He whispered, "I'll take the cuffs off if you want me to."

Steve matched his voice to that of his former teammate. "Leave them on. I don't want you to get into any more trouble than you're going to be."

Steve asked about Bernie's wife and children by name as they began their journey. He imagined Detective Long giving Bernie the stink-eye as they conversed freely.

When talk of family played out, Bernie asked, "What's it like being a PI?"

"It's good because I have a brilliant partner. I was lucky to have Leo and just as lucky to work with Heather."

"I hear she's rich."

"Rich doesn't come close to describing her wealth. She's also smart. I have a hard time keeping up with her."

"A real looker, too. The way her auburn hair framed her face gave me a hot flash like my wife gets."

Detective Long's voice barked out. "Would you two give it a

rest? We have two hours to go and I don't want to hear you codgers talk about hot flashes."

"How about prostates and getting up three times in the night?" asked Steve.

"Four times for me," said Bernie. He then chuckled.

"He's right," said Steve. "Let's talk about the case. Did you know Hermann Park isn't the original crime scene?"

"You're crazy," said Detective Long.

"Perhaps, but that doesn't change the fact that someone killed Amanda on the campus of Rice University and your lieutenant will have egg all over his handsome face. Heather and I have proof."

"You're lying."

Bernie shot back a stern response. "If Steve says the killing took place at Rice University and he has proof, that's good enough for me." After a few seconds of silence, Bernie said, "Holy smoke. This isn't our case. The university police department should be in charge of the investigation."

"They are now." said Steve. "That's one reason you'll receive a phone call and have to take me back to Mattherson."

"In your dreams," said Long. "We did a thorough investigation and have plenty to convict Brian Mattherson."

"My dreams will be your nightmare."

The junior detective's phone rang. He pulled the SUV off the state road and carried on a conversation punctuated with, "Yes, Sir. Yes, Sir. Right away, Sir."

A string of muffled expletives accompanied the vehicle turning a tight half-circle and accelerating so fast it pressed Steve against the door. Bernie chuckled. "Everything Steve said was true, wasn't it?"

"Shut up."

"You'd better get these cuffs off me," said Steve. "Unless, of course, you want another paragraph in my statement to the press."

Heather opened the door of the SUV for Steve as soon as it came to a stop in the front driveway. She spoke loud enough for her voice to carry to the front seat. "Did you and the boys have a pleasant ride?"

"I found it satisfying," said Steve.

She slammed the rear door and guided him up the front steps.

"Did you get everything arranged for the meeting tomorrow evening?"

"All taken care of. We'll have a full house here at 6:00 p.m."

"Good. Let's go to the kitchen. It's my first time to be arrested. I didn't know being in cuffs stimulates the appetite. Let's go find the excess of pies Sara Jane talked about earlier. I couldn't stop thinking about them on the trip back."

31

To accommodate the crowd, Leon and Sara Jane brought in extra chairs to the parlor. Under Heather's guidance, they arranged the furniture so everyone could see all the members of the gathering. Steve told them not to bother with providing a chair for him; he'd stand in front of the fireplace. Heather knew him well enough to know that at some point he'd want to sit, so she and Leon brought in an overstuffed chair from the billiard room.

At seven minutes after six, Heather leaned into Steve. "Johnny Mattherson still isn't here. Do you want to get started?"

"Not yet. We'll give him until six-fifteen."

Heather made a clockwise scan of the room. Belinda Mattherson chose the largest chair, a high-backed, Spanish inspired, all-wood antique with intricate carvings. All the woman needed was a crown and scepter. Next to Belinda sat an empty chair reserved for her tardy husband, a much smaller chair and of dubious quality.

On the first of two vintage couches sat the Wells family—Leon, Sara Jane, and Traci, who rubbed her protruding midsection.

The sheriff occupied the next chair, a cane-backed rocker. He used one of the vertical back-posts as an impromptu hat rack for his Stetson.

A gap in the seating allowed people to flow into the room and take their assigned seats. Another empty chair, a well-worn club chair, came next.

Continuing the circle, Ryan Mattherson sat on the first cushion of the second couch, directly across from Traci. The middle seat of the couch remained vacant.

Last, but certainly not least, sat the true Mattherson matriarch, Barbara "Babbs" Mattherson. Absent were any of her beloved cats and her normal attire. She came to the meeting wearing tan slacks, a white silk blouse, and a print scarf fastened with a cameo broach. The thatch of gray hair looked professionally tamed, and the appropriate amount of makeup completed the transformation.

Belinda Mattherson exhaled a breath laced with boredom. "Ryan, where's your father?"

He shrugged, but added, "Probably at the 19th hole of some golf course having his third, fourth, or fifth glass of scotch and soda."

She opened her mouth and huffed, but let the opportunity to respond pass.

A few more minutes of uncomfortable silence slipped by before the sound of footsteps in the hall caused most heads to swivel. In walked Johnny Mattherson wearing casual trousers with splatters of mud around the cuffs, soft-soled loafers, a collared knit shirt, and a baseball cap emblazoned with a logo reading, *The Texas Open*. He carried a glass tumbler filled with amber liquid and ice.

"You're late," said Belinda.

"Am I? So sorry, dear. Had to change my shoes." He sat, took the time to give Heather a quick knee to neck inspection, and ran his tongue over his top lip.

Traci further delayed discussion when she let out a muffled yelp. Gazes shifted to her as she rubbed her midsection with her fingertips and blew out a breath from puffed cheeks. "Sorry. A contraction."

Belinda lifted her chin. "The high price of sin."

Babbs gave her daughter an icy stare. "Are any of us without sin?"

Eyes widened, and Johnny spilled part of his drink. Ryan chuckled as he said, "Wow, Babbs. Where did that come from?"

"From now on, if you want me to respond, you are to address me as Grandmother." Her gaze shifted to Belinda and Johnny. "Mother or Barbara will suffice for you two. I've dropped the inappropriate moniker of Babbs."

Belinda's face took on a shade of pink Heather had never seen her wear before. Humility looked good on her.

Steve broke in. "Other guests are arriving. I heard a car pull into the front driveway."

"I didn't hear anything," said Johnny with a slur.

Sara Jane stood. "I'll get the door."

When muffled voices sounded down the hall, Steve announced, "That will be a good friend of mine. His name is Detective Leo Vega. He's a homicide detective from Houston and he has someone you all know with him."

Leo made it to the doorway, nodded a greeting, and stood to one side.

"Brian!" shouted Traci. She wiggled to the edge of the couch, stood, and they met in the center of the room, hugging and talking over each other.

While everyone focused on the young man fresh from jail, Heather concentrated on people's reactions. Leon Wells came to Brian, gave him a half-hearted hug, and said, "Welcome home." He then went back to Sara Jane, who looked on with wide eyes.

Instead of her gaze being fixed on her son, Belinda directed her stare at her husband. He shrugged and mouthed, "I don't know." It appeared to be an answer to an unasked question. Both rose and gingerly walked to where their second son stood in Traci's grasp. Once the youngest people in the room released their hold on each other, Belinda and Johnny moved in for a quick hug.

Belinda spoke first. "Why didn't you call and let us know? How did you..."

"Yeah," said Johnny, as he interrupted. "How did you get out? We haven't been able to gather enough cash to post bail."

Brian and Traci stood shoulder to shoulder. Brian looked at his father. "I noticed."

Traci wasn't so kind. "Isn't it strange that the family with the most property in the county couldn't use that as collateral to secure bond? I thought that's how lawyers helped their client."

Belinda narrowed her eyes. "Young lady, you do not know about the complexities of the law."

Steve broke in. "We have much to discuss this evening. Everyone, take your seats. Brian, you're to sit with your grandmother. Leo, you're across from the sheriff. Everyone else will remain where we asked you to sit." He gave a disarming smile. "Assigned seating is for my benefit. Sometimes voices are hard to distinguish."

Brian sat beside his older brother, who stood to give him a weak hug and an even weaker "Welcome home."

Before he sat, Brian looked at his grandmother. "Babbs? Is that you? You look awesome."

"It's the new me." She patted him on his thigh. "Much has changed since you've been away. Much more will soon change, but we'll weather this storm and sail into sunshine. By the way, my friends will want to welcome you home, too. Come by my bungalow tonight."

Steve cleared his throat, which signaled everyone to listen. "Detective Vega will explain how and why Brian is back home."

Leo hadn't sat down, so he wasted no time in launching into his explanation. "It's simple. He's out on bond. Since this is still an ongoing investigation, I can't divulge anything more."

"Fortunately," said Steve. "Because Heather and I are private investigators, we have much more latitude in what we can say. If you'll bear with us, we'll first give you our take on why someone in this room killed Amanda. It's a long story that begins with Clovis Mattherson."

The figure of a large man appeared in the doorway. "I was told the killer of my daughter is in this room."

"Please come in, Mr. Palmer," said Steve. "I apologize for not inviting you, but I wrongly assumed you'd be too distraught to take in what we have to say. Detective Vega will surrender his seat to you and you may stay as long as you commit to no physical violence. Are you armed?"

"What if I am?"

The sheriff spoke up. "Then I'll take your pistol and give it back to you at your home later tonight."

Belinda pointed a finger at her nemesis, Craig Palmer. "Sheriff, I demand you arrest this man."

Before the sheriff could respond, Barbara Mattherson spoke in a clear voice. "Stuff a sock in that mouth of yours, Belinda. Mr. Palmer made no direct threat against anyone, and carrying a pistol in Texas is now legal." She took in the astonished gazes around the room. "What? Just because I'm old and like cats doesn't mean I don't know what's going on."

Leo and the sheriff stood between Craig and the rest of the gathering. "Don't reach for it," said Leo. "Just tell us where it is and I'll give it to the sheriff."

"Back of my waistband. It's a nine millimeter, semi. Full clip, but nothing in the pipe."

Leo lifted the back of the shirt, eased the pistol out, extracted the clip, and operated the slide to make sure the weapon was unloaded. He handed the pistol to the sheriff, along with the clip.

"Good job, Leo," came a voice from the hallway.

"Captain Price," said Steve. "I thought I heard the front door close. Come in and take my chair." He then introduced his former boss to the occupants of the room.

"Sorry I'm late. Believe it or not, I got pulled over by a highway patrolman for speeding. It took some serious talking to get out of the ticket."

"How's the new knee?" asked Steve.

"Coming along all right, but I had a hard time convincing the patrolman I could drive with a gimpy leg."

Heather asked, "Did you bring clothes to stay the night?"

"Sure did. I even brought my wife like you told me to. Lora Sue's the reason I got out of the ticket. She promised to drive the rest of the way and back to Houston."

Sara Jane sprang from the couch. "Is she outside?"

"She always packs half her wardrobe. Should be on the porch with most of it by now."

Brian rose. "I'll give you a hand."

Heather noted that the elder brother, Ryan, made no move to help.

Steve said, "Since we're going to be delayed, let's take a quick break."

Traci wiggled to the front of the couch again. "There are drinks and snacks in the dining room. Help yourselves."

"Ten minutes only," said Steve. "We have a lot to cover tonight."

32

Heather placed a few vegetables on a small paper plate and stood in a corner of the dining room. She wanted to see how people split into smaller groups. Traci, Brian, and Barbara took full portions and walked toward the kitchen. Steve, Captain Price, and Leo each chose coffee with a slice of pie and retired to the billiard room. The sheriff, Craig Palmer, and Leon Wells never arrived in the dining room, choosing to go instead to the front porch. That left Sara Jane to act as hostess for the three remaining members of the Mattherson clan, Belinda, Johnny, and their eldest son, Ryan.

The two Mattherson men took a full helping of deserts while Belinda cornered Sara Jane. "Where did all these pies come from?"

"Craig and Mindi had so much food delivered by the churches that they asked us to take it. Traci's been delivering most of it to people in need."

The encounter reminded Heather of a cat playing with a mouse before dispatching it.

"I'm sure Traci had help with the deliveries. That explains why your husband hasn't taken the time to prepare and plant my flowerbed like I told him to. I'll need to have a talk with him. It's time for me to reconsider our arrangement. There's plenty of people who'd love to earn what I pay him for part-time work. Tell him I want to speak with him tomorrow afternoon at 2:30."

"But Amanda's funeral starts at 2:00."

"Then Leon has a decision to make, doesn't he?" She took a step closer to Sara Jane. "Like I said, 2:30 tomorrow afternoon or he needn't come at all."

Belinda turned toward Heather and walked with head erect to her. When she drew near enough to keep the conversation semi-private, she said. "I hope you realize this is an imposition on my family."

Heather tilted her head. "We thought you'd want to know the person responsible for having Brian arrested."

"Of course, but why did that blind man mention the founder of the county and city? Is he demented enough to think a man who's been dead for well over a century is responsible?"

Heather shrugged. "I guess we'll find out in a few minutes."

Steve came back into the room. "It's time."

Belinda spoke loud enough that everyone in the room heard her. "This better be a short meeting, Mr. Smiley."

"It all depends on how many times people interrupt us." He turned and walked in the parlor's direction.

It wasn't long before all the participants settled in their assigned seats.

Steve stood before the group and waited until everyone stopped talking. He then waited ten more seconds. "Let me begin at the beginning. I received a request from my former partner, Detective Vega, to assist him with a cold case. The murder occurred in Houston, but involved a young man from Mattherson. The year was 1942. The victim, Rodney Wells, was a talented, motivated, and, from what I've been told, a handsome young man. An all-American boy from a small town, destined for fame and fortune. If, that is, he survived being a pilot in World War II. He fell in love with his high school sweetheart, a stunning beauty and his equal in academics. She attended Rice University after graduation from Mattherson High School." Steve paused. "As Rodney Wells stepped off the train, someone shot him in the back and he died on the platform of Houston's train station."

Belinda spoke up. "What does this have to do with anything today?"

"Good question." Steve shifted his face to where Barbara sat next to Brian. "Tell us who this beautiful woman was."

"That would be my mother, Elsa Dumont-Mattherson. She came from an average family, earned a scholarship, but dropped out after Rodney's death and came back home. Times were hard and her family needed help. Most women marry for love, but that was no longer an option. She married my father and things changed for her family. Everyone who needed a job, or a promotion, got it, thanks to the Matthersons."

Brian turned to his grandmother. "Do you think my great-grandfather killed Rodney Wells?"

"No. He was too shrewd for that. He, or more likely his father, hired someone to do it."

"Ridiculous," said Belinda. "The Matthersons have always been pillars in the community with the highest moral and ethical standards."

Barbara ignored her daughter's outburst. "The man's name was Scotty O'Quinn. He had quite a reputation for drinking, stealing, and violence. An assault charge brought him in front of Judge Mattherson, who allowed him to join the Marines. He eventually died on some island in the Pacific."

"Don't believe her, Brian," said Belinda. "There's no proof and everyone knows Mother makes up things."

Steve spoke next. "Belinda's half right. Physical evidence is virtually non-existent and everyone with direct knowledge is dead. However, it's Belinda and not Barbara who's making up her own version of history. Heather, Leo, and I have done extensive research and everything Barbara said fits with documents we've found. Scotty O'Quinn appeared before Judge Mattherson on a charge of attempted murder. The judge reduced it to simple assault and made his release conditional that he join the Marines."

Captain Price spoke in a deep baritone voice with emphasis that demanded respect. "I examined Detective Vega's case file. There's enough evidence in it for me to stamp it CLOSED. It wouldn't be enough for a court conviction today, but who knows what a good investigation would have uncovered back then."

Belinda scowled. "If you're intent on slandering the Mattherson name, I'm leaving."

"Nobody's leaving," said the sheriff. "Steve gave me a peek at the agenda and we're only getting started."

Steve took over again. "That settles one issue, but let's continue talking about historical events. We need to discuss Clovis Mattherson."

"Why?" demanded Belinda.

"I'll explain later when we talk about Amanda's murder. For now, I need to give background on Mattherson's founder to give context to what's happened through the years. I found it interesting that the local public library gives a sanitized version of Clovis's life. The Mattherson family dedicated an entire room to the history of this county. I understand it was a nice compilation of historical documents. There were many books and documents related to the early founders, especially Clovis. Also, the statue of Clovis in front of the library describes him as the spiritual leader of the community."

Steve pointed to the back of the room. "Leo, what did you discover?"

"I had an assistant at the main branch of Houston's public library help me find everything they could about Clovis Mattherson and the early days of Mattherson County. To sum it up, he was a hard man for hard times. He led a militia that drove Native Americans further west, fought against Santa Anna and the Mexicans at the Battle of San Jacinto, and received a lot of property in return."

"See," said Belinda. "A true Texas hero."

Leo continued. "Clovis performed with zeal in fighting and killing. Unfortunately, there're mounds of documents that tell us he used the same zeal for achieving his desires after Texas gained independence and the land was safe for settlers. By various methods, he took as much land as he was given."

"That's a lie," said Belinda.

Leo kept talking without reacting to her accusation. "Clovis appointed himself as the chief law enforcement officer and the sitting judge. There are plenty of documents showing him selling parcels of land to more than one person. They'd bring their claims to him and he'd rule in favor of who paid him the most. If anyone complained, he'd hold them in contempt of court and deal with them in ways that insured they kept their mouths shut or moved on."

Belinda huffed. "More lies."

"Another thing that was believed about Clovis until recently is that he never married, but reared one male child on his own. Not true. Clovis was married when he came to Texas from Georgia. His wife joined him two years later, and they had a son. They found her and a man Clovis believed to be her paramour shot to death outside the man's cabin. The murder remains unsolved."

"Again, no proof," said Belinda.

"And again," said Steve, "plenty of documentation to convince us that the account is true."

Heather couldn't help herself. "It's called a preponderance

of the evidence. Face it, Belinda, Clovis Mattherson wasn't the man you tried to make him out to be by purging the library of anything that contradicted the legend you fabricated."

For the first time since his arrival, Craig Palmer had something to say. "Detective Vega, can you get me a copy of all the books and documents you found that give an accurate history of this county and Clovis Mattherson?"

"Can do."

"Good." Craig turned his attention to Belinda. "Make sure you attend the next city council meeting. I'll be submitting a motion demanding your dismissal from your role as library supervisor for stealing books and other items. I'll also announce that I plan on acquiring everything on the list Detective Vega gives me and donating them as soon as possible. It's time the citizens of this county have access to accurate history."

"If it's a battle you want, it's a battle you'll—"

Steve shouted over her. "Amanda Palmer." The name of the murdered young woman resonated in the room like the last clash of a cymbal.

33

With the room stunned into silence, Heather rubbed the goose bumps on her arm. Steve had once again taken control and would not allow Belinda to sidetrack the meeting with threats.

"Motive, means, and opportunity," said Steve. "Those are the three basics of any criminal investigation and everything hangs on these three things. I find this case to be unique because it hinges more on motive than the other two. Not that means and opportunity aren't important, as you'll soon discover."

Steve took a deep breath. "When Detective Vega came to me with the cold case involving the murder of Rodney Wells back in 1942, I didn't know it would be a precursor to an equally tragic event some eighty years later. Physical evidence was so sparse that my only option was to go back even further in time to find clues in history that pointed me to a motive. That's what led me to come to Mattherson."

Heather took a half step forward. "I was trying to obtain land for a high-speed rail line that was to run through Mattherson County. Steve and I came together, met with

Belinda and Johnny, and stayed here at the Wells Mansion. Nothing worked out. My subsequent, even more generous proposal, was literally thrown on the floor, and Steve's attempt to use the public library for research didn't happen because the library was closed."

Craig Palmer interrupted, "That reminds me, Belinda. Expect to answer for that, too."

"Let's stay on point," said Steve. "Heather's proposal was not only rejected, but Belinda didn't even read it. That made no sense."

"I read it," said Johnny.

"Be quiet," snapped Belinda as her gaze settled on Steve. "So what if I didn't read it? I read the last one and decided I wasn't interested in selling the land."

"See what I mean?" Steve scratched his chin. "That statement came from a real estate broker, a person who makes their living from property deals. Yet Belinda wouldn't make a counteroffer or even discuss the project. Her refusal would negatively affect many other landowners in the county who had already agreed to sell their land."

"I don't have to have a reason."

Steve nodded. "You're right. All I'm saying is, it made me wonder why. What motive did you have for not wanting others to benefit?"

He raised a hand to stop her, in case Belinda wanted to argue more. "We left Mattherson with more questions than we arrived with. However, it wasn't a total loss. We had a very nice stay here and got to know the Wells family."

Heather spoke next. "We also spoke with Craig, Mindi, and Amanda. That was the last time we saw Amanda alive. We'd been gone several days and were on our way back to Mattherson when we received word that she'd been murdered."

Steve took over again. "Once word was out, people lined up to hire us. Brian was being detained in jail for questioning, so

Belinda and Johnny wanted us to investigate to prove his innocence."

Brian glared at his parents as he restated something he'd said before. "Being bailed the next time they took me to jail would have been nice, but that didn't happen."

Pressing on, Steve said, "Leon and Sara Jane, and even Traci, tried to hire us. Then came the fourth request from an unexpected source."

Barbara raised a thin, vein-streaked hand. "That would be me. Amanda was such a dear child. I had to see justice done, and I knew Brian couldn't have done it. He was ga-ga for Amanda, even though she wasn't so hot-to-trot for him."

"No," said Belinda with emphasis. "It was a simple high school romance that ended when Brian went to the University of Houston." She looked at her youngest son with a challenging stare. "Isn't that right? You told me so yourself."

"I told you what you wanted to hear, but it wasn't the truth and you know it. I had plenty of time to think things through in jail. You're such a control freak. There's no way you didn't know I transferred to Rice to be with Amanda."

Steve interrupted. "We're getting ahead of ourselves. Let's keep the sequence of events in order. As with many business ventures, the high-speed railroad fell through. This allowed Heather and I to devote ourselves to Amanda's murder. Because all the physical evidence was in Houston, we concentrated on means and opportunity, but motive kept me awake at night."

Steve turned to the couch on his left, occupied by the three members of the Wells family. "You three were the first ones that came to mind as suspects."

Leon bristled. "Why us?"

"At one time, your family was every bit as prosperous and influential as the other two families. That drop in wealth and status couldn't have been easy. I can understand how resentment might pass down from one generation to the next."

Leon nodded in agreement. His voice lowered. "You might be right about the three generations that came before me, but not me."

Sara Jane abandoned her mouse-like demeanor. "Leon decided at an early age that he wouldn't allow the past to guide his future."

Steve held up his hands in surrender. "You two are so busy running this B&B, keeping up the other two mansions on this street, and helping others, that I soon dropped you both from my list of suspects."

"What about me?" asked Traci.

"I kept you on the list a while longer."

"Why?"

"I'll explain later."

He moved on without taking a breath. "Barbara 'Babbs' Mattherson didn't earn a mention on my list, even though she pretended to be mentally unstable."

Brian spoke up. "Amanda, Traci, and I knew it was an act. It's how she coped with the stupid feud."

Steve took a step back. "We left town at this point in the investigation and concentrated on Houston. I should mention that one person of interest surfaced. He was a foreign student attending Rice who developed an unhealthy infatuation for Amanda."

Craig Palmer moved to the edge of his seat. "A stalker? Why didn't she tell me?"

Heather responded. "Amanda handled the situation herself by reporting him to the university police. They took appropriate action, which included notifying his parents. He wasn't in the country when Amanda died."

Brian added, "She never saw him again, and he didn't come back for the spring semester."

"You knew about this?" asked Craig.

"She made me promise not to tell you. Didn't want you to

worry."

Steve continued. "Then the police formally charged Brian with killing Amanda, and everything pointed to him as the one responsible. They'd had an argument in the library earlier that day, resulting in both of them being escorted out. The police soon found out that Brian had deceived his parents by pretending to be a student at the University of Houston but he was actually a student at Rice. Amanda's body was found in nearby Hermann Park. The police assumed that's where she was killed. They found her DNA in Brian's car."

"Of course it was," said Brian. "She didn't like to drive in Houston."

"All the same," said Steve. "One more thing against Brian."

Leo added, "Don't forget about the necktie."

"Right," said Steve. "The press didn't report it, but the cops found a necktie with the body. Forensic tests confirm it was used to strangle Amanda, and it belongs to Brian."

Craig stared at Brian, but spoke to Steve. "With all this against Brian, why isn't he still in jail?"

"Because the police stopped looking."

Heather added, "But we kept digging until we discovered Amanda wasn't killed at Hermann Park, but in a parking lot at the university."

Traci asked, "How could the cops make such a mistake? Are you sure?"

"The police are human, and in any other case, I might have stopped looking, too. But Steve insisted we keep digging. Now, I'm glad we kept going."

"Me, too," said Leo.

"What evidence do you have?" asked Johnny.

Steve's top lip twitched. "I'll explain all, but in my own way."

"I don't understand," said Ryan.

"Think about two things: motive and one clue too many."

Belinda rose from her throne-like chair and made what

sounded like a royal pronouncement. "I'm a patient woman, but I've had my fill of verbal assaults on my family name and nonsensical ramblings. My time is much too precious to spend it listening to this babble."

Steve nodded. "You're absolutely right, Belinda. I think it's time you and your husband leave, but only while Heather and I continue our discussion with everyone else. The sheriff will explain where to go."

The sheriff stood. "There's a deputy on the front porch. Johnny, you're to go there until we call you back in."

He hesitated for a couple of seconds, but the steel in the sheriff's voice communicated that refusal wasn't an option. A burly deputy who appeared in the doorway with his forearm resting on his pistol, reinforced the sheriff's command.

Blood rose into Belinda's neck until it turned a deep splotchy pink. "Sheriff, I'm going home and if you think for one minute that I'm not, just watch."

A male and female deputy entered the doorway. The sheriff stood with feet spread, shoulders wide. "Belinda, you're going to the backyard and sit in a chair by the pool. The only question at this point is if you're going with or without handcuffs."

34

Heather scanned the room for reactions from those assembled. Traci clenched her fist, nodded her head, and mouthed a silent "Yes."

Brian received a pat on his hand by his grandmother. She whispered something to him, but it was too low to make out.

Leon and Sara Jane looked at each other. Her lips separated into a wide grin. He returned one of his own and patted her on the thigh.

Craig Palmer was the most vocal of the group. "So far, I like what I'm seeing and hearing. I hope it means what I think it will."

Steve didn't respond. Instead, he turned to the eldest Mattherson son. "Ryan, it's my understanding you desire to work for Ms. McBlythe this summer. Is that correct?"

"I'm seriously considering it."

"Spoken like a future attorney. Never a straight answer unless absolutely necessary." Steve waved a hand at the chair Ryan's mother had vacated. "Have a seat up here where everyone can see you better. Ms. McBlythe will conduct your next interview."

Steve stepped to the side as Heather walked to the fireplace. "Yes, I want everyone to have a good look at Ryan as he answers my questions."

She turned to Ryan, who remained on the couch in stunned silence. "You didn't expect the interviews to get easier, did you? I want to see how you respond to pressure. Pretend you're in court." What she didn't say was that he'd be in court as a defendant if he insisted on lying.

Ryan rose from the couch and gingerly lowered himself into the chair vacated by his mother.

Steve stood off to the side while Heather gave Ryan her most comforting smile. "Relax. We're going to pick up where we left off at my office."

He issued a weak smile.

She began with a series of softball questions, which he fielded and was soon playing a game of verbal catch with her. This ended when she said, "Tell me again why you were in Houston on the day Amanda died."

Out of the corner of her eye, Heather saw Craig Palmer stiffen.

Ryan remained calm. "Like I told you, I had an interview with a law firm. It was a summer intern job. Also, Dad was in town playing golf. He, Brian, and I had dinner together, and I drove back to Austin."

"Refresh my memory," said Heather. "What was the name of the law firm?"

"King and Weaver."

"That's odd," said Heather. "I called Tommy Weaver and he assured me you didn't have a meeting with anyone from the firm on that day. How do you explain that?"

Ryan squirmed like he was trying to get comfortable, but he looked more like a worm on a hook. "Oh, yeah. I remember. They canceled my interview while I was driving in from Austin."

Heather turned to the gathering. "Pretend you're on a jury. Ryan is testifying. He says they canceled his meeting. Raise your hand if you think he's telling the truth."

Only one hand went up halfway before Sara Jane lowered it.

Heather shook her head and made a tsk-tsk sound. "A word of advice. A good attorney knows the answer to almost every question they ask someone they're deposing or call to testify. Don't think you can make up answers on the fly and get by with it."

She took a breath and hit him with another question. "Did you wear a suit and tie to Houston on the day Amanda died?"

"Yes."

"Why did you get dressed up for a meeting with your brother?"

"Well, I, uh—"

Heather cut him off. "This would be much easier if you'd tell the truth. Remember, Steve and I already know the answers."

Ryan puffed his cheeks and blew air out. "Dad called and told me how to dress."

"Did he also have you call Brian and arrange dinner?"

"Yes."

"Did you?"

"Yes."

"Was Amanda supposed to be there?"

"She didn't come."

"What did you talk about?"

He shrugged. "This and that."

Steve took two steps forward and raised his voice to something just under a shout. "That's not good enough, Ryan. Heather's giving you a chance to save yourself from jail, and you're too self-assured to realize what's going on. I know you're not used to telling the truth, but do it now or suffer the consequences." .

Ryan's Adam's apple bobbed as he swallowed. "All right. Dad and I told Brian he needed to break off his relationship with Amanda before Mom came down on him. Somehow, she found out he'd changed universities."

Steve turned toward the crowd. "Truth or lie?"

As if in one voice, those gathered said, "Truth."

Heather gave Ryan a smile as a reward for his veracity. "See. That wasn't so hard. Let's keep going, now that we're on a roll. What are your plans for after you graduate next year?"

His shoulders rose and fell. "I was hoping to intern with you this summer and make a good enough impression that you'd want to hire me next year. I guess I blew that."

Heather didn't respond, but hit him with another question. "What are your mother's plans for your future?"

"She wants me here in Mattherson. She has everything planned out. I'm to take over Dad's office, go into politics after a few years, marry someone of her choosing, and carry on the family name."

"And what do you want?"

"Austin, Houston, or Dallas. I can't imagine living here now that I'm used to concerts, real sporting events, coffee shops, top quality restaurants, and a nightlife that doesn't include watching fireflies on the front porch."

"You didn't mention a smorgasbord of women."

"That, too."

Barbara spoke up. "I know what he means about staying here. I had to leave, too." She looked with sympathy at her grandson. "Be careful, Ryan. Those bright lights can burn your heart."

Heather brought Ryan back around to the matter at hand with her next question. "Did you go to Hermann Park while you were in Houston?"

"No."

"What about Rice University?"

"No."

"Did your father?"

"I don't know. I drove straight back to Austin after dinner."

"How did Brian react when you and your father confronted him about his relationship with Amanda?"

"He told us to mind our own business."

"Was he angry?"

"Determined. Not angry. Brian can get angry, but this time he didn't."

"Do you think your father killed Amanda?"

The response didn't come at once. "I've been asking myself that very question. On one hand, he's lazy. On the other, he's easy to manipulate."

"Is it possible he killed Amanda to please your mother?"

"That's another question I've been asking myself."

"Have you considered your mother as a suspect in Amanda's murder?"

"She wouldn't do it herself."

"Finish that thought."

"I think you know what I mean. Mom finds people to accomplish what she wants done."

"Like your father?"

"I wouldn't restrict it to him."

"One more question and I'm through. When was the last time you rode in either your mother or father's SUV?"

Ryan looked at the ceiling for long seconds. "I don't think I've been in either of them. They bought new ones for Christmas and those yachts with four wheels aren't for me."

Steve took a step forward. "Ryan, we want you to trade places with your father. You're not free to leave, and the deputy will make sure you stay."

STEVE TOOK OVER THE QUESTIONING WHEN JOHNNY CAME INTO the room. He moved back to the chair he'd previously occupied and sat down with his right leg draped over his left knee.

"You were in Houston on the night Amanda died," said Steve in a no-nonsense tone.

"Are you accusing me of killing her?"

"Not yet, but the night is young. This is your opportunity to tell your side. Why did you go to Rice University?"

"Who says I was there?"

"Before I tell you that, has Amanda ever ridden in your vehicle?"

"Are you serious? Of course she hasn't."

Steve lowered his voice. "I warn you not to play games with us. A young woman with incredible potential to do good in this world is dead and your Cadillac is on video surveillance footage. That Cadillac SUV is now with a team of forensic specialists. Believe me when I say they'll find evidence of Amanda being in your vehicle."

Johnny's eyes shot back and forth. His eyebrows raised as a response hit him. "It may be my SUV, but I wasn't driving it."

Steve softened his voice. "You realize that if Belinda doesn't back you up, the police won't believe you. You'd better come up with a name or your next night's sleep will take place in one of Houston's jail cells."

Brian broke his silence. "You can have the one I was in. It's obvious you and Mom didn't mind leaving me there."

"Not a bad idea," said Steve, as he turned his attention back to Johnny. "Let me help you. We know you had dinner with your two sons. At that dinner, you and Ryan carried out orders from Belinda to tell Brian he was in deep trouble for changing schools and continuing his relationship with Amanda."

Steve allowed silence to fill the room for at least fifteen

seconds. "I'm glad you didn't deny it. Both of your sons have made statements, and they've had no contact with each other since the police arrested Brian."

Steve snapped his fingers as if he just remembered something. "One thing I'd like to know. Why did you tell Ryan to wear a suit and tie?"

"Belinda said she wanted him to look like a successful attorney."

"Interesting. A necktie was used to strangle Amanda. But I'm sure you have plenty of ties also, or you could have grabbed one of Brian's."

Desperation filled Johnny's voice. "I didn't go near Hermann Park or Rice University while I was in Houston. I swear it."

"A name. Give us a name of who was in your SUV."

"It was Belinda. Her SUV was dirty and mine was clean, so she told me to take hers to Houston. She's trying to frame both me and Ryan."

Steve smiled. "Bring Belinda and Ryan back in."

35

Belinda entered a full minute behind Ryan and wasted a dagger stare on Steve. Heather concluded that the soothing waters of the pool's fountain had done nothing to decrease the vitriol within the self-appointed matriarch of family, city and county.

"This is nothing less than kidnapping. If it takes every penny I own, I'll make sure you two pay for what you've done." She turned to face the sheriff. "I demand you arrest these two."

"Belinda." He let her name hang in the air. "For once in your life, sit down and shut up."

Her mouth gaped open, but it wasn't long before words spewed forth. "Include yourself in the lawsuit."

Steve spoke before she could continue. "The interesting thing about motive is that it doesn't have to make sense to anyone but the person committing the crime. This crime wasn't particularly difficult to solve once we focused on motive."

Heather covered a smile with her hand. It was Steve Smiley at his best. He took a volatile person and hit her with what appeared to be something out of left field. Next, he'd bend it back with facts until he glued together the entire case.

Steve went on. "Let's consider Clovis Mattherson. He killed his wife and the man he thought was her lover. There's no historical evidence they were anything but neighbors. Then there's the murder of Rodney Wells. We have a good idea of the why and who murdered him. A special word of thanks goes out to Barbara, who provided information about her mother and father."

Barbara sat straight and spoke in a clear voice. "My father was another entitled Mattherson man. He wanted a woman already spoken for and the family paid someone to shed innocent blood to get her."

Steve nodded in agreement. "Skip ahead a few generations, and we have the same family and another seemingly senseless murder. If you haven't figured out the common thread to each of these murders, let me help you. Every third or fourth generation, there's a Mattherson who believes this town and county are their personal possession. The problem today is we have four people named Mattherson, and they're all pointing at each other."

"Who's the fourth?" asked Barbara, the true matriarch of the family.

"That would be Brian," said Steve. "He was the first to be blamed, and with good reason. We allowed you to believe they released him from jail because he's innocent. That remains to be seen."

"I don't understand," said Barbara.

Heather spoke up. "I posted bond for him so there wouldn't be anyone from the Mattherson family missing tonight."

Steve faced Belinda. "I believe you left Brian in jail because you're willing to sacrifice him."

"I don't care what you think."

Brian spoke up. "That's the same conclusion I came to. She could have posted bond for my release, but she didn't. The chosen child is Ryan. I'm expendable."

"Speaking of Ryan," said Steve as he faced Belinda. "You'll be interested in learning what he and your husband had to say while you were by the pool. I'll start with Ryan. His intentions after college are to move to a major metropolitan area, work for a big law firm and live the high life. How does that fit into your well-constructed plans?"

Belinda responded with a snort. "You're lying. Ryan knows his place and what's expected of him."

Barbara pointed an arthritic finger. "Open your eyes, daughter. There's not enough action in this town to satisfy Ryan. He'll be sowing wild oats until he burns out or comes to his senses, and it won't be here. The only question is, which will come first?"

Belinda used her most mocking tone. "So says the crazy cat lady."

Heather spoke up. "I'd be glad to furnish you the video recording of Ryan when I interviewed him for a summer intern position. Steve's telling the truth. Ryan has no intention of moving back to Mattherson."

Ryan shrugged. "Sorry Mom. I can't think of anything worse than living here again."

Instead of getting upset, Belinda dismissed her son's words. "You're the next true Mattherson. You'll come around by the time you're ready to practice law."

Steve's next question caused Belinda to blink before she answered. "What did you think about Amanda Palmer?"

"What do you mean?"

"It's common knowledge that Amanda was the smartest person Mattherson ever produced."

"That's not true."

Undeterred, Steve continued on. "What I find interesting is that Amanda played the stock market with her father when most girls her age couldn't spell Wall Street. You saw the

Palmer's wealth rise at an alarming rate." Steve turned his head. "Isn't that right, Craig?"

"She processed information with a speed that left my head spinning. It was like living with a super-computer. She'd tell me what to buy and when to sell. It was nothing more than a child's game to her."

Steve verbally hammered Belinda again. "You still own a significant amount of land, but your grip on the city and county is slipping. You couldn't allow this county to grow and prosper. That's why you blocked Heather's attempt to buy land for a new high-speed rail line. It meant change.

"Motive and history," said Steve with emphasis, as he took a step toward Belinda. "If you remember, I said this case was stronger on motive than most cases. It also has a lot to do with history and control. You read the tea leaves. It wouldn't be long before Amanda Palmer helped her father make so much money he could transform this county into something new and exciting. Something that didn't have the Mattherson brand on it."

"The lake project is only the beginning," said Craig.

Steve modulated his voice down to a more conversational level. "Belinda, there's something that came up in our talk with your husband. He said he traded vehicles with you on the day he went to Houston to play golf and meet with your two sons. Is that correct?"

"That's a lie. Leon failed to follow my instructions and didn't wash my vehicle. We went in Johnny's because it was clean and had a full tank of gas."

"So you and Johnny went to Houston in his SUV. Did he bring his golf clubs?"

"He goes nowhere without them, but he didn't play."

"What time did you leave town?"

"It was early afternoon."

Steve ran his hand through his hair. "I've only seen Johnny

wearing clothes suitable for a day on the links. Didn't he look a little dressed down with Ryan in a nice suit?"

Belinda issued another of her haughty snorts. "I told him to make himself presentable with a coat and tie."

"What did you do while he met with your two sons?"

"I went shopping and then had dinner."

"Alone?"

"Johnny said he wanted to spend time with the boys. You know. It was that male bonding thing."

"Did you call Amanda and make arrangements to meet her?"

"Absolutely not."

Heather stepped forward and cast her gaze over the gathering. "Let's vote again. Was that last statement the truth or a lie?"

The word *lie* rang out with no dissension.

Belinda recoiled. "What kind of trick are you trying to pull?"

"No trick," said Steve. "These citizens of Mattherson voted and found you to be a liar." He pointed to her eldest son, but Steve meant it for her. "We didn't single you out as a liar. They thought the same thing about Ryan."

Steve took a step to his left. "Let's see if you can be more truthful from here on out. Johnny tried to cover for you by not mentioning you went to Houston with him. By your own admission, you were with your husband on the night Amanda died. Who drove?"

"He always drives when we go someplace together. That's the way my parents raised me."

Heather issued a mostly inaudible, "Gotcha."

Steve made no outward sign that Belinda had all but sealed her fate and kept talking. "Johnny had a hard time explaining the fact that we know his SUV was on the campus of Rice University that night. Were you with him?"

She hesitated a second too long. "Of course not. Why would I be on that campus?"

"She's lying again," said Johnny.

"I told you to stay quiet." Belinda's words came out like a rifle shot. "I can handle this blind nobody and ten more like him."

Steve ignored the insult and shifted his attention to Johnny. "Are you sure Belinda was with you in the north parking lot at Rice University?"

"Don't you dare say another word," said Belinda. She rocked back and forth.

As Johnny stood and put distance between him and his wife, he said, "It's too late. He knows everything. They have video of my Caddy on campus. Your DNA is in the back seat. They didn't know I wore a coat and tie before you told them. You made sure the tie I put on was one of Brian's. That means you tried to set up both me and Brian."

Steve interrupted. "The tie. That was the one clue too many that I mentioned earlier."

Belinda blinked even more and continued rocking.

Johnny shifted his gaze to Steve. "She said we were going to the campus to talk to Amanda. That's all, talk. She had me text her to meet on the street outside her housing unit. She didn't want us to double park, so we agreed to meet her in the north parking lot. Belinda told me the tie made me look old and stuffy, so I took off the jacket and tie and put them in the back seat. When Amanda came to the car, Belinda got in the back seat and Amanda sat in front. Belinda tried to bully her into not seeing Brian. She laughed at Belinda and called her a pitiful old woman. Belinda couldn't take it when Amanda laughed at her."

Belinda's hands covered her ears. She shut her eyes and continued to rock.

Craig Palmer sprung to his feet. "Why didn't you stop her? You had to know she's the crazy one in the family?"

Johnny had no answer.

The sheriff put a hand up to stop Craig from advancing any further. "Go home, but come see me tomorrow. I'll need a formal statement. Write it tonight. It will help if you get it out and onto paper."

The sound of Craig slamming the front door echoed through the cavernous house as Heather brought Steve to stand before the sheriff.

The sheriff motioned to his three deputies to come forward. He pointed at Johnny. "Take Mr. Mattherson to jail. Call an ambulance for Mrs. Mattherson."

Sara Jane came over and draped an arm around her neighbor. "Let's take her to the poolroom. There's a nice couch she can lay on."

Belinda rocked back and forth as she allowed Sara Jane to lead her.

When Johnny and Belinda were out of sight, Steve spoke again. "Sheriff, I have a favor to ask."

"Ask away."

"I'd like to have a few minutes with several of these people with no law enforcement. There's one bit of unfinished business we need to address."

"Are we talking about more people going to jail?"

Heather answered. "It should be a civil matter if we play our cards right."

HEATHER TOOK CARE OF ASKING THE THREE MEMBERS OF THE Wells family to stay. They exchanged furtive glances, but each nodded. Next, she went to the opposite couch and made the same request. Ryan objected until his grandmother told him his final year of law school depended on him sitting and listening a while longer. Otherwise, the room cleared as Leo and Captain Price went to their rooms after Steve promised them the meeting wouldn't last long and he and Heather would meet them at the Dairy Queen for a late supper.

With the door shut, Steve began. "I hate to leave a case with a loose end dangling in the air. I have one question for Traci. Depending on her answer, I may ask one more and then Heather will take over."

Traci righted herself on the couch as Steve took in a deep breath. "Is the child you're carrying the result of a consensual relationship?"

Her head dipped. "No."

"I didn't think so. Is it your intention to file criminal charges on the man?"

"No."

Steve took a seat as Heather assumed his spot in front of the fireplace and looked at Traci. "You have multiple options. The first is to do nothing. This may sound like a good course to take, but there's no guarantee the child's father won't come back at a later date and claim paternity. That usually results in custody and child support issues."

Traci set her jaw. "Can't I get him to sign away his rights?"

Heather nodded. "That's possible, but in situations like this, most men want to be relieved of the burden of supporting the child in trade for making no claim to the child."

Barbara tried to speak, but had to clear her throat. "I believe I have a solution. What if the man, or a relative, or even a friend of the man established a trust for the child that was acceptable to the woman? That way, the financial burden of raising the child would be eased and the cad who's responsible could live the life he thinks he wants."

Traci said, "Two conditions. The amount would need to be

generous, but not extravagant. Next, I don't want my child to have anything to do with him. Ever."

Heather gave a word of caution. "He'd have to agree in writing."

Everyone but Steve focused on Ryan. Barbara spoke in a stern voice as she glared at her eldest grandson. "This is when you say, 'I'll agree to whatever is reasonable.'"

Ryan nodded. "I agree... and I apologize."

Barbara stared at her grandson. "Don't think this is a free ride. You'll budget for repayment into the trust with your first paycheck after you pass the bar and get a job."

"One more thing," said Steve. "The telescope in Ryan's room has to go."

36

After a full day in heels, Heather moaned in delight as she kicked them off at the door of her condo. As she passed the dining room table, she heard the cat door flap open and heard Steve say, "Leo's here. Come over."

"I'll be there as soon as I change." It was time to let the silk dress hit the floor in a crumpled pile. Tonight she'd wear black leggings and an extra-large T-shirt. After all, it was only Steve and Leo.

Barefooted, she padded her way next door and entered Steve's condo without knocking. She found Steve and Leo at the dining room table, each with a bottle of beer in front of them.

"Come join us," said Steve. "We're celebrating."

Heather was already on her way to the refrigerator to retrieve her own bottle of brew when she asked, "What's the occasion?"

Leo beamed. "They released me from purgatory."

Steve echoed the news. "He's back at his old desk in Homicide, where he belongs."

Heather took her first swig and issued a low moan of

delight. She tore off a paper towel, folded it in half and used it as a coaster as she took a seat at the table. "What took so long? It's been over a month since we returned from Mattherson."

"Captain Price is a slow healer. He wanted to take care of things in his own way and couldn't do it until they medically cleared him to come back to work."

"This sounds interesting."

"It was," said Steve.

Heather shifted her gaze. "You were there?"

Steve grinned. "It was my first time back. Of course, I could see everyone's ugly faces then. Now I can imagine they look better."

"No chance of that," said Leo.

The insistent plea from a four-legged feline brought her attention to the floor. "Max." Heather scooted back and patted her lap. "Come see your mama."

Even though the Maine Coon cat weighed two to three times as much as a normal feline, he made the leap with ease. Heather stroked his head and Max responded with baritone purrs.

"Before you ask," said Steve. "I fed him, and let him lick my plate."

Heather contemplated chastising Steve again for spoiling Max, but refrained because she wanted to hear Leo's story of redemption. Besides, chastising Steve didn't stop him from putting his plate or bowl on the floor as a treat for Max.

"It was great," said Leo. "The captain didn't tell anyone Steve and I were coming this morning. He called everyone together and laid it on thick about how much he appreciated me taking the initiative to include all available resources to solve not just the cold case, but the murder of Amanda Palmer."

Steve interrupted. "That's you and me, Heather. We're what's called 'available resources.'"

Leo rolled his eyes. "It's a shame your attempts at humor haven't improved with age."

"Don't let him interrupt you like that, Leo, or we'll be here all night."

"Like I was saying, the captain laid it on thick. That's when he announced I'd be returning and he assigned me a new junior partner. Guess who."

Heather shook her head. Then a revelation hit her. "He didn't."

"He did. My new partner is none other than Detective Long. I'll have the pleasure of breaking him in, like Steve did me."

Heather looked at Leo. "Something tells me there are a lot of stories you could tell."

"He ran me ragged doing all the things he didn't want to do."

"Get back to your story about today," said Steve.

"See?" said Leo. "He still has to be in charge."

"Anyway, the captain then gave everyone a lecture on how the new pups needed to learn from the old dogs."

Steve added, "I thought he balanced it out well by telling the old dogs that if they stopped hunting, it was time to move on."

Heather asked, "Won't Detective Long try to undermine you as long as Lieutenant Chase is still your immediate supervisor?"

Leo grinned. "That's the best news. There's a new lieutenant in Cold Cases. Lieutenant Jim Bounds couldn't stand it anymore and found a cushy job with a private security firm. That left a vacancy, and since Lieutenant Chase botched the Palmer case, the decision makers put him in time out without having to go through all the hassle of disciplinary procedures."

Leo added, "The captain had pity on him and didn't announce it until after the meeting."

Steve held up his bottle as a salute. "Here's to Leo. And to justice, karma, divine intervention, and anything else that puts wrongs right."

After the toast, Steve shifted his attention to Heather. "How was your trip to Mattherson?"

"Everyone there was mad at me for not bringing you. Especially Traci."

"How is she?"

"Seven pounds, five ounces lighter. She named the baby Amanda. It was a surprise because she thought it would be a boy."

Steve swallowed hard.

Heather kept talking. "When they arrested Brian, Rice University expelled him. After the arrests, he decided it was time for a new direction. He's already finished the course work to be a real estate agent and is waiting to take the test. Craig Palmer's broker will supervise him so he can keep his mother's office open. Traci is right behind him in following the same career."

"Did you talk to Mindi Palmer?"

"Only for a minute. She came to bring a stack of presents for baby Amanda. I think she's coping with the grief through retail therapy."

"What about your new project?" asked Steve.

"It's promising. Craig's doing a great job on developing property around the lake, but he didn't have enough land nearby for a golf course, condos, and a resort. That's my project. Barbara and I agreed on a land deal that will compliment Craig's property. In a few years, it will be a vacation destination within driving distance of Houston and Dallas."

Steve ran his fingers down the bottle. "Everything is coming full circle."

Leo looked at Heather. She shrugged, showing she didn't know what Steve meant.

"I don't follow," said Leo.

"Mattherson is back to where it started. Three families working together for the good of everyone. I call that success."

––––––––––

Thank you for reading *Murder Down The Line*. I hope it kept you turning the pages to find out whodunit!

I want to give a shout out to my readers who are part of my Mystery Insiders community. I needed help on naming the town I would use in this book and they came through in a big way! I received many great names and after narrowing them down a couple of times, I settled on Mattherson. A big *Thank You* to Lorraine who suggested the name.

If you would like to get in on the fun that surrounds the writing of my books, and receive a free short story, scan below to join my mailing list. You may also go to brucehammack.com to sign up.

Ready for your next book?
If you like police procedurals with a side of mystery, you'll enjoy the Star of Justice series.

Turn the page for a preview of *Long Road to Justice*.

All that was stolen from his family haunts David Harper
every day...and revenge is calling him.

For sixteen long years David Harper has wanted justice for his
murdered mother. In order to prove his father's innocence, he
must find her killer. If he doesn't stop them, his father will be
next.

Long Road to Justice
Excerpt

APPEAL GOES TO HIGHEST COURT
Lake Jackson Man Maintains Innocence.

By SIMON SAMS
Staff Writer, Angleton Times

*The Texas Court of Criminal Appeals heard testimony today in the
case of Robert Quisenheimer, a former mechanical engineer at Dow
Chemical Company, convicted of the brutal murder of his wife. In
the original trial, sixteen years ago, a Brazoria County jury needed
only an hour and fifty-seven minutes to return a guilty verdict.*

Officers in dress uniforms joined a crowd under a sweltering
late morning sun for the graveside service. Family, the elderly,
and a few others found refuge under a white canopy where CJ
sat with folded hands, staring at the small coffin.

Linked arm in arm, she and David took short, labored steps
to the black limousine with Grace and LeRoy. A caravan of cars

snaked behind them. Upon arrival at their home, a line of construction workers, each scrubbed and dressed in the best clothes they had, greeted CJ with a rose and words of condolence, mostly in Spanish.

The barn filled with voices and food. The benevolence committee from church outdid themselves as covered dishes filled tables until they threatened to break under the weight. The workers produced two saw horses and a sheet of plywood for a makeshift table, averting a small disaster. Lids from a row of ice chests raised and lowered in salutes, providing much needed liquid refreshment on the unusually hot day. Gradually, and thankfully, the crowd thinned.

CJ saw David's senior captain take a phone call. Something like a tourniquet gripped her gut when the two men retreated to a distant corner of the barn.

The pull on David's sleeve took him by surprise. He led Captain Crow to a shadowy corner of the barn, as far away from the gathering as they could get.

The elder lawman removed his hat, stroked his graying hair and returned the Stetson to his head. "The timing of this stinks. I wish I could put it off, but it's going to be on the evening news and in all the papers tomorrow morning."

David gave his head a nod and steeled himself as best he could.

With a flat voice the pronouncement came. "The decision from the Court of Criminal Appeals is in. It's what we expected, and more. They reversed the guilty verdict and remanded the case back to District Court. They took an extra step and issued instructions to the district judge to find the defendant not guilty. He'll soon be a free man."

The world spun. David's knees buckled.

"Hold on there."

David righted himself and looked at some point beyond his supervisor.

"There could be no other verdict after the court admitted the DNA evidence." He paused. "There's more."

David's gaze shot to the eyes of the man facing him.

"We got a hit from the DNA data base. His name is Samuel Barcroft. He's a second offender doing twenty for aggravated assault with a deadly weapon."

"Where is he?" asked David through clenched teeth.

"Clemens Unit. Brazoria County."

"Not more than fifteen miles from where he..."

Captain Crow narrowed his gaze. "Listen to me. I know what you're thinking. You want to take your sniper's rifle and get revenge. No matter how much you want it, revenge won't work. You'll wind up in jail. What would it do to CJ?"

David stared into the distance, every muscle in his body coiled and his mind awash in fury.

Captain Crow continued, "The director called. You're not to go anywhere near this case. We'll handle it."

David remained silent, his jaw flexing.

The senior ranger issued an icy stare. "You're not to get within five miles of that prison farm. Is that understood?"

David gave a sharp nod. "Wasn't there DNA on two people?"

"The second is not in the data base."

"All this fancy technology we have today and it still can't tell us what we need to know."

Ranger Crow looked away from angry eyes. "We'll find out. Let us handle it."

David took a deep breath and blew it out slowly. "Who do you have assigned to interrogate this Samuel Barcroft?"

"Quint Fowler."

"Quint's a good man."

"He's already had one session. Barcroft is a savvy convict

and a tough nut to crack. Quint reports he's wearing him down and should have the name of the other person soon."

The senior captain stood straight for his next announcement. "In the meantime, you're off duty for a week, more if you need it. You've been through too much lately. Take care of CJ and build your house. I'll keep you posted if anything important breaks on the case."

David's face hardened. "What about the suppression of evidence at the original trial and the stonewalling by the DA for the past two years?"

The ranger supervisor snapped back, "That's two questions too many." He softened, but only marginally. "I can't tell you anything else at this time."

David stared into the ranger's steely eyes.

The captain glanced away then met David's gaze again. He sighed and said, "We're trying to uncover a den of snakes in Brazoria County. The one thing we don't need is you storming in with guns blazing."

WHAT REVIEWERS ARE SAYING...

"Took off from page one and didn't land till the last sentence."

"Refreshingly exciting!"

"Stayed up till 3am, could not put it down..."

The Star of Justice Series is clean read crime fiction full of mystery, action and suspense. Available in eBook at your favorite online retailer and in paperback on Amazon.

The idea for *Murder Down The Line* began to germinate with
me after a stay at a small Texas town's B&B to celebrate my
wife's birthday. We chose a place with a lot of history that
neither one of us had visited. As we sat around the breakfast
table having coffee with our host, he regaled us with tales of
summer mansions built in the early 20th century by bankers,
businessmen, and oil and cattle barons. His gift for storytelling
painted a vivid picture of the town in its hey-day. My wife and I
walked away that morning with ideas flying between us.

As we made our way around the town we viewed many of the
mansions built in the town's boom period. The perfection of
the town as a book setting began to gel within me. I didn't know
exactly when I would use the setting, but I knew I would.

"Small towns can have big secrets." Steve Smiley didn't grow up
in a small town, but many of you, like my wife and I, did. Most
of those towns, like Mattherson, were run by two or three very
influential families, generation after generation. The founding
families of Mattherson are fictional versions of families I have
known personally or were influenced by our B&B host's stories.

There was one character I chose to model after someone I
knew well. I drew Rodney Wells out of my own family history.
My dad, Ross, like Rodney, was an officer in the Army Air
Corps. After high school graduation, my dad enrolled in a local
college. The rumbling of World War II began and he decided
he wanted to join the newly-formed Army Air Corps. (At that
time, there was no Air Force branch of the U.S. military
service.) To increase his chances of being chosen, he got a job at
a local air field, applied for the Air Corps and then waited until

he was called. He attended Officers Candidate School (OCS) and became a bomber pilot serving in the Mediterranean Theatre of Operations. Thankfully, unlike my character Rodney, my dad lived through the war and returned home to my mom. A photo of the twenty-year-old version of my dad hangs in a glass display case in our home, surrounded by the medals Rodney never had the chance to earn.

Starting with tiny seeds planted on that weekend retreat, and my own life experiences, I wanted to explore, in story form, the question of generational influences on people today. My mind went to a passage from the Bible, Exodus 34:7. The second part of the verse speaks of the sins of the fathers visiting their offspring to the third and fourth generation. Thus came the idea of a cold case, an unsolved murder that happened during World War II. How could this long-forgotten killing influence a modern-day family? This was one of many times in the writing process where I took the bit out of the mouth of my imagination and allowed it to run free. I envisioned three families who were once good friends and trusted business partners until...

You've read the story, so you know the rest.

Thanks for coming along as Steve and Heather unraveled their latest case. Stay tuned for the next one!

About The Author

Drawing from his extensive background in criminal justice, Bruce Hammack writes contemporary, clean read detective and crime mysteries. He is the author of the Smiley and McBlythe Mystery series and the Star of Justice series. Having lived in eighteen cities around the world, he now lives in the Texas hill country with his wife of thirty-plus years.

Follow Bruce on Bookbub and Goodreads for the latest new release info and recommendations. Learn more at brucehammack.com.

Thank you for reading one of my books. I hope the mystery satisfied your appetite for a good 'whodunit.' I would be very grateful if you would take a minute to leave a review at your favorite retail site, Bookbub or Goodreads. Reviews help authors keep churning out stories for you to enjoy.

Happy Reading!

Bruce

Made in the USA
Las Vegas, NV
17 June 2022

50310311R00156